Dead Wreckoning

Sylvia Dickey Smith

L & L Dreamspell
Spring, Texas

Cover and Interior Design by L & L Dreamspell

Copyright © 2009 Sylvia Dickey Smith. All rights reserved. No part of this publication may be reproduced, stored in a retrieval system or transmitted in any form or by any means, electronic, mechanical, photocopying, recording or otherwise without the prior written permission of the copyright holder, except for brief quotations used in a review.

This is a work of fiction, and is produced from the author's imagination. People, places and things mentioned in this novel are used in a fictional manner.

ISBN: 978-1-60318-138-9

Library of Congress Control Number: 2009923170

Visit us on the web at www.lldreamspell.com

Published by L & L Dreamspell
Printed in the United States of America

In Appreciation

Writing this book turned into absolute fun because of the help and encouragement offered by so many people who know so much about so many subjects.

D. C. Campbell	David Ciambrone
Lonnie Cruse	Pete Dickey
Helen Ginger	Joan Upton Hall
Penny Leleux	Bruce Lockett
Joy Nord	Randy Rawls
Jaime Roton	Manfred Reimann
Sam Kittrell	Earl Staggs

Also, thanks to the owners of L & L Dreamspell, Lisa Smith and Linda Houle, who show confidence in my ability to pull it off. And to my Bill, William M. Smith (U.S Army Col. Ret.) who gives me constant encouragement, puts up with my weird writing schedule, and thanks me every single day for marrying him.

For Penny Leleux. A true Southeast Texas woman who inspires and supports my work and introduces me to exciting ghosts that haunt southeast Texas.

and

For Arthlee (Lee) Talbert (deceased) a man who climbed aboard a pirate ship in the swamps of Orange, Texas and whose adventure inspired this story.

Few people receive the truth in a complete, on the spot, sight-blinding beam of light. Most learn it one tiny step at a time, and sometimes, even after we've learned it, we find ourselves learning the same lesson all over again, but in an even deeper, more intuitive way.

Sidra Smart

One

Sidra Smart sat with her back to the desk staring out the window, watching traces of pink crawl across the southeast Texas sky. A soft click echoed in the office as her index finger flicked across one corner of the envelope in her hand. She shifted her gaze from the brightening sky back down to the letter. The muscles in her shoulders cramped, begging to relax their vigil on her emotions, but she dared not move. Not yet, not with so much at stake. After working under the tutelage of licensed private eye George Léger, she now held the results of her state board exam, and her future, in the palm of her hand, afraid to open the stupid envelope.

"This isn't the craziest thing you've ever done, Sidra Smart," she said, admonishing herself. "But it sure ranks right up at the top with a couple of other doozies. Whoever heard of a woman, married to a preacher for thirty years, divorcing the guy and then inheriting a private detective business?"

But she had done just that and found not a hen scratch of similarity between the two worlds.

In the first one, her self-appointed instructor-husband required that she be the subservient, inferior wife and play by rules written by the superior gender. Striving for perfection within that role left her with so many religious wounds she felt like she'd survived the Christian Chainsaw Massacre.

In this second world—the private eye one—she'd learned she didn't have to be perfect and didn't have to act like she was, that she had an opinion worth as much as any man's, and she no longer had to act like a lady 24-7 and sit with her knees together. She'd also been shot at, half-drowned, and hung by her wrists—naked—like a beef carcass ready for butchering.

And she'd take this second world any day of the week.

Slider romped into the room. The half-paranoid, half-Chesapeake Bay retriever's snoring had kept her up half the night, but now he pranced in with the energy of a newborn colt.

"Look here, Slider. My test results came in."

He sauntered over, sniffed the envelope, and lifted his head in the air like some snotty-nosed critter too good to eat dog food. And that part wasn't an act.

"So you think I'm crazy, eh? You think I should forget all of this private eye stuff and take the easy way out. Marry Ben and let him take care of me?"

Slider's front end wagged one way while the back half wagged the other. His tail tried to keep up.

Sid loved Ben Hillerman, but she never should have accepted the engagement ring he slipped on her finger one night. A few weeks later she'd taken it off and stuck it in a drawer when he started talking about her closing the private eye business. With her lack of experience, he said, it was far too dangerous. She'd get herself killed. Well, she too struggled with the thought of a gruesome death.

Then again, she'd never felt so alive.

If her office across the street from the courthouse hadn't been firebombed, she'd still be working there instead of at Annie's ghost-active house, built in the 1850s and known then as the Catfish Hotel. Sid swore that the aroma of fried catfish still wafted down the halls. Which ghost did the cooking—and whether or not they competed with Aunt Annie, the self-proclaimed best cook in the south—hadn't yet been determined. What Annie meant, of course, was she cooked better than anyone on the planet.

Slider barked and sniffed at the envelope still in Sid's hand. The envelope that started this whole recall of the craziest things she'd ever done.

"Okay, okay! I'll open it." Holding her breath, she tore into the packet, yanked out the letter and read.

"Seventy-six, Slider, seventy-six!" She chucked him under the chin. "Not bad for a fifty-year old."

Slider glared at her and barked, not once, but twice.

"Okay, okay, fifty-two. Come on, let's go show Annie."

Sid always swore she'd sleep on a bed of fire ants before moving in with her meddlesome, bossy, outlandish-dressing aunt. But when necessity demanded, she'd moved in, and still hadn't slept on that bed of fire ants. She sprinted out of the office and headed to the kitchen, the good news in her hand and Slider at her heels.

"Annie, where are you, sweetheart? Look what came in the mail."

With a patience that put Job to shame, Aunt Annie stood at the stove stirring the dark brown roux for a chicken and sausage gumbo. The heat from the stove left her cropped, bottle-red hair lying in soft curls alongside heavily rouged cheeks. Chesterfield, Annie's cat-with-an-attitude, lay at her feet curled into a fluffy orange ball.

Her aunt wore a bright yellow, long-sleeved top, banded at both wrists and just below her thick belly. Mid-calf-length brown stretch pants clung to spindly legs. Gold-colored tennis shoes completed the picture. Once again, Big Bird had invaded their kitchen.

King Cat—as Sid referred to Chesterfield—half-opened his eyes, apparently irritated at the interruption of one of his many naps of the day. He and Slider barely tolerated each other, knowing if they didn't, they'd be banished—the dog outside and the cat to a room by himself. Being alone didn't bother Chesterfield nearly as much as outside bothered Slider, but they'd settled into a grudgingly endured love-hate relationship. The hate usually won out.

Annie gave the contents of the cast iron skillet one more stir and half-turned toward Sid. "What is it, Siddie? I can't stop right now. If I burn this roux, I'll have to start all over again."

"Look! I passed the exam. I'm now licensed in the state of Texas." She rattled the sheet of paper in front of Annie, who gave it a quick scan.

"Seventy-six. Humph. You passed all right, but just by the skin of your teeth. Wasn't 75 the cut-off?"

A few months ago, the comment would have sucked the wind right out of Sid's enthusiasm, but not this time. "Hey, the way I see it, passing is passing." She snatched the paper back and stared at it one more time.

"So what does that mean?" Annie turned off the fire and slowly spooned the roux into the large stock pot. It bubbled, sizzled and splattered all over the stove. Startled, the cat hissed and sprinted out of the kitchen, cursing all three of them.

"It means as soon as the insurance money comes in, I can rebuild the office."

"That's what I was afraid of." Annie stared into the pot, stirring fast and rhythmically, her displeasure filling the room. "I was kind of hoping you'd keep the office here. I like having you nearby." She adjusted the fire to simmer, lidded the pot and wiped her hands on a bright orange kitchen towel. The hot brown mixture released a smell so good it would make a milquetoast slap his pappy.

"I know, sweetheart, and I hate to break your heart by relocating my office, but..." Sid headed over to the coffee pot and poured a cup. Not that she hadn't had enough caffeine for the day, but if she didn't do something, the black hole descending on the room might swallow her whole. "It'll be okay. You'll see." She took a sip of the strong hot liquid.

Instead of responding to Sid's last remark, Annie hummed and stuck her head in the refrigerator, the message clear. Don't expect her to support the move.

Collecting a stick of butter, Annie closed the refrigerator, marched over to the stove and started into her usual tirade. "And for God's sake, Sid put some color on that white flour hair of yours and, for heaven's sakes, go to the beauty parlor. Cutting your hair with pinking shears is just asking for wood rot."

Sid spun on her heels, certain she'd spilt a couple drops of coffee, but since she was in no mood to look, much less clean it up, she marched straight back to her office. There, for several marvelous minutes, she sat and stared at the letter, letting every glorious word on the page burrow deep into her opinion of herself.

She was now bona fide. A full-fledged private investigator who, at times, still had no idea what the hell she was doing. She wondered if she had enough years left to ever feel qualified in this strange new world she'd chosen. Then sometimes she felt like she hadn't chosen it at all, that it had chosen her.

As luck would have it, Annie walked in a few minutes later with the newspaper and an attitude. "Wanna see the morning paper?" She offered Sid the bundle, her words as stiff as her back.

"No, not yet, thanks. I'll look at it later. Right now, I've got to make some order out of this desk."

Annie tossed the paper aside and collected a stack of unopened mail. Without stopping to read the return address, she rammed the letter opener through the flap on an envelope, slit it open, and slapped it in front of Sid. "I thought you were happy here," she said, sniffling, her bottom lip stuck out halfway to Mars.

"Oh, honey, don't be like that," Sid said. "You know I've got to do what's best for the business. Folks just don't know we're here. The Third Eye needs visibility, or I'll never make a go of it."

"But this works so well for *me*. I can cook and help you in the office at the same time."

Sid picked up the top envelope, pulled out the enclosure and stared at it slack-jawed. "Speaking of insurance, they finally came through. Here's my settlement check. Now I have a choice—keep my office here and make you happy, or rebuild and… Of course, I could just delay the rebuild and let the interest accumulate."

Encouraged, Sid pulled out the enclosure from the second envelope and scanned the letter. "Well, I guess the decision is made for us. This is a notice from the city. Seems a detective office can't be in a residence. It's against a city zoning ordinance. I have fifteen days to show serious intent to relocate."

Out of arguments, Annie turned and stalked out of the room, taking with her the vacuum she'd created when she'd entered a few minutes earlier.

Eager to deposit the check, Sid drove straight to Orange Savings Bank, and after conducting her business, paused long enough to admire the numerals on the deposit slip. Clarity of decision sat on her shoulders as firmly as it had the day she'd walked away from her marriage to Sam and his denomination.

She headed home, eager to make an appointment with a contractor, amazed at how her attitude had changed since she first awakened that morning, and amazed at the difference a few zeros made.

In early June in southeast Texas, summer often arrived earlier than the calendar, and this was one of those days. As soon she pulled into her driveway and stepped out of the air conditioned vehicle, tiny beads of perspiration coated her skin. Overhead, birds whistled at her from the sycamore tree, and she laughed up at them. "Don't think that flattery is going to keep you out of trouble if you dump on my car," she advised, shaking her finger at them just as a faded-blue jalopy of a truck sputtered up.

The vehicle turned into the driveway, left fender dragging the curb, and by the time it came to stop mere inches away from Sid's vehicle, her mind had already racked up mounting repair bills.

She headed down the driveway peering through the truck's filthy windshield. "Durwood? I thought that was your truck."

Durwood had been one of her first clients. His case had been one of those she almost didn't survive. Now he greeted her with a smile and stuck his hand out the window. She clasped it in hers, taking great care not to squeeze. Arthritis had twisted his fingers so much they even looked painful. She hadn't seen him since she'd closed his case a few months ago, and yes, the omnipresent tobacco juice still coated the corners of his mouth.

"I was hoping to talk to you, but it looks like you're heading out somewhere."

"No, just getting back. What can I do for you?"

The gristly old man opened the truck door and climbed out, stopping long enough to swipe his spit 'n polish black leather shoes on the back legs of his overalls. His furrowed brow told her something bothered him.

"You okay?" she asked.

"It's that dang sheriff."

"You mean the new one, Sheriff Quade Burns?"

Durwood nodded, fidgeting. "He's scared my friend Boo Murphy half to death. Keeps questioning her about the pirate ship she saw out in the swamp behind her house. I need you to come talk to her, calm her down. She's afraid he's going to arrest her."

"For seeing a pirate ship?" She laughed. "That's not against the law."

"No, no, Sid, for murder. Dang it, you know what I meant."

"I'm sorry, sweetheart. I shouldn't make light of your friend's situation. Come on in and let's talk about it." Sid took his elbow and tried to steer him toward the house, but the soles of his shiny black shoes stayed glued to the driveway.

"No, Sid, we need to go to her house right now, before she has a coronary. She's an old woman what likes the outdoors. She won't make it locked away behind bars."

"Can we sit and talk first?"

"We can sit in my truck and talk on the way over there. Come on. Climb in."

Giving in to the stubborn old coot was easier than arguing with him. She walked around the front of the dilapidated truck and popped open the screeching door.

The condition of the cab almost made her change her mind. Stuffing stuck out of holes in the upholstery. Duct tape tried to keep the seat together and a tear across the back still had residue where one piece had abandoned its responsibility. The floorboard held an unopened can of motor oil, and a wooden box full of assorted tools and oily red rags. On the dash lay a well-worn copy of *Lafitte the Pirate*.

Gingerly, trying to climb in without touching anything, Sid wished she'd chosen blue jeans earlier that morning. Her white linen slacks would never be the same. When the buzz of an insect caught her attention, she turned toward the sound and saw a spider web in the corner of the window. A bee fought for a way out of the trap, but was unsuccessful.

She knew that feeling.

The truck backfired and skipped down the road, forcing Sid to glance in the rearview mirror. Just as she suspected, dark smoke billowed out behind them.

"Okay, catch me up," she said, hoping to get the ride over quickly.

"Here's what I know." Durwood stared straight ahead, his blue, watery eyes focused on the road. "Boo went squirrel hunting out in the swamp just like she always does, but this time she found a pirate ship stuck up out of the water. The next day, she took Sasha out to see it."

"A pirate ship? Who's Sasha?"

"Boo's second cousin, twice removed. She's going crazy thinking folks believe she killed him."

"Sasha?"

"No, dang it. Not Sasha—Boo. Keep up, Sid."

"Believe me, I'm trying to. You need to slow down, Durwood. I can't make sense of what you're saying."

"Best I can tell, she came home and told Sasha—"

"Her second cousin, twice removed," Sid said, suppressing a grin.

Durwood nodded again, seemingly pleased that she was catching up. "Sasha went into hysterics, bellowing about how Boo killed Zeke."

"Whoa, whoa." Sid's head swam. "Who's Zeke?"

"Sasha's husband, or was—till yesterday."

No wonder she couldn't keep up, she first had to translate the man's language. For he put an I in yesterday and took out the R and the A—as in *yistedy*.

"Okay, okay, I get the picture. A man is dead, and Boo thinks she'll be arrested for the murder."

"And if she's arrested, she's gonna plead guilty. Only thing is, she ain't killed nobody, Sid. That's what I'm trying to tell you." Agitation took his eyes off the road just as a mangy cur dog claimed his pedestrian rights. Sid yelped and threw on her own brakes, fearful her feet might go through the rusted-out floorboard. The floor held, although her brakes didn't. Durwood didn't touch his. He simply swerved, tossing Sid against the door, while the dog ignored them and continued his saunter across the street.

Durwood turned off on a winding dirt road that eventually led to the river. Water tupelo, cypress, and pine trees stood tall and resolute between two unpainted houses. A wide, hard-packed dirt yard separated the two. Each house, catty-corner to the other, sat on concrete blocks, while rough-hewn steps led up to their front porches. Odds and ends of junk lay in big piles under a shed between and underneath the houses.

"She knows you're coming." Durwood reached across Sid—smelling like he'd spent the night in a tobacco barn—and yanked the handle until the door opened.

"She knows? Is she psychic or something?"

"I told her I was bringing you back here with me."

"Pretty sure of yourself, weren't you?"

"Sure about you," he said, his grin showing off brown-stained teeth.

Just as they got out and closed the doors, an elderly woman with wiry gray hair, rounded shoulders and sun-leathered face, stepped out the screen door and started yelling and raising a fist in the air.

"Dadgum it, Durwood, I told you not to bring that woman here. Don't think just 'cause you did, you're gonna get in my pants!"

Durwood looked at Sid with a big grin on his face. "Ain't she cute?" Then he turned back to the big-fisted woman. "Now Boo, I told you that ain't what I'm after. I'm just trying to help."

"Then why'd you bring that Myra whore by here last week if you ain't wanting her to teach me the tricks of her trade?"

"Good lord, Boo, that ain't why me and Myra came to see you. She's my friend. I just wanted you two to meet. People judge her for what she does for a living, but she's just as human as you and me."

"Friend, huh? Well, I hear tell she's got lots of friends and they're all men."

By now Durwood had taken Sid's elbow and led her up the front steps—or maybe pulled would be more like it.

"This here Ms. Smart is a dang good detective, and she can help find out who killed Zeke."

"Meddling old fool," Boo mumbled. "Well, now that you're here you might as well come on in and sit a spell." Boo opened the door wide and gave Sid the onceover as she passed through the doorway. The room's furnishings were simple. Ancestral photos sat on table tops and a sideboard, while the wall held faded pictures of pirate ships—schooners of various models. Sid headed to a straight-backed chair and sat.

"One thing I can tell you for sure," Boo said to Sid, stationing her own chair as far away from Durwood as possible and still be in the same room with him. "I ain't killed Zeke. I didn't like him none, but so what? I only know two people in the whole world that did like him, and that was his mama and God. Course they ain't got much choice." Boo chuckled at her own joke, and then the laughter turned to tears. She covered her face with her hands and her shoulders shook.

Sid felt like a giant tsunami sucked her toward Boo. "Excuse me, ma'am, but Durwood said you'd seen a ship out in the swamp. Are you up to talking about it?"

The veil of misery that had filled the old woman's eyes dropped away. In its place, diamond beams of delight glistened out, transforming her from a tired, grief-stricken old woman into a young girl sparked with the excitement offered by a pirate ship. Her voice bubbled over like that of a small child.

"I never seen nothing the likes of before in my life. It was big, big I tell you, and I just knew it had treasure down in the captain's cabin, but I never got down that far. When this dang soda water bottle rolled across the deck, I just about messed my pants." She pointed a finger at Durwood. "And if you laugh, I'm gonna kick your ass outta my house."

"I ain't laughing," he said, obviously suppressing a snicker.

"Weren't nobody else out there to see it, so I finally gave up and come home, but I was so excited about it I couldn't wait to tell Sasha. When I docked, I spied Zeke out in his garden hoeing them shriveled-up cucumbers. 'Morning, Zeke, where's Sasha?' I says, right nice like. Well, he clams up and won't say nothing. He just takes off his straw hat and fans his face, looks over at me with them glaring eyes, and then turns back to his hoeing.

"'Zeke,' I says to him, 'you make me so dang mad, I could…'" Boo grew silent, staring at her hands.

"What did you do then?" Sid scooted forward in her chair.

"Well, I raised my gun, pulled back the hammer, and fired."

Two

"You shot him?" Sid looked from Boo to Durwood.

"Don't pay her no never mind, Sid, she exaggerates." He shook his finger at Boo, "Dang it, woman, be serious."

"I ain't making it up. I did shoot, just not to hit him. The bullet went right over his head, just like I intended. Heck, if I'd a wanted to kill the bastard, I dang sure could've. Well, Sasha heard the shot and came running out of her house wiping her hands on her apron yelling I killed her husband. 'He ain't hurt,' I says. 'I just parted his dang hair.' Then Sasha smarted off something about me scaring the dang chickens outta laying."

"And?" Sid asked, now hooked by the old woman's countrified ways.

"I told her about this pirate ship sticking up out of the water, that I knowed it must be Jean Lafitte's. But she couldn't go out with me that day, said she had a doctor's appointment that afternoon, could we go tomorrow. Eager as I was, I figured it'd still be there the next day."

Sid straightened her back and waited while Boo stopped to catch her breath.

"Late that afternoon, while Sasha was still gone to the doctor's office—and knowing her, probably by the mall to buy pretties—I seen Zeke get in his boat and head off into the swamp, but I never seen him come back. If he did, I figure it must've been during Wheel of Fortune. I never miss that show.

"Anyway, me and Sasha and my Brownie box camera headed

out the next morning at daybreak. We hadn't found the ship yet, but then, when we seen Zeke..." Boo closed her eyes and shuddered. "Next thing I know, Sasha's gone into hysterics. I liked to've never got her calmed down enough so's I could get us back to shore."

Boo's *figure* lacked a U in the pronunciation, and her *here,* as if it were spelled close to *heaunh,* with some kind of nasal-guttural thing used on the last part of the word. Sid doubted she'd ever be able to duplicate the woman's manner of speech—and saw no reason to try. But how anyone could think this woman might have committed murder was beyond Sid. "So who called Sheriff Burns?" she asked.

"I reckon the ambulance people did. I called them to take care of Sasha. I just knew she was having a coronary. The sheriff and the ambulance people got there about the same time. Sasha started yelling about me going out there the evening before and killing him 'cause I didn't want him to see my pirate ship. I kept telling the sheriff I didn't, but after I took him out to the site, and they found Zeke with my shirt around his neck, they commenced to thinking maybe Sasha was right. She even told them I tried to kill him the morning before."

"And we both know if you'd have wanted to kill him, you would have." Sid smiled sweetly, her hands folded in her lap.

A quick grin sliced across Boo's face. "Durwood, I take it back. This here's a smart woman!"

"Course she is. That's her name!" Durwood slapped his thigh with glee.

"Okay, so let me recap. You went out in the swamp, saw an old ship, came back, and shot over Zeke's head. That evening you saw him take his boat out. But surely you suspected he went to find the schooner, yet you didn't follow him. Why is that?"

Boo shook her head. "Nah, even if he did go look for it, I knew he wouldn't find it. If you locked that man in a closet, he couldn't find his ass with both hands."

Durwood and Sid both laughed at that comment, and Boo

didn't seem to mind, for she laughed with them.

"It's true, I never seen anything like it. I never seen him come in that night, but I know when Sasha got home. Her headlights shined in my living room while I was watching Boston Legal. I love that show, don't you?"

Sid nodded. "Especially James Spader."

"Not me, I like William Shatner. I love it when he says, *Denny Crane*. One of these nights, you come over, Ms. Smart, and you and me will watch it together, then we'll sit out here on my front porch and smoke us a cigar and drink us a glass of Scotch. You like Scotch, huh?"

"Sounds like fun to me." Sid didn't tell Boo she'd never tasted Scotch, nor smoked a cigarette, much less a cigar. But hey, her life had begun anew, so…

"Go on," she said, encouraging Boo.

"Anyway, I never did see Zeke again. The next morning when Sasha got to my place, she said she left Zeke still asleep in his bedroom—they got separate rooms 'cause of Zeke's snoring—said when she got home, he'd already taken to his bed, or that's what she thought, so she just let him sleep. He always got mad at her if she ever woke him up, or even went in his room, so she took to letting sleeping dogs lie, if you get my drift."

"So you didn't go back out until you and Sasha went the next morning?"

Boo nodded, her head propped in her hands again, elbows on her knees.

"Who else knew about the ship?"

"I never told no one but Sasha and her donkey-poke husband."

"Do you have a lawyer, Ms. Murphy?" It sounded to Sid like Boo would soon need one.

Boo swiped her nose on her sleeve and shook her head. "I'm poor, Miss Sid. All I got coming in is my little Social Security check once a month. Where in the world am I going to get enough money to pay for a lawyer?"

"I called my lawyer, Marv Bledsoe," Durwood volunteered.

"What did he say?" Sid assumed if Boo couldn't afford a lawyer, there was little likelihood she could afford a private investigator.

"He checked on it and called us back. Said he don't think the sheriff's got a case—even though, 'cording to the sheriff, they have proof the shirt was Boo's, and plus—"

"Course the shirt was mine, I dang told him it was, but that don't mean I killed him. Lot a good that'll do since I ain't got money to prove it. I might's well go ahead and plead guilty and get it—"

"Plus, now they're saying she made up the whole thing about seeing the *Hot Spur*." Durwood finished.

"The Hot Spur? Is that the name of the schooner?" Sid's education grew by the minute.

"I swear it was one of Lafitte's ships. I studied them for years, I know my pirate ships." The octave of Boo's voice elevated almost to the sound of panic.

"Ma'am, you okay?" Sid reached over and placed her hands on Boo's.

"Yeah, I'm okay. I'm just tired talking about all this."

Sid stood. "Durwood, I think we need to let Boo rest a while. I truly doubt anything's going to come of this. I don't think they're going to arrest her for Zeke's death based on a shirt. A murder conviction requires a lot more evidence than what it seems they've found."

When Durwood didn't move, she looked over to see that he looked almost as pathetic as Boo, sitting with his head bowed, staring at his shoes. He'd barely said two words throughout the whole conversation.

He caught Sid looking at him. "So what do you think?"

"Well, if she goes in and pleads guilty like she says—that's not good."

"Guilty? She ain't done it, Sid. I tell you she ain't killed nobody."

"But if she pleads guilty there's not much… Well, maybe you can get Marv to help her. He'll know what to do."

Durwood leapt to his feet, challenging her. "Now Sid, you know I like Marv, but remember, he ain't no criminal investigator."

"That's true. But right now, Durwood, Boo needs to rest. Come on. Take me back to my house. We can talk more about this on the way. Boo, you take care. Everything will work out okay. You'll see." She got Boo a glass of ice water, helped put her feet up, and then took Durwood's arm and led him to the front door.

Down in the mouth over his friend's plight, Durwood said little on the ride back to Sid's office. She knew he was upset that she had not readily taken on Boo's case, but the woman was as poor as a mouse kicked out of church, plus, it wasn't a case yet. No one had arrested Boo.

Besides, if he could see Sid's stack of bills, he'd understand. But even his truck didn't seem to buy her argument, sputtering even heavier as they chugged down the road.

Durwood tapped the dashboard. "This thing says I'm 'bout empty. It ain't right one time outta ten, but I better not take a chance." He swung into a Diamond Shamrock station and slammed on the brakes. "It won't take me but a minute."

"Hmm," Sid responded, anxious to get home, but in no mood to walk there.

He yanked on the door, pushed it open with his shoulder, and leaving it to swing on its hinges, limped inside to pay in advance.

Sid stared out the passenger window while she waited.

"What the hell's going on, Sid?" Her brother's voice echoed inside her head—her dead brother's voice.

"I wish I knew, Warren, I sure wish I knew."

Three

Nathalee Sweeney's breath came in quick, short puffs as her feet pounded the unpaved road alongside Sabine Lake. She loved to run, her long blond ponytail swishing across her bare shoulders, the wind tickling her face. The early morning sun filtered through the treetops, making a lacy pattern of sunlight and shadow dance on the roadbed in front of her. It reminded her of her own speckled life, and that of her family's, and the sense of control she'd gained from jogging. Just the simple act of movement, of abandoning herself to the exertion, of pushing through the pain, had taught her that life didn't have to be one of constant vigilance, fearful the law watched their activities, or that the cartel might get their hands on the family business.

Funny how the simple act of discipline had freed her of the demons she carried inside, and of the expectations she forced upon herself simply because of her bloodline.

How this simple activity had brought her to the biggest decision of her life. She hoped she'd survive it, but if not…

She didn't see the men crouched in the bushes until they leapt out at her.

The smell of stale hay and sweat roused Nathalee from a stupor to the pressure of something big and heavy ramming itself between her legs. By an act of pure will, she forced her eyes open and realized she lay nude, in some kind of stall, her hands tied over her head, and her feet tied spread-eagle. A heavy-set man lay on top of her, pounding away, yet she felt nothing long and hard forced inside her. How long he'd been at it, she hadn't a clue, but the profuse sweat dripping off his face and into hers hinted he'd long passed his ability to maintain an erection.

She fought hard against the looming black hole threatening her again, a hole so deep nothing survived. But the over-powering specter crept behind her eyelids and sucked her inside again.

Four

Boo's situation played out in Sid's head half the night. The woman didn't have a cent to her name, yet Sid felt strangely pulled into the story. Even Slider got concerned when she gave up on sleep, got out of bed and paced the floor. When she crawled back in between the sheets an hour later, he climbed in beside her and propped his head on her belly and kept it there until the alarm went off at six.

Throughout breakfast Annie barely spoke a word, and she stayed out of the office all morning long. Sid wasn't sure which was worse, Annie in the office bugging the hell out of her, or Annie *not in the office* but still managing to bug the hell out of her.

The morning passed quickly as Sid closed up loose ends on the case with the pot-bellied, bald-headed, belching—but wealthy—husband certain his twenty-something sex kitten wife cheated on him with some young stud. As it turned out he'd been correct, but Sid discovered the young man had more money than did her client. Now the case headed to divorce court. Sid predicted Mrs. Sex Kitten would end up richer than both men put together.

She headed over to the file cabinet, tucked the folder away and gave the drawer a shove with her hip just as her office door opened and George Léger stuck his head around the side.

"Got a minute, Sid?"

"George, come in," she said, her invitation matching the warmth she felt every time she saw the guy.

From the first time she walked into his PI office and he'd

agreed to sponsor her until she got her license, she'd fallen in love with his easy ways and the big belly that hung over his belt. It seemed he carried his Cajun accent in his pocket and pulled it out whenever he wanted. Sid never had figured out what triggered his mood for using it. One thing for certain, she might not be able to trust some folks, but she could him. She'd stake her life on that.

"Hey, Sha, nice quarters you got here." George peppered his conversation with the affectionate Sha, the Cajun-shortened version of the French cherié.

"That's right, you haven't been here since the relocation have you?"

"Been meaning to come by, but you know how full the days get." He pulled a chair over and sat in front of the desk. The seating arrangement felt weird, for Sid had always sat on the guest-side of George's desk, not this way.

"I heard you got your license. Guess you won't need me now that you know what you're doing."

On that, a guttural laugh spewed out of Sid's mouth. "Well, looking like, quacking like, and smelling like a duck doesn't convince the duck she is one. How'd you hear so soon? I just got the letter."

"Association newsletter. It lists the names of those who passed the test, sometimes they get those out before they do the test grades. Got your ID card and all?"

"Yep," she held it up to him.

"Well, little lady, with your record of solved cases—difficult ones, I might add—you've done gone and made a name for yourself in this town. You'll do fine on your own. I'll just miss bossing you around, though," he said, chortling. "So does this mean you're going to rebuild the burned out office across the street from the courthouse?"

"That's exactly what it means. I got a notice from the city that says having it here goes against the zoning code. Within fifteen days, I've got to show serious intent to relocate. Lucky for me, the insurance money came at the same time. That should cover a big part of the rebuilding cost." Sid crossed her fingers at George. "With just a couple of paying clients a month, I think I can swing it."

"Well, this is your lucky day, Sha. Hope it stays that way." George glanced around the office. "Now that you got your license, don't think you can't stay in touch with me."

She sensed something preyed on his mind, but instead of saying what it was, he just fidgeted in his chair. She'd never known him to fidget.

"So, George, what brings you here? Run out of whiskey for your coffee? If so, you're out of luck. I'm fresh out."

"No, no, just thought it was time I came by to check on you—to pay you a neighborly visit." He hesitated, as if unsure where to go from there, which certainly wasn't like him either. When a light bulb seemed to go off in his head, he said, "It's Martha. She's bugging me to get you and Ben over for supper tonight. She's making her secret recipe Cajun Crawfish Pie." He patted his stomach.

"Sounds delicious, and how could I refuse an offer like that? If you have a minute, I'll call Ben and see."

"Sure, go ahead. Then I've got something I need to tell you."

After a quick call to Ben, they agreed on dinner, or supper, as the locals called it, at George and Martha's that evening around six.

"Good, I completed my wife-given assignment, now…" He crossed his legs and folded his arms over his chest. "I read about your license right before I planned to come over and tell you I couldn't supervise you anymore."

"Oh, really?" Sid fell back in her chair. That wasn't like George either.

"Yeah, something's come up that I expect will take a lot of my time over the next few months. I didn't think I could do you justice."

"Okay. It sounds mighty serious. Anything I can help you with?" Her gut told her this topic, and not the dinner invitation, was the real reason for the visit.

He pulled out a big pearl-handled pocketknife and proceeded to clean his fingernails. The blade made a slight click on each exit. "Nah, but thanks. I can't really talk about it."

"Okay," she said again, feeling like a parrot at a loss for words. She'd never known any topic the two of them couldn't discuss. Something about what George said, and how he said it, just didn't gel. But he'd invited them to his house for dinner—or supper—so maybe it was all her imagination.

"Well, I gotta go see a dog about a man, but if you get in a real tight, call me." He closed the knife and put it back into his pocket and stepped out onto the porch, calling over his shoulder. "We'll see you and Ben tonight."

He'd been gone a few minutes when Sid realized she hadn't asked if they could bring something to contribute to the meal. She pulled up his home number on her speed dial and called. Martha answered. "Hi, Martha, this is Sid. George just stopped by. Thanks for inviting us over for supper tonight. I forgot to ask him if we could bring anything."

"Hi, Sid. Excuse me, but George said what?"

"Sorry Martha, I guess I called before he had a chance to let you know we accepted the dinner invitation for crawfish pie at your house tonight."

"Dinner?" Martha sounded clueless.

"Oh, I mean supper."

"Supper? Tonight? Oh yeah, Sid, we'd love to have you over. I'll run down to Market Basket and get the makings. What time did he say?"

"Six, but are you sure? Sounds like…"

"Oh, yes, I'm sure. It'll be fine. I'll just put up this quilting. You guys come on. We'd love to see you."

Sid said goodbye, disconnected the call, and then sat and stared off into space, wondering what the hell was going on.

Relieved when the clock finally flashed twelve, Sid headed to the kitchen for lunch and found that Annie had made them both a tuna salad sandwich. She now sat at the head of the table staring at her plate, hands in her lap, waiting. Sid sat on Annie's right and attempted to make light conversation while they ate. "I found this new pickle recipe the other day. You'd probably like them because they look spicy. What do you think? Should I make us a few jars?"

Annie answered with grunts and nods, chewing her food in tight, hard bites.

After the tense lunch that seemed to last forever, Sid carried her dishes to the sink and opened the dishwasher. Slider roused and followed along behind.

"Don't you worry about those dishes, Siddie," Annie admonished in her best, high-pitched voice, shoving her chair away from the table. She bustled over to the sink, straightening a bright orange top over her belly. "I've got all afternoon to do these dishes. I know you've got more important things to do if you're going to find enough customers to pay for that new building." She snatched the plate out of Sid's hands and scraped the crumbs into the disposal. Her back looked like someone had rammed a rod down it.

"Annie, I've—"

"Never mind about me, you two just get." She motioned a scoot at Sid and Slider. "I've got things to do now that I don't have a stakeout to work on and probably never will again. Besides, I've got an appointment with a woman at Jerry Hughes Realty. I'm putting the farm in Buna up for sale. You never can tell, I might just ask them, if I get my realtors license can I go to work for them."

Drama Queen, Drama Queen, Drama Queen. Without another word, Sid spun on her heels and headed back to her office. Behind her, Slider scratched and slid across the laminate wood flooring, caught up and passed her, eager to escape the control freak in the kitchen.

She snickered. "In a hurry, eh, bud?" She glanced through the lace-covered windows on her right, carrying hope that a customer stood outside, then sighed when all she saw was an empty sidewalk.

When she stepped into her office, she couldn't help feeling that the harsh mid-day sun streaming through the window behind her desk looked more inviting than had the cool kitchen with its green ferns hanging in the bay window and the cold shoulder at the sink.

Sid had no idea Annie considered selling the farm out in Buna. She and Uncle Frank had bought the hundred-acres fifty years ago and he had worked it ever since, up until his death a few months ago. After that, Annie hired a neighbor to feed and water the chickens and the pigs, and sold the mare at an auction, but perhaps the place still created a burden—or held too many painful memories. Poor thing, Sid shouldn't be so sensitive to Annie's comments. What would she have done without Annie's help? Annie had even bought this house and moved to town to help Sid out when she needed help the most. She made a quick resolve to be more patient with Annie.

The afternoon kept her busy with a couple of phone calls from other investigators congratulating her on passing the board exam, and another from a local mystery writers' group looking for a program speaker. She'd spoken to enough church groups that a public presentation didn't bother her, but a room full of mystery authors sure did. She'd agreed anyway, and they booked a date. After that, she closed her office a little early and headed into the cold kitchen.

"Hey, sweetheart," she said to Annie, who sat at the table perusing recipes. "Remember, I'm going out with Ben tonight."

"George and Martha's, so you said."

"Okay. I'm heading upstairs to dress."

Annie gave no response.

Sid walked out. "Be that way then," she said under her breath.

An hour later, she'd showered and dressed and was on her

way downstairs when the doorbell rang. She opened it to Ben, dressed in a dark-chocolate shirt unbuttoned at the neck, and tan Dockers. She loved his promptness—that and how he smelled when he leaned over and planted a soft kiss on her lips. She responded in kind.

"Sid, you drive a man wild," he said, smiling, undeniable longing on his face. He cupped her chin in his hand. "It's been a long time. When you coming for a sleepover?"

"Actually, it hasn't been that long—when was it? Oh yes, just last week."

"A week's a long time for a horny guy, you know."

"She reached behind him and patted him on the butt. "Get over it, bud!" She laughed and headed into the living room, Ben in tow.

Together, they sat on the sofa, thighs touching, hands clasped. Ben fingered the engagement ring on Sid's finger—the ring she'd put on when she'd dressed for the evening. "Haven't heard much from you in the last couple of days. You been busy?"

"A little bit," Sid admitted, knowing he preferred her corralling kids in a classroom rather than working as a private detective. These days, she wondered which of the two jobs carried the least danger.

Annie walked in and flashed Ben a saccharin smile. "Hey, Ben. When you going to make an honorable woman out of Sid? I keep asking her if she's set a date yet, but she won't tell me nothing."

Ben stood and hugged Annie. "She doesn't tell me anything either, Annie, and truth be known, I think she's happier without honor—if honor requires the M word."

Sid shifted the conversation away from her to the weather, always a safer topic. "Think it's going to rain?"

"She's trying to change the subject, Annie. What should I do with her?" Ben clucked his tongue.

"If you find out, would you let me know? Now she's talking about building her office back over there where it was before it burned."

He looked at Sid, puzzlement in his eyes. "Across from the courthouse? Really?"

"I received a letter from the city zoning board. It seems having it here puts me outside some zoning code."

Annie's eyes sparkled with anticipation of her next bombshell waiting to be dropped on Ben—news of Sid's state license.

Sid beat her to it. "I also received word that I passed my state board exam."

"Congratulations! Then I guess this evening is your celebratory dinner, huh?"

"I wasn't sure you'd be happy to hear that, since you don't want me in the business."

"No, no, I'm happy for you." He frowned and looked at his watch. "We better get on the way or we'll be late for dinner."

Soon as they were in the car, Ben pushed a CD in the player and turned up the volume on Neil Diamond. Neither of them said a word the whole way, but when she noticed his white knuckles clasping the steering wheel, her heels dug into the floor. Passing the exam and rebuilding the office left no doubt of her intentions.

Ben said little on the drive over to George and Martha's, not that he didn't want to tell Sid how he felt, but he just couldn't find the words to explain it. God he loved her, couldn't imagine life without her in it, but he had to be so careful not to scare her away. He'd almost done that before. He had to accept her as a private investigator. She loved it, although he wasn't sure she even knew that herself yet. Her wounds went deep, lack of self esteem, lack of even an identity of who she was. Lord if she only knew. He admired her strength of character, her compassion for those in need, and willingness to jump in feet first, the way she viewed the world and everyone in it.

Who would have thought that religious wounds would go so deep? He'd never before thought about the importance of loving someone just as they are, instead of that love being used as a tool—weapon—to *get them into heaven.*

He did love her for who she was, and that included being a private eye if she damn well wanted to be. Whatever fear he held in his gut, he'd just have to accept, and not pass that fear on as control, trying to put her on a pillow in a basket he could carry around. She definitely wasn't a trophy wife. She may have been the preacher's trophy, building him up by staying down herself. "That's sick," he whispered out loud, causing her to stir. He held his breath fearing he'd awakened her. Right now all he wanted to do was breathe her in. He knew now he couldn't ever tell her of the fear he carried for her in that job. How every time he saw her climb a wall, he climbed it, too.

When they walked into George and Martha's, the aroma of Cajun spices, tangy seafood, and hot pastry filled the small living room that already overflowed with a country-style décor. Several dolls dressed in white frilly lace sat around on tiny sofas and inside glass cases. Family photographs adorned the walls. Throw pillows and afghans piled on the furniture. The result was a room that offered comfort and crowded friendliness.

"Martha will be here directly," George said, scooting aside a pillow so Sid could sit on the red plaid sofa. "She's chopping salad at the moment."

"Maybe I can help her," Sid offered, shaking off an old memory of Sam shaming her when, in his opinion, she hadn't jumped up as quickly as he thought she should to help a church member preparing Sunday dinner. In those days, with a full-term baby in her belly, she didn't do anything fast, except maybe head to the bathroom.

George waved her off. "Nah, she's almost done. Said to keep you company and she'd be here directly."

No sooner had he spoken than Martha entered from the back of the house and through the dining room where a large table, set with white square plates and a vase of fresh-cut, multi-colored zinnias, awaited them.

"Sid, nice to see you again, honey." Martha stood on tiptoe, kissed Sid on the cheek and hugged her tightly. "And I hear congratulations are in order. George says you passed your state board exam. That's fantastic!"

Even though she sensed Ben stiffen behind her, at least Sid had broken the news to him, and not Martha.

Martha slipped off her apron, patted her dark hair, and invited them to sit at the table. "Crawfish pie is hot and ready. Hope you two are hungry. George, why don't you pour the wine while I get the pie?"

Ben held Sid's chair, calling out to Martha in the kitchen, "If we weren't hungry before, we sure are now. Something smells mighty good."

Martha bustled back into the room with a steaming deep-dish pie plate with a rich, golden brown top crust. "So, Sid, George also said now that you have your license, you'll be rebuilding the Third Eye. I'm thrilled for you, and I know your late brother, Warren, would be ecstatic. He sure loved the Third Eye, and it seems he made the right decision when he left the business to you." Martha filled Sid's plate with a big slice of the pie.

"Yes, I am. As a matter of fact I received my insurance check this morning."

After raves over the food, and appetite satiation, Sid, Martha and Ben chatted from one topic to another. Sid brought them up to date on her children, Chrissy and Chad, both grown and out on their own. Martha confessed her attempts to make George take early retirement. Ben bragged about his daughter's big promotion and her moving from Dallas to Fort Worth, while George kept excusing himself and talking to someone on the phone most of the evening. Sid apologized again for the short notice of guests for supper.

"Don't worry about it, honey. That's not like George, but he hadn't been himself lately anyway. Not sure what's going on. But if anyone owes me an apology, it's George. Besides, it's great to see you two again."

Enjoying the conversation, mouth-watering food, and wine,

Sid stalled a trip to the little girl's room as long as she dared. "Martha, I'm afraid I need to use your powder room if you don't mind," she said, scooting her chair back.

"Sure, honey, you know where it is. Help yourself. You may need to turn on the hall light. If you do, the switch is there on your left. Ben and I will entertain each other while you're gone. It looks like George is going to be on the phone all night." Irritation at her husband's rudeness crept into her voice.

Sid headed through the living room and stopped when she reached the darkened hallway. Running her hand over the wall, she rummaged around for the light switch, not realizing George stood in the bedroom across the hall from her until she heard him whispering to someone. It startled her, for she'd never heard a whisper out of the loud-mouthed Cajun.

Where was the dang light switch? Should she clear her throat, say something?

"No, the name's not Leger, it's Léger, like Layjay. Okay, I'll be there tomorrow at two. Yeah, I know the place. Simmons Drive, pink building on the left. Be sure my money is in twenties or smaller, or I'm done."

The click of a closed cell phone occurred half a second after she found the light switch and George stepped out into the glare. When he saw her, he jerked back as if hoping for an instant replay with an altered outcome. His facial expression reminded her of her son, Chad, caught with his hand in the proverbial cookie jar. "Shit!" he said under his breath, then "Sid, I-I didn't see you there," he said, stuttering.

"The bathroom—I'm headed to the bathroom," she mumbled, pointing, wondering if she should claim she hadn't overheard his conversation.

After bustling inside, she closed the door and leaned against it until she heard George walk off, and after her racing heart settled down.

What the hell was that? Whatever it was, he didn't want her, or anyone else in the house, to hear him—that was obvious.

Five

A woman with a huge stack of coal-black hair stuck her head around Sid's office door. "Ms. Smart?"

"Yes, come in," Sid said, startled. It was nearly nine o'clock, and she'd been at her desk since seven-thirty, going over her notes about a child custody case. She'd been so wrapped up in it she hadn't heard the door open.

"Good morning. My name is Myra Black. I'm a friend of Mr. Durwood's. I was talking to him about something, and he said I should come see you."

"Have a seat." Sid indicated a chair. "Yes, Mr. Durwood is a fine man."

By the time Myra walked across to a chair and Sid got a better view of how the woman sat, dressed, and smelled—drowning in cheap perfume—she remembered Boo's comment about his friend, Myra. A 'professional' woman, Boo indicated, working outside the law. A hooker. Sid had never been this close to one—not that she knew of, at least. "How can I help you?" she asked.

"Oh, I'm not looking for a private investigator," Myra said, waving her hand. "This is more personal. It may be nothing, or all in my imagination, but… there's this—this guy. A—a client, you might say. He calls himself Rodriguez—that's all I know. I think he's Mexican—I mean, Mexican Mexican—like from Mexico. He's bad."

"Has he hurt you, Myra?" Sid leaned forward and stretched

her hand across the desk, wishing to comfort the distressed-looking woman.

"Look at this and then ask me that." Myra opened her mouth to reveal several missing teeth.

"He knocked your teeth out?"

"His kind always does."

"Then you don't need me, you need to go to the police."

"Now how am I going to do something like that?" Myra smirked.

"Oh, that's right. I guess that isn't much of an option for you." Sid laughed, nervous as all get out.

"Anyway, that's the downside of the profession, but that's not why I came to see you. This Rodriguez is bad news. Drugs, maybe gun running, some type of smuggling or… I don't know, maybe he's a terrorist. Lord, I hope not. The other day after he finished with me and went into the bathroom, his cell phone started ringing. It was on the bed next to me, and I couldn't help but see the caller ID." Myra paused, staring at her fingers twisting in her lap.

"Why are you telling me about Rodriguez, Myra?"

"It's not about Rodriguez. Durwood said you were a decent person and you should know that someone you know is doing business with him."

"Someone I know? Who?"

"That Léger guy—you know, the other PI in town?"

"That's impossible he wouldn't…" She couldn't finish the sentence. What reason might George have for calling Rodriguez? "You know where he hangs out?" Sid squirmed in her chair. She had her license now, but good god, she wasn't ready to spy on her former supervisor.

"The Pink Slipper, out on Simmons Drive."

Simmons Drive, pink building on the left. Sid fiddled with her car keys on her desk, "You work out of there?"

"Most of the time. On slow nights, I'll go check out other places."

"Do you ever go there in the afternoons?"

"Sure, all the time. Most people think we just work nights, but we work anytime we can get the business."

Sid looked at the clock. "How about at two this afternoon? Can you get there by then?"

Myra had crossed her legs when she sat. Now, the top leg started kicking the air. "You mean, at the Pink Slipper? To spy?"

"That's exactly what I mean. Just go be there, watch and see who comes in and what they say or do. Then call me. Can you do that?"

"Sure. I have a few more teeth left." She sneered.

Sid pulled a couple of bills out of her wallet and handed them to Myra. In one smooth, practiced motion, she took them from Sid and tucked them in her bra.

Myra stayed another fifteen minutes. After she left, Sid sat perfectly still in her chair for half an hour, unable to move and unable to believe what she'd heard.

George Léger squinted into the sun as he stepped out the door of his private eye office, a bright yellow prefab building on Sixteenth Street. Fronds from the palm trees on each side of the parking lot rustled in the warm breeze. For a second, he recalled the carefree days of childhood summers and wished he were a child again. Anything was better than what he had gotten himself into. He looked at his watch. He had fifteen minutes to get to his appointment.

He rammed his hand down into the pocket of his blue jeans, found the keys and clicked the remote as he headed to his black Dodge Ram truck. Inside the hot cab, he sat deep in thought, oblivious to the perspiration wetting the front of his green plaid shirt. Then, he shook his head and started the motor.

Turning left at Green Avenue, he cruised past the small quaint building that housed the Chamber of Commerce. Painted along the side of the building, an art deco style mural of miniature orange trees bloomed. His fingers drummed a nervous rhythm on the steering wheel. Sneakiness crawled up his backbone and over his shoulders, causing him to run his hand over his forehead and down the back of his balding pate. Why had he let himself get involved in this in the first place?

After turning onto Simmons Drive and going north for a mile or so, he spied the dingy building on the left. Mildew grew rampant on the pink stucco walls as if power washers didn't exist. In actuality, no one cared.

Signaling a turn, he flipped down the visor to block the sun's reflection off the windshield of an oncoming car, but when he glanced at himself in the visor mirror, the eyes of a stranger stared back at him. He'd never seen that look in his eyes before. It scared the hell out of him. He wondered how far he'd go with this. Promises of wealth always tempted a man his age with a wife ready for him to retire and a bank account that said he needed to work for the next sixty years.

At this time of day there wasn't another car in the front parking lot. The rear end of a dark green Hummer peeked around the corner at the back of the building. Rodriguez's, he assumed. He headed toward it, wishing the tires didn't crunch so damn loudly across the shell driveway.

Reaching into the center console for one last swig of coffee laced with Black Jack, he switched off the engine and hopped out, pausing long enough to take a deep breath, refasten a couple of buttons over his belly, and tuck in his shirttail. Then, out of delaying tactics, he ducked his head and headed to the back door.

Inside the darkened bar-cum-brothel, he glanced at the empty tables scattered throughout the room, picturing what happened in here after dark. He hadn't been in a bar since his best friend Warren Chadwick died. It just wasn't the same anymore. He loved Warren's sister, Sid, but he couldn't have the same relationship with her as he had with Warren. And now, even his relationship with Sid would change.

The air in the room smelled of stale whiskey and women. A lone woman stood at the bar. She turned and smiled at him as he walked in. Her hair was dyed a jet black and her makeup looked like she'd applied it with a pallet knife. She wore a red, cheap-looking dress with a low cut top and a high cut bottom, black mesh hose and spike heels. He knew she wasn't an undercover cop—they had all their teeth. This woman's mouth had gaps where several of her teeth should have been.

He didn't spot his contact until the dark-complexioned man in the back booth struck a match and lit a cigarette. Light from the flames distorted his face, but George recognized him. George sauntered over and slid into the booth across from the man. "Sorry I'm late."

"No one followed you, did they?" Rodriguez spoke with the voice of a heavy smoker.

"You take me for a dunce?"

"Just asking. We can't be too careful. Your Homeland Security would love to get their hands on us. Hell, these days, even my own government would."

"Well, it's obvious she's not one of them." George indicated the prostitute at the bar chatting up the bartender.

"Nah, that's just Myra. She's not good, but she's cheap, and she knows how to keep her mouth shut. Come on over here, baby," he called out, motioning Myra over. "Get me a beer and keep the change." He tented a twenty dollar bill over his index finger and held it out to her. She took it, tucked it in her bra and sauntered to the bar.

"Did you get the arrangements made?"

Rodriguez nodded. "My men are prepared. Soon as we get word that our next ship is set to dock, we'll put the plan into operation. We'd rather not have to hide the crystal collection until we're ready to transport it. We hit, grab, and before the curator even knows the collection is missing, we have it on its way to an eager customer, who, by the way, doesn't want half a collection. It is all or nothing."

"We'll get in, I'll make sure of that."

"Tell me again how you plan to do that?"

"To what, make sure?" George raised his eyebrows for effect. He fiddled with his car keys, hoping it made him look unconcerned.

"Yeah, how do you plan on getting us into the Stark Museum undetected?"

"I'm personal friends with the museum's head of security. I've offered him a percentage of my take if we can get your guys in long enough to short circuit the cameras. That's where your experts take over." Fingers of guilt pecked around the edges of George's conscience, but he shoved the guilt aside. No time for second guesses.

Rodriguez shoved a brown envelope across the table. "We'll hold up our end of the bargain, don't you worry about that."

George opened the envelope and looked inside, made a couple of mental calculations, and stuck the package in his pocket, glancing over at Myra, crossing the room, as he did so.

Myra slapped the beer on the table and made to leave, but Rodriguez pulled her down and buried his face in her cleavage, groaned, and came up for air. "Sweet!" he said, then turned back to George. "We've got another little job we're working on as well. If it pans out like I think, we may can use you."

"With what?" George asked, curious to know more.

"Coast Guard holds a tighter coastline than it did seven years ago. Some of the locals were having trouble getting through, so we've taken to using Adams Bayou to get our goods out. The other day, one of my men saw what looked like a pirate schooner sitting up out of the water in the middle of the swamp. If it's what we think it is, it could well contain a document our customer has wanted for decades. He's willing to pay more than you earn in a lifetime, plus a couple of zeros."

George waved off the idea with his hand. "I wouldn't put much stock in a schooner story."

"Why?"

"They're legend, pure and simple. When you've live in this area all your life, you learn not to pay any attention to them. The only ones who get excited anymore are kids who've watched one too many pirate movies, and folks hoping to get rich quick. Old-timers like me? We're old enough and ugly enough to know that ain't gonna happen."

"Well, it might, if you do what you say you can." The man waved his hand in dismissal. "I better stop there. May not be anything—may be something. We're checking it out. Keep your cell phone with you."

"I always do." George stood, tipped his fingertips to his forehead at Myra and headed out the way he'd come.

Just as he opened the door to the Dodge Ram, the wave that had been building in his gut chose that moment to erupt. He leaned over and emptied the contents of his stomach on the ground until only dry heaves remained.

Then, spent, he climbed into the cab, hoping to hold his stomach in check at least until he reached his office. As he rounded the ugly pink building on the right, he saw Myra standing under a shade tree talking on her cell phone. She smiled and waved at him as he drove past.

Sid sat at her desk and watched the clock tick off another minute. Two-twenty-seven. She hadn't moved a voluntary muscle for the last half hour or so. Slider waited with her, his eye on the phone as if he, too, waited for it to ring. When it did, they both jumped. She snatched at it, eager to hear her suspicions were wrong.

Without preamble, she asked into the receiver, "He just leave?" Her voice cracked with tension. "Okay, yeah, who was the man? Did you get a name?" She cleared her throat, writing as the voice on the other line continued. "So it was Rodriguez. And what did they say?" More scribbling. "Did this Rodriguez fellow give him anything, like a package or an envelope? I see. Okay, what else?"

She paused, listening, making a couple more notes. After she'd finished, she tossed the pen on the desk in disgust. "Thank you, Myra. Yes, if I need you again, I know where you live."

The phone back on the base, she banged her fist on the desk. "Dammit, George, what are you involved in? Is it a case, or are you on the take?"

The thought of the second option made her sick.

Six

The next morning, Sid roused from sleep to the sound of rain pounding on the roof. The dark clouds outside made her snuggle back down into the covers, telling herself no one would be out wanting to hire a detective in this weather anyway.

A whine near the edge of the bed forced her eyes open again. Slider's nose almost touched hers, his body squirming. She threw back the covers and swung her feet off the bed. "So, all this rain reminds you of your full bladder, huh? Well, me too. Hold it until I empty mine and we'll head downstairs."

Standing on the back porch, Sid waited while Slider found a spot protected from the downpour and did his business. She wrapped her arms around herself to keep off the chilly wetness and recalled the conversation with Myra, and the similarity between the schooner Boo Murphy had seen out in the swamp and the one Rodriguez mentioned to George. "Well, there certainly couldn't be two of them that resurrected simultaneously, Slider," she said as he finished his business and she headed upstairs to shower and dress.

After she finished her morning ablutions, she and Slider headed to the office, leaving Annie and King Cat to fight over territorial rights to the rest of the house. The first thing she did was flip on the lights, power up the computer and cross the room to unlock the outside entrance. But as soon as she shoved back the deadbolt, someone splashed up on the porch as if they watched until the office lights came on before making a mad dash through the rain.

With a blast, George blew inside, rain dripping off the edges of his umbrella.

Slider jumped to his feet, hackles raised, and a growl in his throat.

"Slider! Settle down," she said. But except for the growl, Sid's reaction felt the same as his. Dammit, had she grown so suspect of George's behavior that she'd lost her trust in him?

Or was it guilt she felt? All she'd done was pay a hooker to spy on her best friend.

Autonomic reflex kicked in and forced her to breathe, and with the fresh oxygen she remembered. George was her friend—not someone to fear.

Hopefully.

He indicated her coffee cup. "Got another cup of that to take away the chill?"

She stalled, unsure how to relate to him until she figured this out. Of course she wasn't privy to his every case. Perhaps this was one of those he hadn't shared with her. The direct approach, to come right out and ask him if he were involved in something illegal, might work. Then again, he'd probably laugh her out of her own office.

"Sid? Maybe you can add a nip to it?"

She pulled her thoughts back to the moment. "Sorry, fresh out. It'll have to be a virgin."

"Nah, I never cared much for virgins." He waved her back to her chair while he pulled up another one.

Sid walked behind her desk and sat on the edge of her chair. "Ben and I had a great time the other night. You were right about Martha's cooking."

"Martha and I sure enjoyed it too." He crossed his legs at the ankle, clasped his hands in his lap and twiddled his thumbs.

Broach the subject, Sid, or you'll never get any peace. "About that night in the hallway at your house, I'm sorry I startled—"

"That's a good crawfish pie recipe for sure. It's won a couple of contests." George flashed a tight smile.

Sid tried again. "I don't mean to pry into your—"

"I promised Martha next time I'd give her better notice before I invite someone over," he said, squirming in his chair.

Obviously he didn't want to talk about the other night in the hallway at his house, or the phone conversation she'd overheard, but his furrowed brow professed he worried about something. Okay sweetheart, she thought, you've got the talking stick.

A couple of minutes passed before he spoke.

"I had a phone call early this morning."

"Oh? Someone I know?"

"Yeah, one of your old clients."

"Mine?

"Durwood."

Uh oh. Something told Sid she wasn't going to like where this conversation headed.

"He called me to take Boo Murphy's case. Said he wanted you, but you turned her down. He thinks you walk on water, you know."

"But George, they haven't even arrested Boo yet, and if they do, she says she's pleading guilty and getting it over with. You can't help someone who doesn't want to be helped."

"Good," he said with such force that Sid flinched. "I hoped you wouldn't get involved in that case."

"Why?"

"I wouldn't touch it with a ten foot pole, and I don't advise you to either, but I hear the sheriff is about to issue a warrant for her arrest, and she ain't pleading guilty. Durwood's done talked her out of it." A Cajun flavor crept into his last sentence.

"Then I guess her lawyer will advise her on that sort of thing."

George stood, rattling coins in his pocket. "I suppose so, but it ain't your worry, Sha. Long as you don't take on the case, I'm happy."

She couldn't resist asking, "What is it about this case that makes you leery?"

George shook his head. "Can't say." He hurried to the door, grabbed his umbrella, and stepped out. "But don't take it, you hear?" He called back at her.

What did her mentor know about this case that he hadn't told her? She glanced at the brown potshard lying on her desk. George had given it to her earlier when he'd pushed her to take a case. This time, he'd pushed her not to take one. She picked up the piece of dried clay, rubbed the smooth, hard surface and tossed it back on her desk.

Evidently, George didn't know her as well as he thought. Where he made his mistake was in telling her what not to do. Her birth sign, Taurus, didn't respond well to that.

Slider walked over, whining, and plopped a paw in her lap. When she looked down to rub the top of his head, his eyes bore into hers. "You need to go outside again so soon? It's pouring down. Oh, all right, come on."

He headed to the door just exited by George, but instead of waiting for her to open the door he lay down in front of it, blocking the way. He whined again, and scratched at the floor with his front paws, twitched his ears and shook his head.

"You feel it too, huh? Something's definitely going on with George. He's involved in something he shouldn't be, or he wouldn't act so weird."

She flopped in her chair. "But I promised myself the first thing I would do this morning is call a couple of contractors and get bids on the new office." She shoved George and Durwood and Boo out of her mind for the moment, collected the phone book and scooted her chair closer to her desk. Flipping through pages until she found what she wanted, she grabbed a pen and paper and scribbled the number of the association of building contractors, hoping they had a list of names and numbers of local businesses.

Just as she started to close the book, another listing caught her eye. She opened the directory again and read out the name of a local volunteer archaeology group.

Had they heard the story about the resurrected schooner?

The possibility of the sea giving back what it had taken so long ago triggered memories of her childhood, when she'd pretended she was her paternal ancestor. stowing away on the *Nancy* in 1767, as it set sail from Belfast, Ireland, and then the bright new world of promise when the ship landed at Charleston, South Carolina. So many times she'd sat, literally, at her Scots-Irish grandfather's feet as he recounted the tale, pride beaming in his eyes.

Okay, back to the task at hand.

After she'd called, obtained the names and numbers of a couple of local builders, she made appointments with them, then leaned back in her chair, relieved that the city zoning board had made the decision on the rebuild of her office. She'd gone back and forth on it so much she felt like a porch swing on a Saturday night.

Fingering the sticky-note pad where she'd written the number for the volunteer archaeology group, she toyed with the idea of calling them. Earlier civilizations had always fascinated her, but a resurrected schooner represented a whole new ballgame—if the ship even existed. But now she'd heard of the same schooner from two totally different sources. Her chest fluttered just thinking about the possibility.

And since she'd just decided to take Boo's case…

She picked up the phone and dialed.

"Shipwreck." The husky voice sounded like the man had a mouth full of gravel.

Not comprehending what he said, Sid stuttered, embarrassed. "Excuse me…I…I…"

A belly laugh blared across the line. "Oh, not to worry, most folks don't get it on the first go-round anyway. My name's Ed Stephens, but everybody calls me Shipwreck."

Sid laughed, warming to the guy. "That's what I thought you said. To tell the truth, I'm surprised folks don't call *me* that, since

I've been accused of acting like one."

He chuckled. "Yeah, my wife says all I ever think about is finding sunken vessels. Now, what can I do for you this bright beautiful morning?"

His comment made her glance outside. The sun wasn't shining, but at least the rain had slowed to a drizzle.

She introduced herself and recounted the story she'd heard of the resurrected schooner and the new case she'd just accepted, unofficially at least.

"As a matter of fact, we heard about it too, and we were just talking about it.

"So you think the story's true?"

"No reason not to."

"Why is that?"

"Well, for one thing, old-timers around here have been seeing things like that for years. My grandpa used to tell about a brass covered bow of an old ship out in the marshes of Louisiana. Him and his buddies would stop near it and have lunch, then proceed into the marsh to trap and hunt. Then one day they went out after a storm and the old ship wasn't there anymore."

"But a brass bow? Did those early ships really use brass?"

"Sure, during the 17th and 18th centuries. The brass protected the bow when they rammed other schooners.

"Wow, sounds like some Hollywood pirate movie."

"Well, ma'am, if this story's true, its better'n any movie, I can assure you of that. You probably heard how Jean Lafitte and his men worked this area. They stole slaves from plantation owners in Barbados, shipped them here and locked them up in shacks out there in Deweyville till they could sell them to plantation owners back east. So yep, that schooner might well be out there, just like the old woman said. If it's Lafitte's brass-bowed *Hotspur*, there's no telling what kind of treasures might still be on board."

The man's enthusiasm bubbled over into his words.

"Or it could be the *Santa Rosa*. Tales are that schooner carried bars of silver worth more than six million bucks."

Sid snorted at the idea. "That must set a treasure hunter's teeth on edge. Have you been out to see if you can find the schooner?"

"As a matter of fact, we're going out first thing in the morning. The sheriff and his men don't believe she saw one, but it could have sunk back down into the mire. When conditions are just right, things have a way of doing that. The bottom is muddy and deep. Ships can sink and rise in the mire, and people sometimes get out of their boats and wade around. Of course the woman might have got the location mixed up, too. Those swamps tend to look a lot alike unless you really know your way around out there."

While he talked, a connecting thread began to weave itself through the events of the last few days. Soon as he stopped to catch his breath, she blurted out, "Do you ever take visitors out with you?"

"Sure. We use all the help we can get. Remember, we're just a bunch of volunteers who're passionate about what we do."

"Then could I go out with you tomorrow? You have room?"

Sid heard a slight pause before Shipwreck said, "I see no reason why you can't. The boat's big enough, but you'll need to bring a pair of rubber hip boots."

"Great! I don't have a pair, but I'll beg, borrow or steal, or go out and buy my own pair. Tell me where to meet you, and what time. I'll be easy to recognize. I'll be the one with bells on." She laughed, but she'd never been more serious in her life.

Add Boo's arrest for murder to the discovery of a sunken pirate ship. Multiply that by George's involvement with a shady character interested in what may be on the schooner, and the results added up to much more than a coincidence.

No way in hell was she going to sit back and not follow that thread.

Seven

Eager for the excursion with Shipwreck, Sid arose early, grabbed a quick breakfast of cereal and a cup of coffee hot enough to match the predicted high for the day, and selected a pair of loose-fitting blue jeans and long sleeved shirt. She'd be sweltering by noon, but if she didn't cover as much skin as possible, she'd be eaten alive—not by alligators, but by billions of mosquitoes.

Leaving Slider to face his own battles with *King Cat* and *Queen Bee*, she headed out, following the directions from Shipwreck that led to Bridge City and then left on Round Bunch Road. Soon she spotted a meandering branch of the Neches River which, she'd learned, intersected the Sabine and ended up in the brackish Sabine Lake and on to the Gulf of Mexico.

Along the coastline on her right, she passed crabbers standing along the river bank holding long-handled fishing nets in one hand, and in the other, the end of a long string dangling down in the water. She'd learned from Marv Bledsoe that the crabber had first tied a chicken neck or some other piece of raw meat to the end in the water.

Each person, man, woman, or child, stared at the water, watching for a blue crab to latch onto the raw meat. Soon as one did, they eased the net underneath the crab, scooped it up and dumped it into a large ice chest beside them.

"Good eating in their house tonight." Sid laughed, almost tasting the seafood gumbo served in a bowl of rice with a large spoon of potato salad dumped on top. That's the part that blew her mind—potato salad *in* the gumbo! Regardless, it worked. But she still hadn't sucked the heads of boiled crawfish. *That* activity might take her awhile.

Her two favorite places in town were the brand new world class Shangri La Botanical Gardens and Nature Center on Sixteenth, and the Lutcher Stark Museum of Art on Green Avenue.

The museum's Decorative Arts collection displayed Dorothy Doughty's entire series of porcelain birds. Until her divorce, Sid collected porcelain birds and one of Doughty's, wrapped and boxed, was in a storage unit in Houston with everything else from the division of property. Sam had refused any part of it, said he didn't want anything that reminded him of her. Cut out the eye that offends and act like it never existed, and then spend the rest of your life stumbling around in the dark wondering why someone turned off the lights.

A few minutes later, Capt'n Richard's Charter and Guide Services came into view on her right. Unsure what to expect, the humility of the place impressed her more than anything. A variety of boats surrounded by weeds lay propped on their sides awaiting repair. Others bobbed at water's edge. One boat, a white fiberglass with a canopy on top, looked the most seaworthy. She hoped that boat was the one reserved for them.

She turned into an oyster shell parking lot that looked like it had been laid down by the Atakapa Indians thousands of years ago. Throughout the area, heavy patches of grass popped their green tendrils through the shell. A sign dangling from the eaves of a white building with a tin roof announced fresh seafood and groceries.

No sooner had she parked her Xterra, collected her rubber boots, and exited the vehicle, than a large, red-faced man in faded blue jeans and a long-sleeve khaki shirt strode over, followed by two other men in similar attire.

The first man stuck a giant hand out to her. "Sid? I'm Shipwreck. This here's Pete Baxter," he said, indicating the older of the two. "When he's not volunteering with me, he works at the Stark Museum."

Pete offered Sid his hand. He was one of those average-looking men who wouldn't stand out in a crowd, despite a big nose and a sunburned complexion.

"Curator?"

"Security."

Security? Sid's internal alarm went off. That night at George's when he was on the phone he said something about being friends with the museum's head of security. Was Pete in charge of it, or just a drone?

Shipwreck continued Pete's introduction. "Capt'n Richard is the guy that owns this place, knows these waters better than anybody, but he's out on a charter today. Pete here is our next best bet. He took off work today just to take us out to the site. The bayou can be treacherous, with sunken logs, trees, boats, and other trash. Pete knows how to navigate around them, and he knows how to spot alligators better'n anybody."

Shipwreck thumbed from the older man to the younger. "And this here is his son. Everyone calls him *Repete*, for obvious reasons." Except for a full head of hair and a less ruddy complexion, Repete stood a younger duplicate of the other.

The men made quick, polite conversation, inquiring about Sid's line of work and her interest in sunken vessels. She explained how she'd inherited a detective agency upon her brother's death and moved here from Houston to run it. Now, she'd been approached by Boo Murphy to find out who had murdered her neighbor, Zeke Harris. After a couple more minutes of small talk, the men grew antsy, shuffled their feet, and checked the rising sun against their watches.

Pete walked off dialing his cell phone while Repete's thumbs texted a message to someone, a girlfriend, Sid figured.

"Looks like the deputy won't make it in time to go out with us." Shipwreck said. "If he was coming, he'd be here by now. I'd hoped he could show us the way, but I think I know where they're talking about. The sheriff's still out there. Soon as Pete finishes his call, we'll head on out and see if we can find the location by ourselves."

A good five minutes later, Pete rejoined them. They climbed into the boat, Pete at the wheel. Shipwreck settled on the first bench, Sid behind him on the second, and Repete behind her.

Pete adjusted the throttle, checked and double checked the gas gauge, while the rest of the team settled in with bottles of water, boots, hats and long metal poles.

Anticipation crept up Sid's gut. What if Boo's story was true and they did find a resurrected pirate ship? What would it look like? What spirits might still be on board? In the last few months, every belief she'd ever held about life, death, and life hereafter had been shot to hell. One thing she did know for sure, she didn't *know* diddlysquat about any of it, and neither did anyone else. Faith was faith, and fact was fact, and fact appeared to be as changeable as faith.

Shipwreck plopped his boots on the bottom of the boat and dropped an overstuffed backpack next to them.

Sid raised her voice over the increasing noise of the motor. "I know I asked you this before, but what do you make of the woman's story about seeing a pirate ship?"

"You mean if I think it could be true?"

Sid nodded. "Yeah, not just that something sits out there in the water, but could it be as old as folks say?"

"Sure it could."

Pete pulled a bright orange life jacket out from under the front hull and handed it back to Sid. "Ma'am, you best put this on just in case." He handed jackets to the others and after everyone had them on and tied, he revved the motor and backed away from the dock.

Shipwreck turned in his seat and yelled over the noise. "When these sightings occur, it stirs up treasure hunters of all kinds, ready to go find their fortune. We've got more stories of buried treasure around here than you might think." He pointed to locations along the bank as he talked. "You walk alongside the Neches and Sabine Rivers, and just under the surface may lie thousands and hundreds of thousands of dollars in gold, silver, and historical artifacts. While the treasures are important, the stories behind the treasures are priceless." Shipwreck turned to look at Sid, his eyes twinkling. "Despite what they tell us in the movies, *Davy Jones* still holds the key to his locker."

Sid laughed, enjoying the man's contagious passion.

"But remember, what the sea takes, one day it gives back. It's the treasure that keeps the stories alive. When we do talks, and I see the sparkle in the kids' eyes, that's worth more than any treasure I find.

"Pirates used not only brass on the bow, but they also used other metals on the hull to help preserve parts below the water line. Remember, pirates liked flashy things like gold and brass." Shipwreck chuckled. "Gold particularly. Because of the gulf's warm water, some vessels were even copper-plated up to the water line to prevent wormwood infestation. Galveston to New Orleans was a main run. Lots of ships wrecked along that route because of sudden storms. River ports such as Orange, Sabine Pass and Liberty. They all have tons of shipwreck stories told by old-timers."

The gleam in the man's eyes convinced Sid that folks had been right when they'd nicknamed the guy. Sid even felt giddy herself, like a child with a treasure map marked with a big X.

At first, Pete drove slowly through the twists and turns of the bayou, which pleased Sid. This was her first trip of the summer, when all the trees and shrubs and wildflowers were in full bloom. It looked like a whole different world from what she'd seen in the fall and winter, when the bald cypress trees were bare, their knobby knees poking through the mud at the base. She recalled that her guide then had told her that the knees were root extensions and helped brace the cypress against high winds and provided oxygen to the submerged roots.

Shipwreck pulled several packets out of his pocket and handed one back to Sid. "Here," he called out over the noise of the motor, "you better wipe this repellant cloth anywhere you have exposed skin. If you don't, when we get back you'll look like you have the measles."

She took one and wiped the moist, chemical-smelling cloth across her face, hands, ankles, ears and throat and tucked the paper in her pocket just as Pete yelled, "Hold on, we're gonna throw pedal to the metal," and shifted gears. The boat shot out into the open waterway. Exhilarated by the wind blowing her hair and the spray on her face, Sid decided right then and there that as soon as she could afford one, she would buy her own boat and motor.

"Been out here before?" Pete asked when he turned away from the wheel for a second and looked back at what must be an enraptured expression on her face.

"Couple of times," she yelled over the noise, "but not in summer, and not in a motor boat. I love this! You feel so free."

"You know this land first had cannibals living along the shores, huh?" He asked the question while yelling back over this shoulder. "They lived on oysters and other shell fish in the area. They pried them open, got the meat out, dumped the empty shells in a particular area, and ending up with mounds of shell. Or middens, as some folks call them. And since the water table was too high to bury them in the ground, they buried their dead down inside the piles of shell. Look, there are a couple of middens right over there. See?" He pointed.

Sid nodded. She'd learned the tales of the Atakapa Indians on earlier excursions into the swamp, but Pete seemed delighted in repeating it, so she listened while he talked. When a lull in the conversation presented itself, she took advantage of it and altered the subject. "When you find a wrecked ship, how do you know how old it is? How do you date it?"

Shipwreck called out over the wind. "Certain items tell you what you've got, the type of material, the kind of wood, whether its white oak, cypress or cedar. Also you look at the thickness of the beams. Does the vessel have an inner and outer hull? What type of propulsion? Is it a stern paddle wheel, side paddle or screw propeller?"

That made sense. A paddle wheel would indicate steam boats, of course.

"Bolts and screws can also give you some idea of what you've got. Because the vessels have broken down in the water, it's necessary to measure them from bow to stern and to get the depth or draft of a wreck. This can help you when you don't have other identification marks such as a name plate, or a bell with the name of the ship on it."

"Okay, so a sunken ship is found," Sid said. "Say, a Cottonclad, one of those steamboats the South lined with cotton bales during the Civil War, or even a pirate ship. Who does it belong to now?"

Repete leaned over Sid's shoulder, jumping into the conversation for the first time. "Jurisdiction is determined by what kind it is, and its identification. If it's a Navy ship, no matter how old, it still belongs to the Navy. Maritime ordinates can still be active on the ship, so you approach it with respect and care. There are over 2000 sunken vessels just on the Texas coast and inland water ways. We know of 16,000 steamboats built, and only a 100 survive today. That means out there somewhere, lie the remains of 15,900 wrecks with gold, silver and historical items aboard."

Shipwreck picked up the conversation again. It seemed the men needed little encouragement to talk about their passion. "The Sabine River's got 85 recorded wrecks and it may have as many 200 that are still unrecorded. There's at least 25 million bucks worth of artifacts less than 20 feet below the water."

"Wow." Sid's mouth dropped open. "Why has no one come in and tried to resurrect them?"

"One reason is that the water has less than a foot visibility. It's what we call dark-water diving—more feel than sight. Makes it more risky. More expensive, too."

"But how do you even get started?" Sid felt her explorer-juices begin to flow.

"We search through data on the history of the area, old newspapers on microfilm, that sort of stuff. These accounts usually have stories of shipwrecks in some detail. The information will relate the name of the ship, the course of action that took place, such as burned, foundered, or exploded on the river, or simply lost at sea with all hands. Another good source is the local library and the historical society."

Excitement squirreled around inside Sid's belly. "What's the first thing you'll do when we get there?"

"If we find it, we'll start taking samples, scrapings, that sort of thing. We hope to go down inside eventually, but first we've got to be sure it won't sink on us. We'll have to get some ropes on it to get it secured before we do something like that." His eyes sparkled as he looked from Sid to the direction in which they headed. "We're so fired up, I don't think any of us slept last night. We been waiting for a chance like this since we got started years ago. Just think, this could be the find of the century."

"If we find it," she reminded him.

"And that's a big if. Miss Murphy said she climbed up on it, but as far as I know, she's the only one that's sighted it."

Rodriguez had said one of his men had seen the schooner. She pondered who that might be, but for now, kept her mouth shut.

In time, Pete slowed the boat, wending his way through tight bends and low water. The smell of nature changed from fresh air to that of rotting vegetation. Not too unlike that of a backed up toilet. But somehow, this smelled rich—alien, and at the same time, strangely familiar.

By the time they arrived at the site, Sheriff Quade Burns and his deputies were taking down the yellow crime scene tape. He called out across the boats. "Hey, Shipwreck, I heard you were coming to see if you could find the schooner."

"If it's out here, we'll find it," Shipwreck yelled back.

"I hope you do, sure would make my job easier. I'll do my best to keep treasure hunters out of here as long as I can, but they're a savage, determined bunch, you know." He chuckled. "Oh, by the way, some guy from Texas A & M called. If we find the schooner, he'll come over and help us out. But I suspect you won't find it. My sense is the whole story's a ruse to disguise a murder."

Sid leaned around Shipwreck and waved at the sheriff. "Do you really think an old woman such as Boo would have the strength to tie her shirt around her neighbor's neck and pull until she killed him?"

"Well, look who's wormed her way in again? Why am I not surprised?" Quade laughed, lifting his hat and running his hand through his sandy blonde flattop.

"And hello to you, too." She smiled right back. "Look who's talking. You wormed your way into the vacated sheriff's position. But you don't have a chance in hell winning the election."

"Yeah, yeah, you just watch me. You'll be eating my dust."

"I'm sure I will, but I can make your life miserable in the process." She teased right back. Then, "Seriously, I haven't had a chance to congratulate you and Robin on your new baby girl, or your new appointment. You'll do a great job with both. Oh, and by the way, Boo Murphy's afraid you're going to arrest her for Zeke Harris's murder. I didn't figure you would, since you've never been one for lost causes, and as far as I can see, you don't have enough evidence for a conviction."

"Well, that might be what she and her friend Durwood think, but they don't know the half of it."

"And that is?"

"The fact is, I simply went to question her. Today, it's more serious. My deputies have an arrest warrant for her. By the time we get back, she'll be locked up in county jail."

Sid stopped pulling on the hip boots she'd borrowed from Martha Léger. "Jesus Christ, Quade, that old woman couldn't kill anyone."

"Well, I don't arrest folks unless I got a pretty airtight case. Plus, I'm getting a lot of pressure from the mayor. He wants this whole thing done and over with. The city's trying to lure more tourists, not crazed treasure hunters who come in and tear the place apart, destroying the environment and pitting one against the other."

"But..."

He turned from Sid to her companion. "Say, Shipwreck, do you really think she saw the *Hotspur*? Folks around town are convinced she did. I'm having a hell of a time keeping them away. They're all convinced they'll find it, along with Napoleon's riches on board."

"Could be, Sheriff, from what I've heard, it sure could be. But whether or not Napoleon's riches are on it is anybody's guess. Story goes, he buried those things across the river over near what's today called Money Hill, but, heck, he could've dug 'em up and been moving 'em again when the *Hotspur* ran aground."

"Yep, sure could've. Well, we're out of here for now. If you find anything, let us know."

Pete putted their boat through bends in the river and marshy areas where Spanish moss brushed the water's surface, leaving in its wake tiny, liquid trails. Wild hyacinth, with its blue, tubular-shaped flowers bloomed along the edge of the water.

Sid turned to Shipwreck. "Who's this 'he' Quade was talking about?"

"Jean Lafitte, privateer during the 1800s."

"Isn't he the one that supposedly helped the U.S. win the Battle of 1812?"

"One and the same. Man, it'd be dreams come true if the Murphy woman really did see the Hotspur, but I ain't counting my chickens. Lafitte patterned it after an earlier one by the same name, attacked off the coast of Cuba by the Spanish. Lafitte's Captain Campbell almost lost his life in that skirmish. So, I guess as a reward, he let Campbell be in charge of naming the new one being built. I figure Campbell named this second ship the Hotspur in an attempt to change his luck. The new vessel was what was called a hermaphrodite—a topsail schooner. History describes it as all wings and no feet. The foremast was square-rigged on the fore and mainmasts, and it flew a number of jibs and topsails."

"Jibs? What are jibs?" Sid hated to sound dumb, but the topic fascinated her.

"Jibs are the hoists."

"Oh, I see." She didn't really, but she had a vague idea.

The sun crept to its zenith while they continued searching the area, when they heard a launch heading their way.

Repete drew their attention away from the approaching launch when he yelled with excitement. "Hey, Shipwreck, look over here. Looks like an 18 pound cannon. And it looks old enough to have been on a ship from that time period. Guess it could've been on the wreck and fallen off."

Shipwreck slapped Repete on the back. "Good eyes, boy, we almost drove right past it."

"And look here." Repete and Shipwreck jumped off the boat and waded through the water to a stack of rusty round objects. "Here's the cannon balls," Repete said, glee filling his voice.

"Yep, but that sure don't make a brass-bowed Hotspur." Shipwreck's words brought the excitement down a notch or two.

As the thrill subsided, the launch came into view and a tall, slender man, his head shaved and polished to a high shine, stood at the helm. Everyone watched him maneuver their way.

Pete shook his head and sucked through his teeth. "Great, just what we need, a greedy treasure hunter wanting to get his hands on sunken treasure."

Eight

The fiftyish, bald-headed man idled the boat motor and coasted alongside theirs. Smiling real friendly like, he flashed a mouthful of teeth so white they must have been veneer. "Morning, ma'am, I'm looking for whoever's in charge here. Is that you, or one of the others?" The man indicated Pete, still at the wheel.

"Who wants to know?" She'd learned to offer no more information than asked for, and then only when she knew *who* did the asking.

"Pardon me. Name's Professor Faulkner, Hoke Faulkner."

"Professor?" Shipwreck sloshed over, apprehension edging his voice.

"Yes, I'm the new marine archeology professor over at Texas A & M. My boss sent me to check out the site."

"Castigliano?"

"Pardon me?"

"Head of the department—your boss?"

"Oh, yes, Castigliano. He heard about the schooner sighting and told me to come check it out. You guys with the local volunteer group?"

"Yep."

"He said I'd probably find you here, and for now, that we should work cooperatively."

Shipwreck bristled. "Nice of him. Been nicer had he let me know you were coming."

"He tried, couldn't get through. I believe he left a message with your wife, said her name was… was…"

"Abigail."

"Yes, that's the name, Abigail." He pointed to the gun moored in the mud. "She sure looks like she's from the same time period, but where's the schooner? News reports said the woman had actually climbed up on the bow and even gone down inside the captain's cabin." He shook his head. "Wow, what I wouldn't give to board one." Hoke stood up in the boat and scanned the area. "Where is it? All I see is that cannon."

"Not much to see but this." Shipwreck waded back over and rubbed his hand down the gun's length. Mud plopped off and into the water. "And your news source stretched the information a little. The woman said she climbed up on the bow, but she didn't say she went down inside."

"So this is all you've found?"

"That's about it. Not sure the woman's story is even true. I'm surprised the university sent you over here just on a reported sighting. There's been several of those stories going around through the years, but none that held up for long. This one may just be the result of an old woman's imagination."

Pete rubbed sweat off his brow and wiped his hand on his shirt sleeve. "Oh, it's out here all right. The question is *where*? It could still even be up closer to the Mermentau River, over in Louisiana."

"Whatever you find, you'll have to turn it over to me—to the university, that is. The local government and the state usually give us jurisdiction over these finds, you know."

Irritation crept into Shipwreck's voice. "Tell me, did you come to help us, or treat us like we're stupid?"

Faulkner turned red-faced, and looked like he might be biting his tongue.

Except for the soft lap of water and an occasional bird call, Sid heard only a pulse beat in her ear. She looked from the stoic professor to Shipwreck, whose jaw muscles made knots on the sides of his face. By the time she glanced back at the professor, his demeanor had changed to one of friendly persuasion.

"Sorry folks, didn't mean to be rude. I've come to help—not cause you a problem. I know you guys been working the 'sunkens' in this area for quite a while, and you know your stuff. The university just wants to be sure you get the expertise you need. This could be an important find."

"Well, duh. We certainly didn't need you here to tell us that." Repete waded over from the canon, his face flushed with irritation.

Shipwreck put his arm around the boy's shoulder. "It's okay, buddy. Take a deep breath. I'm sure Professor Faulkner didn't mean to offend us." He pushed his way through the waist deep water and shook hands with the newcomer. "Forgive us if we're a little testy, Professor. We're excited. It's not often we get firsthand accounts of something like this. Yep, we're well aware of the significance of this find. We welcome your professional help. You know a lot more about this than we do."

Faulkner leaned over the side of his boat, shook hands with the other men, then turned to Sid. "Let's start this day over again. Morning, Ma'am, Faulkner's the name."

She clasped his hand in a tight squeeze. "Sid Smart."

"Wow, powerful shake you have there. So, you're a part of this investigative team, huh? I hadn't heard they had a woman member, but I'm glad to see it. We need the woman's touch in these things. Women see things we men miss."

"I'm just along for the ride."

"Sid's a private eye," Shipwreck piped up.

Faulkner's eyebrows arched in surprise. "You don't say. I'd never have guessed. Sorry, Ma'am, but you don't look much like a private detective."

"And you don't look much like a college professor either," Sid snapped back.

"Pardon me, but I meant that as a compliment, not an offense."

"So did I," she said, just as innocently.

His mouth gaped a second too long before he closed it and turned back toward the cannon. "Look at that. Isn't she a beauty? Think she's off the Hotspur?"

"Could well be. She fits that time period." Sid smirked at herself for talking like she knew of what she spoke. Hell, if he could, she could.

The realization hit her—subconsciously she'd dubbed him a phony or a blowhard, and she detested both.

Accelerating the motor a little, Faulkner guided the aluminum hull over to a tall cypress knee and looped his rope around the trunk. Without looking at the others, he pulled on a pair of hip boots stashed in the bottom of the boat and climbed over the side.

Not to be outdone, Sid pulled on hers.

"You know there were two schooners called the Hotspur," Faulkner said over his shoulder as he headed to the cannon. "Second one was called a hermaphrodite brig because the builders sacrificed cargo space for speed. In nautical lingo—"

Sid tried to stop herself from interrupting, but the words came out anyway. "Yes, we do know that. These men may be volunteers, but they know enough to be professionals."

Faulkner changed the subject. "Say, I heard they found a dead man out here. You guys know him?"

The men shrugged, shook their heads, and continued what they were doing.

The professor turned from the men back to Sid. "You said you were a private eye, ma'am. Did you say you were investigating the murder?"

"No, I didn't say that."

"Well, let's get busy and see what we find." Faulkner collected a long metal pole from his boat and waded over to Shipwreck. "If the cannon didn't wash up from a distance, the schooner could well be nearby. The tide looks like it's rising again. If it is here, and the swamp gases and the ocean tides work against us, it will soon be too late."

No shit, Sherlock, Sid thought. She glanced over at Shipwreck and the two Petes. Their expressions said Sid's thoughts echoed theirs.

Repete cut a long branch from a tree, shaved off the leaves and vine clusters, and handed it to Sid. The others used long metal poles similar to Faulkner's.

For what seemed like hours, they plowed through waist-deep swamp, each sounding out the bottom of the bayou with the poles, hoping to hit something hard and definitive. Occasionally, one of them would come upon a hunk of rusted metal or a rotted piece of wood, and the others rushed over, only to be disappointed. For all they found were rubber tires, bicycles, another rusted cannon ball, and odd pieces of junk that had accumulated over the years.

The sun rose higher and steamier, without the slightest breeze to cool the perspiration on their skin. Sid swiped her shirt sleeve across her forehead, thankful she didn't have long hair down her back.

The professor had stuck a crumpled hat on his bald pate, but periodically took it off and wiped his head with a handkerchief he'd pulled from his back pocket.

"Wow, most fun I've ever had," Sid answered, when Shipwreck asked her how she was holding up.

Frustrated and growing a mite bored with searching for a pirate schooner that didn't exist, Sid wandered away from the others, taking in the feral water garden's acrid smell of rotting vegetation mingled with the sweet aroma of wild yellow honeysuckle and blue hyacinth. Swamp vapors rose from the water's surface like the breath of a giant on a cold winter morning. Despite the subtropic temperature, goose bumps popped out on her arms.

But when she rounded a bend, the goose bumps turned into boulders.

For just above the surface of the water, a schooner, the description of which she'd just learned from Shipwreck, glided across the expanse and through a low-lying ground fog. It carried a square-rigged foremast and schooner-rigged fore and mainmasts. Numerous jibs and brilliant-white topsails puffed in the wind. The faint image of a buxom, flame-haired beauty dressed in dark pantaloons and white ruffled shirt stood at the bow and stared off in the distance, her breasts bared, and a broadsword in her hand.

Paralyzed, Sid tried to yell to the others, but as if in a dream, no sound erupted from her throat. Helpless, unable to move, barely able to breathe, she watched the schooner fade from view, and as it did, the numbness left her body. She swirled around, hoping to see something—anything—to confirm she'd seen what she'd seen.

Instead, the smooth liquid road stretched out before her, leaving no witness of movement in the water except hers and the v-shaped wake left behind by an alligator snapping turtle.

Certifiable—absolutely positively certifiable—that's what she'd be called if she told the guys what she'd just seen—or imagined. Seeing a ghost was one thing—but a whole frigging pirate ship? Come on, Sid!

Following the path she'd taken a few minutes earlier, she soon rejoined the men.

Repete stood away from the others, bent over, digging in the mud. But when he stood, he held a handful of bones. "Looks like a skeleton over here."

"Human?" Shipwreck headed toward him.

"I thought it was at first, but, no, looks like some critter." He dropped the bones back into the water. "Things around here seem stirred up a bit, but I guess that's because the sheriff and his deputies been searching."

"I reckon so, son." Shipwreck put his arm around the boy's shoulder. "Come on, let's head back to the boat and call it a day." He waved Pete their way.

When they reached Sid, standing next to the boat, Shipwreck laced his fingers together and leaned over. "Here, Sid, you got short legs, let me give you a boost."

She placed her muddy boot in his hands and scratched and crawled her way up and over, taking the same bench as earlier.

By then, Pete had rejoined the group. Disbelief creased his forehead. "If there *was* a ship here, we'd dang well have seen it by now. We've covered every square inch of this place."

Not every inch, Sid thought.

She glanced over at Professor Faulkner, whose face had turned the color of cigarette ash. He shook his head in disbelief. "You think that Murphy woman lied about seeing it just to cover the murder?"

"I don't know, but I'm with Pete." Shipwreck motioned the others in. "If it were here, we'd have found it by now. Mud's been shoved around so bad, it's no telling where…"

Faulkner, now back in his own boat, asked, "Did the sheriff's team take anything from the site?"

"Not that I know of—but I doubt it. Sheriff's expecting me to keep an eye out for anything he might have missed."

"And that crazy woman, what's her name?" Faulkner looked from one to the other.

Sid puffed out an indignant chest. "Are you referring to Boo Murphy? If so, the woman is not crazy—she's just old."

"She's old all right, old as Methuselah, from what I hear, and she claims to have stood on the bow of a non-existent ship. If that's not crazy, I don't know what is, since it's obvious there isn't a schooner out here."

The others in the boat ignored the man, but not Sid. She told herself to shut up—that she didn't need to defend the woman— but events of the day had rattled her self-control. Besides, the man's arrogance reminded her of her ex-husband Sam. When she'd left him, she made the decision to never listen to another shaming comment about a woman without speaking up. So, no way in hell would she shut her mouth now. "I'll believe her before I believe you, Mr. Faulkner."

Shipwreck finally spoke, interrupting the exchange. "That's what she said, but then when she came back the next day with her cousin, she says they never saw it. All they found was the other's husband, choked to death."

"Yeah, with a shirt that Miss Boo just happened to have lost the day before. Mighty convenient, don't you think? My boss is going to be madder than hell when he learns this trip was a waste."

"Can't help you there, buddy," Pete said, starting the motor. He revved the engine, circled around and headed home, leaving Hoke Faulkner and his boat, in their wake.

They all sat in silence as they headed back to the dock. Sid guessed none of them were sure what to make of Boo's story, including her.

When they reached the dock, Shipwreck climbed out and held Sid's hand while she climbed out. "I'm glad you came out with us, Sid," he said, a big smile twinkling in his eyes. "I enjoy a woman with spunk, and lady, you got it. Any time you want to go out with us again, just give me a call. Sorry we didn't see anything. Maybe next time."

Yeah, maybe next time, she thought, still rattled by what she had seen this time.

She'd never felt so uncertain about anything.

Maybe she'd been a victim of a swamp-like illusion. No, delusion was more like it.

Maybe Boo had, too. Or maybe Boo had been set up.

Or maybe Sid had.

After she thanked the men for the trip, she headed to her car. But as she started the engine, what she had seen, or at least thought she'd seen in the swamp niggled at the back of her mind. She pulled out of the gravel parking lot in a daze, processing everything she'd heard and seen, when a foot-stomping version of *The Battle of New Orleans* blared. Startled, she reached over to turn off the radio and realized the radio was in the off position. The music played in her head.

Nine

Up early the next morning, Sid sat in her office and puzzled over events of the last few days, when she spied a note left on her desk by Annie. Durwood had called, in a panic, saying the sheriff arrested Boo last night. Could Sid please hurry?

Her fingers drummed the desk, while her brain hummed the tune to *The Battle of New Orleans*. She'd loved the song and the way Johnny Horton sang it, but she hadn't heard, or even thought of it, in years. Now the dang thing wouldn't get out of her head. The music and lyrics, she recalled, were written by a history teacher wanting to teach his students about the last major battle in The War of 1812.

Who tried to teach her what, and why?

They hadn't found any trace of Boo's schooner the day before, but dammit, Sid had seen her own. Not a real live one, but certainly *something* sailed above the water. She wasn't crazy, nor had she imagined it. However, if Boo's sighting matched Sid's, she certainly couldn't have climbed up on it, like she'd said.

But someone murdered Zeke, unless of course he did it to himself.

According to Myra, she overheard Rodriguez mention a resurrected schooner in Adams Bayou. What if they had all seen a ghost ship? But that didn't make sense. Even if she believed in the things, why in the world would it be plying the backwaters? The whole situation smelled as rank as a sewer.

Sid called the jail and found out she could visit Boo, so she headed there, eager to find out how the old woman held up, her first night locked in a jail cell.

Taking only her wallet and badge for identity, she locked her bag and Glock in the back of the car, tucked her keys in her pocket and headed inside.

The jail lobby consisted of a small room with a recruitment poster for the U. S. Army, a couple of chairs and one internal window she assumed someone monitored from the other side. She rang a buzzer beside a door, and a woman's voice came over the intercom. Sid explained who she was and what she wanted, and a deputy opened a metal door and ushered her into a tiny interview room containing a modern-looking desk and two straight-back chairs. A surveillance camera in a corner of the ceiling spied down on her. Sid wondered who watched.

The deputy asked for Sid's keys and did a quick pat-down for weapons, and left.

After a ten minute wait, a deputy ushered Boo into the room. Dressed in black and white stripes, Boo's steel-gray ringlets curled around a sallow complexion. Her dull eyes gave the smallest hint of a sparkle when she saw Sid waiting for her.

The chains around Boo's hands and feet jangled as she shuffled to the table and sat sideways on the chair. By the way she looked, she hadn't a grain of fight left.

"Guard, can't you take these off while she's in here with me? My god, the woman isn't going anywhere."

The deputy closed the door behind her as if she hadn't heard Sid's plea.

"Okay, Boo, I guess this is the best we can get. Let's talk. Have you been arraigned yet?"

Boo nodded. "Last night."

"Does Durwood know you've been arrested?"

She nodded. "He was at my house when the sheriff came by."

"Okay, good, then has a lawyer been notified?"

"Don't need no lawyer, I'm pleading guilty and getting it over with."

"What? You can't do that, Boo."

"Don't worry, the judge said I had to have a lawyer, and if'n I couldn't afford one, he'd appoint one for me."

The old woman cleared her throat then spoke in a voice so low Sid wasn't sure if she spoke to her, or if she thought out loud. "I heard this morning that he appointed me the same lawyer as Durwood's, but he ain't come in yet. Reckon he'll be here directly. Guess it don't make no never mind. It won't do no good to get out. They'll just end up sticking me back in here till I die."

"Well, that's a pity party if ever I heard one." Sid got out of her chair and stomped around the small room for effect. "Whether you've given up or not, if I'm going to help you, it sure would be a lot simpler if you at least tried. Now suck it up—and tell me you're not going to plead guilty. If you do that, I'm wasting my time—and I don't like to waste my time. Do you understand?"

Boo nodded, tried to grin, but the effort came out sickly-looking.

"Are you guilty or not? Did you kill Zeke?"

"I ain't never killed nothing 'cepting critters for dinner."

"Then why do you intend to plead guilty?"

"Ma'am, no offense, but I'd just as soon have 'em put me in the chair as to live in this place, no light of day, no nothin'."

"Well, I've got news for you, Boo Murphy. Texas doesn't use the chair anymore." Sid emphasized *chair* for effect. "They stick needles in your arm."

The room grew quiet except for Boo's heavy breathing. When she shuddered, Sid realized she'd hit a nerve. The woman feared needles.

"And besides, it takes many years before the entire appeal process ends. You could well spend the rest of your life locked behind bars. So if you're banking on something quick, easy, and painless, you better think again."

She felt bad, talking so rough to the old woman, but someone needed to shake some sense into her thick attitude.

Boo drew her mouth into a clamped-shut line and stuck out her chin.

"Okay, I'm done." Exasperated as hell, Sid opened the door to the waiting deputy. She turned back to Boo. "I'll tell you what I will do. I'll go by your lawyer's office and see why he hasn't come by yet. Meanwhile, you think about what I've said. If you plead guilty, you don't need my help, and hardly that of a lawyer, regardless of what Durwood thinks."

Every time Sid walked into Marv Bledsoe's office she snickered with the memory of the first time she'd come to see him and found a young redhead astraddle his lap. As if that wasn't embarrassment enough, after the girl left, Sid deepened her humiliation by breaking into hysterical laughter at what she had interrupted. Despite a rocky start, however, he'd earned her respect with his assistance in her last case, albeit, rather late in the process.

Marv's regular assistant, Evelyn, had been out sick that first day. Today, she sat with her white head bent over her computer keyboard, which relieved Sid of one worry. Marv wouldn't have a young thing on his lap today, and even if he did, Evelyn wouldn't let Sid barge into his private office and make a fool of herself.

"Morning, Evelyn. Is Marv in this morning?"

Evelyn looked up as Sid entered, adding a bright smile to her greeting. "Hello, Ms. Smart, good to see you. Yes, he's here—and alone, I might add." She flashed a quick, colluding smile and winked at Sid.

So Evelyn had heard the story of the redhead who entertained her boss while she was out sick. Sid wondered who told her. Certainly not Marv, and certainly not Sid. Maybe someone from the temp agency.

"He's in, let me check and see if he has a few minutes." She rose with arthritic slowness and headed to Marv's private office. At the door, she rapped sharply and entered, returning a couple of seconds later to invite Sid inside.

"Sid, it's good to see you." Marv's round red face beamed when he saw her. He stood and walked around his desk sticking out his baseball mitt of a hand. A sprig of sandy blond hair had fallen over his forehead, making him look like he'd been deep into a case before she'd interrupted him. "You and Ben still an item, or do I still have a chance?" He gave her a hug and kissed her on the cheek.

"Sorry, Marv, looks like you missed out. So far, Ben and I are hanging in there." Moving the conversation away from her love life and towards Boo Murphy, she said, "I hear Boo needed a public defender, and the judge appointed you to her case."

"Much to my dissatisfaction," he replied, sucking through his teeth. He headed to a small refrigerator, collected a couple bottles of water and handed one to her then perched one leg over the corner of his desk. "I swear that judge gives me more pro bono cases than anyone in this town. How the hell am I going to make a living doing all these free gigs?"

She took a quick drink from the bottle of water and laughed. "I sure understand that. It seems like everyone who needs a private detective can't afford one."

"Let me get this straight. You're working on this case, too?"

"Not really, although I know it looks like it."

"Why? Judges don't order you to take a pro bono."

Sid smirked. "It's Durwood. Seems he's got a sweet thing going for Boo."

"Well I'll be damned," he said, grinning. "Love, or lust, will make us do all kinds of crazy things, eh? I guess I'm not the only one who gets caught in the 'raging hormone trap,' as you women call it."

"Doesn't look so. Personally, I think he's got it bad, not sure about Boo."

Marv walked back around his desk and sat. "Oh well, the case shouldn't last long. She insists on pleading guilty to first degree murder."

"First degree? Marv, that leads to the death penalty, and you know how Texas courts hand down those judgments and carry out that sentence. She's an old woman, for chrisake."

Marv shrugged and rubbed the back of his head. "Best thing I can do is try to get her life."

"Well, it sure as hell won't take long for her to complete that sentence." Sid spat the words into the room, frustration building in her chest. "She didn't kill the man, dammit."

He stiffened, grabbed a pen and piddled it back and forth on the top of his desk. A look crossed his face that Sid couldn't read.

"What is it, Marv?"

"Oh hell, Sid, I don't have time for your interference. I know you. If you take on Boo's case, you'll get so much shit stirred up and delay this case until it consumes all my time. It's pro bono, for God's sake. The woman said she did it—she did it."

Irritation charged up Sid's backbone. "Have you even been out to the site?"

"Didn't figure there was a need since the woman wants to plead guilty, and from what I hear, there isn't a single clue that she saw a schooner, much less climbed up on it. And if she'd lie about that, she'd sure as hell lie about murder."

"What if she didn't do it? What if she's just given up and has a lawyer who doesn't give a rat's ass? What if she's innocent? That means someone else committed the murder, and if so, why? What's at stake? What was so valuable out there that someone killed a man? Or maybe Zeke's death was an accident, or even a suicide."

"Oh hell, who knows? People go crazy when they think there may be a treasure buried nearby. Their imagination causes them to do all kinds of weird things."

Sid stood her ground. "Are you going to defend her or not? I need to know. The poor thing needs someone fighting on her side, but if you plead her guilty, there's nothing anyone can do that'll make a difference."

His face a mask, Marv stared at Sid without saying another word.

She stood, slapped the bottle of water back into his hand and headed to the door. "Durwood called and asked me to meet him at the county jail at three o'clock this afternoon. If you change your mind, give me a call. I'll be on my cell phone."

Halfway across the room, she stopped and turned back to Marv. "You almost got me killed once before. You screw this up, or keep something from me, and I'll…I'll… Just plead the woman not guilty, okay?" She slammed the door on her way out.

The warm day now matched the heat under her collar, and her shirt didn't even have a collar. She clicked the remote to unlock the car door, but before she reached the vehicle, a tall, debonair-looking man stepped toward her. The unusual cut of his black suit, set off by a white shirt with ruffles for cuffs, made him look like he came from an earlier century. Tan skin indicated a life spent outdoors, but he didn't smell like he had. For when he stepped closer and bowed, the scent of flowery cologne reminded her that before the mid 1800s, men and women wore the same fragrances.

"Madam may you and I kindly have a brief conversation of a most urgent matter?"

Sid almost opened her purse for change, but the guy didn't look like a beggar. Actually, his clothes indicated a certain wealth, albeit greatly out of style.

"It is of the utmost importance to me that you find the document. Many search, but many are unworthy. They look for it with greed behind their eyes."

She glanced around to see if anyone else saw the man, but the only person in sight was a woman with spiked hair across the street in front of Farmers Mercantile, loading bags of feed onto the back of a flatbed pickup.

"What document?" She asked, still looking at the woman across the street. That felt more comfortable than looking into the black eyes of the handsome, strange-looking man. "What are you talking about?"

When he didn't answer, she forced herself to look back his way.

No man stood before her, only a lingering whiff of flowery cologne.

Ten

Shaken by the man's sudden appearance and disappearance, plus his concern over some unknown document, and his plea that Sid find it, made not one drop of sense to her. His come-and-go act didn't either. She got in her car and locked the doors as if that would keep out a ghost. Hell, she didn't even believe in the things, even though now it seemed, she'd seen both a ship and man without substance. But that's what he had to be—that's the only explanation that made any sense. If he wasn't, then he must be one of the many homeless crazies. But he sure didn't look the type.

In most towns, the residents got familiar with the homeless, and even learned them by first name. Once when she'd visited Austin, she saw a bearded, lanky, hairy-legged man named Leslie who walked the streets in high heels and pink, string bikini.

But this guy?

Reminding herself to check with the local police department about the known local homeless, she put aside the man's admonition until she could make better sense of it, and headed off to meet with a contractor about rebuilding her office.

At straight-up three, she walked back into county jail. The duty officer behind the window shuffled papers on his desk, looking up when she walked in. A teenage boy slouched in the corner next to distraught parents, while Durwood sat at a small industrial-looking desk sipping coffee with a Denzel Washington look-alike. Despite her feelings for Ben, the perfect-specimen made her heart flutter. A lot of men didn't interest her, but Denzel wasn't one of them.

She thought about asking where they got the coffee, but when she got close enough to see inside the cups, she decided the men sipped melted asphalt.

"Hey Sid, this is Jackie," Durwood announced when he saw Sid enter the room.

"He's a bail bondsman, and he's here to help me get Boo out of jail. I paid her bail. As soon as we finish this paperwork, and Jackie talks with her, she'll be free to go."

Denzel—Jackie rose to his feet and offered his hand to Sid. "Pleased to meet you ma'am."

"And you." Sid stuttered when he looked her in the eye. His big hand delivered a firm grip before he sat and returned to the paperwork. Meanwhile, Durwood kept defending his actions to Sid, none of which made sense. "You mean they are releasing her on bail this quick, even though she pled guilty to first degree murder? I didn't think they'd do that."

"Well, that's not exactly what happened. You see—"

Okay, here it came, the soft-shoe-shuffle.

"I got here early, just before Marv came to take her before the judge, and I talked her into pleading not guilty. Told her I knew she ain't killed nobody, and she weren't taking the blame for something somebody else did, and that me and you'd be right here beside her. Lord, Sid, she sure is a purty woman when she smiles. She just don't do it often enough. I told her that."

What luck! She might have known she'd get caught smack in the middle of a love-affair between two old codgers.

"What did Marv say when he got here and found out you'd just made his life more difficult?" That thought made her smile.

"Well, he weren't too happy 'bout it, but tough nuggies is all I got to say. She ain't killed nobody. By gum, I ain't letting her say she did." Durwood pounded his fist on his knee.

"So let me get this straight—she and Marv went before the judge, she changed her plea, the judge ruled she wasn't a flight risk and set bail."

"In a nutshell, yeah."

"And you've posted bond." How the hell much money did the guy have under his mattress? "So what more do you want—me to take her case?"

Durwood snickered behind his hand. "Yep, that's about it. That, plus, can you help me get her home? I know she'll feel better with a woman there to comfort her."

Yeah, right, you manipulating old coot. "Sorry, I've got a full day ahead of me. I'm sure you can get her home okay. It's not like she's an invalid or anything."

No way would she outright say she was taking Boo's case. Not the way this guy worked.

"Okay, okay. I hear you. But then why'd you show up here today? You must be having second thoughts, I figure."

Shit. The man could read her mind.

"I'll wait with you until she comes out. Then you can take her wherever you or she wants to go." She smiled and hummed a ditty in her head to block any psychic ability the man might have.

Jackie left to go meet with Boo while Sid and Durwood waited. Durwood was fit to be tied. He stood, he paced the floor, he dusted off his shoes, he went outdoors to spit out the cud of tobacco he'd been rolling back and forth between cheek and gum.

But when he came back in with a proud—but guilty—grin on his face, she knew he'd done something.

He sat next to Sid and leaned in towards her. "Your car's got a flat tire."

"A what? Oh come on, Durwood, don't tell me you let the air out my tires just so I'd go with you to take Boo home?"

He crossed his heart and held his hand up in the air. "I swear—I didn't do no such thing, Sid. I wouldn't do that to you."

"Yeah, right. But you were glad when you saw it flat, weren't you?"

"Well…" He smiled. "You can't blame me for that."

A few minutes later, Boo and Jackie walked into the lobby. Boo had changed from jail garb to a print dress, probably the one she'd worn when they arrested her, along with white socks and brown brogans. Her gray, wiry hair hung down her back, still in a long, thick plait. Her face looked as white as Jackie's shirt.

He smiled as he handed her over to Durwood, who took her by the arm and sat her down. "She's pretty weak," Jackie said. "You might need to help her to the car. The matron says she hasn't eaten a bite since she's been inside. Swears the food tastes like garbage."

"Now Boo, listen to me." Jackie sat at her side. "Remember, you have to call me every Tuesday without fail. If you miss one time, you forfeit bail, and I cash Mr. Durwood's check. That's a lot of money for a friend to lose. Plus, the sheriff will be coming to your house to pick you up immediately, and you won't get out of jail then until after the trial. That is if you're found innocent of the charges. So don't forget."

"Here's my phone number." Jackie put a business card in Boo's lap then glanced at Sid. "And I'm giving one to Ms. Smart and to Mr. Durwood just in case you misplace yours. Call me, okay?"

Boo nodded, flipping the edge of the card between her thumb and forefinger.

"Call me if you need me." He gave cards to Sid and Durwood, shook hands, and walked out of the building with Sid's racing heart.

"Get me outta this place." Boo said, squirming with impatience.

"The sooner the better, is what I say. Wait here. I'll go pull the truck up to the front door." Durwood wiped a smear of tobacco off the corner of his mouth as he headed outside. As eager to leave as Boo, and knowing she had a flat tire to deal with, Sid walked out right behind him.

His rattle-trap of a truck sat next to her shiny, taxi-cab yellow Xterra. Sure enough, her left front tire sat airless. Darn, she must have driven over a nail or something—or maybe just sitting beside Durwood's truck took the wind out of the tire's sail.

A bright idea gleamed behind his eyes. "If'n you'll ride with me to take Boo home, I'll bring you back here later and help you change your tire."

What a promise. Hell's bells, she could change a tire, but…

Feeling as trapped as the bee in the spider web, Sid relented. "Okay, Durwood, okay."

"Great!" He hurried around and started the truck while Sid went inside and got Boo.

After getting the weary, half-starved woman into the truck and settling her in the middle, Sid climbed in.

But it took a couple of bangs before she got the door closed and locked. For all the good that would do. At any minute the whole vehicle might well fall apart in the middle of the road.

Durwood shifted into first gear, eased on the gas as he released the clutch, and soon they were rumbling down the road.

"You gonna be okay staying all by yourself?" Durwood asked. Although he spoke to Boo, Sid knew the inference was that Sid should get involved.

"Most certainly! Been out there in that house ever day since I came outta my mama! Ain't nobody running me off. I ain't kilt nobody, and I ain't afeared of nobody neither."

The farther they drove, the bigger the knot grew in Sid's gut over getting involved.

Durwood turned onto a hard-packed dirt driveway that ran between two look-alike houses, neither of which had a lick of paint on the walls. Identical concrete slabs led up to weather-beaten porches. Off to the side, brown swamp water lay still as death.

Sid opened the squeaking truck door while Durwood hustled around from the other side. Together, they helped Boo out of the cab and across the dirt-packed yard. Before they reached the porch, a huge mongrel loped toward them, his tongue dangling out the side of his mouth. Sid braced her feet, unable to stop the dog's forward motion or get out of his path.

The dog jumped on them with such force they all three tumbled to the ground, the dog on top. A mass of wriggling arms and legs and wagging tail twisted and turned on each other like a pile of earthworms trying to get out of a rusty tin can.

While the dog slathered Boo's face with his long, wet tongue, Sid scooted out from under the pile. That's when she saw a big gash, still crusted with blood, on the friendly dog's forehead. Boo must have seen it at the same time, for she chucked the dog under his chin and asked, "What happened to you, boy?"

He whined and licked her hand, tail still wagging wildly.

"Here, let's get you inside and settled then I'll clean up his wound for you," Sid said. She and Durwood took Boo by the hand and helped her to her feet.

Before they got inside, however, a car drove into the yard and parked in front of the other house. Sasha's, Sid figured. She turned to see an elderly well-groomed woman get out of the car cradling a Hobby Lobby-looking vase in her arms.

Sid turned back to Boo. "Is that your cousin?"

Boo shot a quick glance across the yard. "That's her all right. Reckon them are Zeke's ashes in that vase. She'll probably put him up on the top shelf in her bedroom closet alongside the ashes of her good-for-nothing brother, *Willie Wino*. Years ago, she dumped Willie in an old shoebox, and if'n she don't stop spilling him on the floor and having to sweep him up, she ain't gonna have enough of him left to spread, if she ever decides where. I'm surprised she spent money on a fancy vase for Zeke. He durn sure wadn't worth it."

Sasha glanced over at them and hurried inside, slamming the screen door behind her.

"Just ignore her." Durwood took Boo by the elbow and ushered her up the steps and across her front porch.

But when they stepped into Boo's front room and switched on the overhead light, chaos lay before them. Tables were upended. A smashed lamp lay beside dishes broken to smithereens. Papers and magazines were strewn across the floor.

"What in tarnation is going on?" Durwood shuffled through the house, his whole demeanor registering the same shock Sid felt as she walked along behind him. In the bedroom, someone had ransacked the drawers and tossed the contents around the room, pulled everything off of the closet shelf and thrown it in a heap.

"Someone believes you did find that pirate ship, Boo, and you got some of the treasure hidden here in your house." Durwood limped around the room picking up women's undergarments between his index finger and thumb and gingerly dropping them on the bed.

Speechless, Sid stared at the mess when a movement out of the corner of her eye caused her to fear they'd surprised the burglar. But it wasn't a thief, it was Boo, fainting and on her way to the floor. Sid grabbed at her, but already unconscious and a dead weight the old woman slid from Sid's grasp and hit the floor. A loud crack sickened Sid's stomach.

Sid dropped to her knees beside her. "Oh Durwood, she's fainted, and look at that bone sticking out of her arm."

"We gotta get her to the hospital." Durwood tried to squat down beside her, but only got halfway down before he gave up and grabbed the bed for assistance back to his feet.

"Look, the phone's over there under the coffee table. See if it's working and if it is, dial 911." Sid eased a pillow under Boo's head, ran to the bathroom for a wet washcloth, and wiped the woman's pale face.

While they waited for the ambulance, Sid dialed Marv's number. When he answered, all she said was, "Your client's house has been vandalized or robbed, and she's fallen and broken her arm. We're taking her to Memorial Herman Hospital. Meet us there," and without waiting for him to say a word, disconnected the call.

By the time the ambulance arrived, Boo had regained consciousness, but when they tried to stabilize her arm, the pain prevented them touching it. They sedated her and she soon lapsed into oblivion. Once prepared for transport, they loaded Boo inside the vehicle. With assistance from the attendants, Durwood crawled up into the ambulance and sat beside the stretcher, one hand caressing Boo's forehead, the other wiping away his own tears.

After the ambulance pulled out, sirens wailing, Sid fed and watered Dog, cleaned his wound, and applied some salve on it from a kitchen drawer that hadn't been upended.

Then she assumed the unenviable task of driving the rickety, stick-shift truck to the hospital. She hoped no one she knew saw her. Hell, she hoped no one saw her, period.

Eleven

After the emergency room staff set Boo's arm and put it in a cast, Boo insisted on going home while the medical staff insisted she stay overnight.

The battle inside the room matched a battle Sid heard going on out in the hall. She let the nurses deal with Boo while she went to investigate, Durwood following on her heels. A contingency of folks had gathered outside the room. One group blathered about the old woman on the other side of the door, wanting confirmation that she'd found the pirate ship. The other, much smaller, group held cameras over their heads and snapped pictures.

A small man with a mass of feral red hair caught Sid's attention. The way he strutted around the hallway reminded Sid of a bantam rooster prancing around claiming he made the sun come up. "Ma'am," he said, leaning into Sid, "we have a right to know about the pirate ship that woman found. It ain't right she gets all the treasure. We demand she tell us where it is and what she done with what she took off it."

From the corner of her eye, Sid saw a nurse pick up the phone and ask for security.

"Yeah, we have a right to know, that bayou's public property." Another man spoke up, feeding off of the confidence of the rooster.

A heavy-set woman, her black skin glistening in the overhead lights, walked over and shoved the man away from Sid. "You men shouldn't be bothering this woman. That ship was one of Lafitte's slave traders come in from Barbados, I'm sure of it. And the good lord told me the ghosts of them slaves was still there in the bowels of the ship awaitin' to be set free. Voodoo, I tell you, is the onliest thing that'll free 'em from their watery grave so's they can go on to their heavenly rewards."

Her 'heavenly' had a B in it instead of a V.

"Ain't no such thing," Rooster said, puffing his chest out. "It's Lafitte's Hotspur, for dang sure, but it ain't got no slaves in its belly. If anything, she's loaded with gold coins from Napoleon's stash. I know she is. My daddy told me how he saw her one day when he was out in the swamp, 'cepting that time it was closer over yonder to Louisiana."

The heavy-set woman stuck her finger in the little man's face. "If you don't get some *gris gris*, things ain't never gonna be made right with them spirits, I'll tell ya that!"

Marv walked up, stepping between Sid and the growing crowd. "It's okay folks. We'll get to the bottom of this," he said. "And the authorities will keep the public informed. Now you folks go on and let us take care of our client. We've got an innocent woman accused of murder. Ya'll know Miss Boo. You've known her all your life. You know she wouldn't kill anyone. Now let's give her a break while the specialists in these kinds of things take over. So give it up, folks, give it up."

The crowd dispersed, grumbling as they stalked away.

Marv leaned over and kissed Sid on the cheek. "Getting yourself in a little trouble, are you? I thought you hadn't taken on this case."

"I haven't. And leave it to you to get here in time to have your photo taken for the newspaper."

"Hey! Free publicity can help make this pro bono case worth my while, and it can help you too, if you'll work it." He pulled up his drooping pants and tucked in his shirttail.

"She's insisting on going home today, Marv, and I don't know what to do with her if she does. She can't stay by herself in this condition, plus in a ransacked house. You should have seen it. It's a mess."

"And hello to you, too, sweet lady. I thought you'd be glad to see me. After all, I dispersed your mob. You haven't even said hello, and here we are almost lovers."

Irritation mingled with her inability to dislike the man. "Give me a break, Marv, you know that's hardly the case, and besides, calling me a lady is editorializing."

"How you figure that?"

"*Lady* describes a woman's behavior. If I were one, I wouldn't be considering punching you in the nose." She stuck the back of her hand up to his face and flashed her engagement ring. "Besides, see, I'm still wearing Ben's ring, so we couldn't be lovers."

"Correction," he said, grabbing her hand. "I said *almost lovers,* and one of these days you're going to wake up and realize what you're missing. And just why is it, every time I see you, you're in a peck of trouble?" He smirked.

Ignoring him, she turned to Durwood. "After that break-in, and now this mob, I'm not sure it's safe for Boo to be home alone. And then there's her cousin Sasha, next door, who thinks Boo killed Zeke. We can't count on her help."

Durwood grunted agreement.

After much harangue between Boo and the emergency room physician, she finally agreed to dismiss Boo with the promise that Boo wouldn't stay alone for the next day or so. Soon they had her in an attendant-guided wheelchair, heading out the door.

Durwood limped along beside Sid as she hurried ahead to open the truck. "I guess we can take her to my house, and she can sleep in my bed. I'll put my old camp cot in the living room and sleep there," he said. Then, with a look of complete despair, he held out his hands. "I don't know what else to do with her, Sid."

"We should have figured this out before we left the hospital with her."

"She didn't give us a chance. She was so gosh darn bent on leaving that place…"

"She sure can't stay alone, and I'm not sure she'd be safe at her house even if she didn't need help." By now, Sid had the truck door open and leaned inside to shift things around to make it more comfortable for Boo and the accompanying pillow for her arm.

Boo slapped at the hands of the attendant, who had reached down to assist her out of the chair. "You two quit talking about me like I ain't here, or like I'm some imbecile who can't understand a word you're saying."

Sid broached the topic with Boo. "Both Durwood and I think it is too dangerous for you to stay out at your place. We're taking you to Durwood's." Then she clenched her teeth while waiting for the onslaught she knew would be coming.

"You ain't doing no such thang, you take me straight home. I ain't sleeping with a man I ain't married to. Heavens to Betsy, what would folks around here think?"

Durwood sucked through his teeth and glanced over at Sid. "Wha'd I tell you. She may be cute, but she sure is a stubborn old coot."

After ten minutes arguing in the hot truck parked in the hospital parking lot, Sid came up with a new suggestion. "I'll tell you what, let me call Marv and see if he thinks you'll be safe at your house. If so, then maybe we can find someone to spend a couple of nights with you. If he says okay, I'll go along with it."

In the back of her mind, Sid played with the idea of Annie staying with Boo for a couple of days. She could always bring King Cat, and that would give Slider a temporary break from the cold war the two waged. But she certainly didn't want to put Annie in danger.

Okay Marv, don't disappoint me here, she thought, punching in his number.

Relieved when he answered, she explained Boo's demands and had no trouble convincing Marv what she needed him to say—that under the circumstances, it wasn't advisable for anyone to be staying out at Boo's house.

But that didn't satisfy Boo. "Gimme that contraption. How do you talk into this thing?"

"Just put this part to your ear, and speak in here." Sid pointed to the tiny microphone and handed the cell phone over to Boo, who listened to Marv, and then handed it back to Sid.

"Here, hang this dang thang up. I don't know how to work these new-fangled contraptions."

Boo's chest puffed up like a toad frog. "Okay, I'll go to Durwood's for a couple a days, but I have to have a chaperone. You know, another woman staying there at night. Otherwise, it don't look right."

"Let me see what I can do." Sid said, thankful they'd at least get the woman past Durwood's front door, although she felt sorry for the man if they couldn't find an attendant.

By the time they reached Durwood's little fishing cabin alongside the Neches River, Sid had called Annie, explained the situation, and Annie had agreed to help out, excited about being involved in another case. Not that Sid had actually accepted Boo as a client yet, but it sure felt like she had.

Annie said she'd pack a bag and Chesterfield and follow Sid's directions to Durwood's. She'd be there within the hour.

By the time Sid got Boo up the front steps and settled in the back bedroom, Durwood had water boiling and finger sandwiches piled on a platter. But he looked pale and winded. Sid reminded herself she also needed to keep an eye on him.

Before they finished the snack, Annie's maroon Oldsmobile screeched to a stop in the driveway.

Sid put her hand on Durwood's arm. "You rest, sweetheart, I'll let her in," she said, and headed to the door. But before she got halfway across the room, Annie bustled in with an armload of cat, yellow roses, and a stack of *Southern Life & Style* magazines.

"Where's that dear lady? I'll take care of her." Annie looked around the room with a big smile on her face—that is until she spied the inch-thick dust on Durwood's furniture. She lifted her nose a couple of degrees and started in. "What we need to do is load Boo in my car and take her home with us."

Durwood cut his eyes over at Sid, "Seems she don't know Boo like we do," he said, grinning as wide as the cat stretched across Annie's arm. "You ain't never gonna get her to agree to that. We had a hard enough time getting her here to my house."

Sid suppressed a smile, hooked her arm around Annie's, and led her to the back bedroom.

Boo bristled when Annie laid the magazines in her lap. "What's these dang things for? I ain't got time to read this nonsense!" She shoved them to the floor, whereby Annie picked them up and plopped them back on the bed.

"They're good to pass the time, Miss Murphy, while you're at my house. You'll like the column in there about Phenomenal Women, bet you know some yourself, heck, I hear tell you are one. Plus, we can cut out recipes and I can cook them while we visit, get to know each other better."

"Humph, name's Boo, not *Miss Murphy*." Boo sneered, trying to cross her arms over her chest until the pain reminded her why the doctor casted one of them.

"You poor dear, you're arm must hurt awful. Here, let me fluff your pillows. We've got time for me to get you some nice cold water. You can take a pain pill before we head out."

"I ain't taking no pills—don't trust 'em—ain't never—ain't starting now. So you can just forget that. And you get away from me. I ain't going nowhere else, I just got settled here."

The room grew silent. Even Whiz, Durwood's dog, stood in the door without making a sound or twitching the fly off his nose.

Sid saw Durwood look first at Boo and then at Annie. She followed suit. Meanwhile Annie had started collecting up Boo's few things and poking them in a plastic grocery bag she'd found lying nearby.

"I ain't going nowhere else, I tell you. Take me back to my

house right now!" Boo swung her legs to the floor.

"Now Boo, you said you'd go along with Marv's advice until he found out..." Durwood grabbed Boo's good shoulder and tried to settle her.

"Oh hell, that lawyer couldn't find his ass with—"

"Boo, hush that." Durwood didn't even try to hide his growing irritation. "These people are a trying to do something nice for you. Don't you make me sorry I talked 'em into it."

"Hush your mouth, you old goat!" But Boo reached for the pile of magazines with her good arm and pulled them up to her chest.

As though she was the creator of perfect timing, Annie chimed in again, "Come on, honey, let's get you to my house and get you settled before dinner. I'm making the best chicken 'n dumplings you ever wrapped them flappy gums around."

That got Boo's attention.

"'S'at so? Well, when I get this dang cast off, I'll cook up a pot of my stewed squirrel, and then we'll see who the best cook is."

Mark one up for Annie.

The two women argued over recipes while Annie got Boo out of bed and ushered her outside to the Olds. Sid started to follow them, but Durwood took her arm and held her back. "I got something I want to ask you."

Glad for the excuse to escape the deadly duo, Sid placed her hand atop Durwood's and settled him on the edge of the bed. He leaned over and wiped a speck of dust off his still-shiny black shoes then sat up and looked Sid square in the eye. "You changed your mind about this case? You ready to take it? You gotta help the poor thing."

"I really need paying cases."

"Ain't you got insurance?"

"Not enough to rebuild and keep body and soul together. Looks like I'm the full support not only for myself, but Annie, too, since Uncle Frank died. Soon as she can get the farm sold, she'll be okay, but right now, bills are piling up."

But the reason Annie was broke, Sid reminded herself, was because she bought a big money-pit of a house and moved to town to help Sid.

He sat staring at Sid, his crusty eyelids red-rimmed and moist.

Dammit, she was tired of taking cases like this—people broke. Reminded her of the commercial where the pre-teen girl says *TNF* to her mother—instant messaging lingo for *that's not fair*. Why was it that, for some folks, everything came easy, good things just multiplying like rabbits?

But for her—plow, plow, plow, and still a half-ass crop.

Twelve

While Annie went to the kitchen to get Boo something to eat, Sid and Durwood helped Boo upstairs and settled her in the blue chintz bedroom across the hall from Annie's.

It wasn't long before Annie bustled in carrying a tray with a steaming bowl of potato soup. "Okay, you two," she said, "Boo's my patient, you all go on and get. Let me do my job. By the time she eats her soup, and I help her get a bath, she'll be ready for a nap. Sid, you did say you'd pick up her prescriptions didn't you?"

Best news Sid had heard in what seemed like forever. "Sure, I've got to go fix a flat tire first then I'll stop by the drug store."

The lines that had creased Durwood's face smoothed out. He straightened up, grunting as he stood. "Come on, Sid, I'll take you to your car and we'll change the tire. Boo, you rest, and behave yourself, okay?" He followed Sid outside.

When they pulled into the parking lot where she'd left her car, the flat tire wasn't flat anymore. Relieved, but stunned, she wondered if her eyes had played tricks on her. But a note under the windshield wiper explained. *Sid, one of my deputies re-inflated your tire. Keep an eye out—may have slow leak. Quade.*

It had a slow leak all right.

Durwood looked as relieved as she felt, and rightly so, since she figured *he* was the slow leak.

He headed on home while Sid headed to the pharmacy.

The prescriptions were ready, but the check-out line had grown to four-shoppers long. Impatient, she picked up a copy of

The County Record. Sure enough, Marv's picture was plastered across the front page.

Geesh, that was fast. Marv will be happy to see he's made the news. She thumbed through articles about the latest teen-aged movie star's DUI antics, a picture of Oprah Winfrey in her front yard playing with her newest puppy, and an op-ed about the rapidly-growing cartels from Central and South America and how they were believed to be involved in smuggling operations off the Texas coast.

Smuggling—she knew it existed, but the reality of the article made her uneasy. Any activity related to cartels threatened everyone. The stranger in front of Marv's office warned her about the unworthy who searched for some document. She wished he had been more specific. What document, and who were the unworthy? Relieved when it was her turn, she stuffed the newspaper under her arm, paid for her purchases and headed home.

Annie stood at the kitchen stove humming and stirring her fabulous-smelling dumplings. Sid wished she could bottle the woman's energy, buy a wagon and hawk it at medicine shows. *Annie's Exciting Energy Elixir. Guaranteed to make you work through the night.*

On second thought, maybe not.

Content, Chesterfield lay curled in a ball at Annie's feet while Slider whined from behind the back door. Sid sucked through her teeth, irritated by Annie's favoritism. When Sid cracked the door, Slider stuck his head in the kitchen and peeked at Annie. When she ignored him, he walked on in and snuggled his head against Sid's leg. In turn, she rubbed the top of his head. "Hey boy, you hungry? Let's see what I can find that you'll eat, I'm fresh out of your favorite brand of yogurt." She opened the pantry and pulled out a bag of dog nuggets. "Looks like this is all we have." She shoved the bag toward him, but he ducked his head and stalked back into the laundry room.

Annie pulled a piece of paper out of her apron pocket and handed it to Sid who had just sat at the kitchen table. "Chrissy wants you to call her. Said she has a favor to ask you."

That didn't sound good. Sid's daughter only called when she needed something, and that something was usually money.

"That woman upstairs is a stubborn old coot," Annie said, changing subjects. "I told her I'd go over and help her get her house straight soon as she feels up to it. I figure that'll be tomorrow—by the way she's talking."

"Tomorrow? Not even. It'll take longer than that for the sheriff to find out what's going on."

"She's not a killer, you know. Ornery cuss, but I'm willing to bet she never hurt a fly. Squirrels maybe, and lots of fish, but not dogs or cats, and definitely not humans. I hope you're taking her case." Annie banged a large spoon against the pot rim.

"She has no money, sweetheart. And we need a *little* bit!"

"Don't worry about that, Siddie. We'll get by."

Not so convinced, Sid stood and said, "I've left Boo's medicine here on the kitchen table. I'm going to go call Chrissy."

Her daughter hadn't called in awhile, not since she'd cried on her mom's shoulder after she'd just told her Baptist preacher father that she'd moved in with Maxx, a high school band teacher. It had taken Sid an hour to smooth Chrissy's feelings and reassure her she was an adult and free to make her own choices—regardless of whether or not her father believed she was living in sin. Now, she dialed the number and waited.

"Chrissy, it's Mom," she said when her daughter answered.

"Mom, thank goodness you called. I don't know what to do."

"Chrissy? You okay? What's wrong?"

"I'm…"

Sid held her breath, for she had already filled in the rest of the sentence.

"…pregnant."

"Oh no! Christine!" Sid flopped back in her chair, as deflated as a grounded hot air balloon.

Annie chose that minute to step into the room. "What? What's happened?" Her henna-painted eyebrows arched upward.

Sid waved at Annie. "Just a minute, let me find out."

"I'm pregnant, and I'm sick," Chrissy wailed.

"You mean morning sickness?"

Annie hustled next to Sid. "She's pregnant? Is the guy going to marry her?"

Although Sid tried to ignore Annie's onslaught of questions, it wasn't easy. Fact of the matter, it was impossible, and on the other end of the line, Chrissy's voice grew higher pitched than Annie's. "Morning sickness, noon sickness, night sickness—all day sickness. Mom, you never told me it would be like this! I've missed so many classes I had to drop out of school, and then—then—they fired me at work."

"They fired you? Why? Because you're pregnant? That's illegal—"

Annie swung Sid's chair around toward her. "Don't tell me she lost her job, too?"

When Sid didn't answer, Annie reached across and punched the speaker button on the phone.

Chrissy voice broadcast into the room.

"No, not because I'm pregnant—because I threw up on a whole table of customers just as I sat their food on the table, and then—then…"

Sid wanted to scream at Chrissy, at Annie, at Maxx, at…

Instead, she held her breath and waited for the next shoe to drop, unsure whose shoe it might be, Annie's or her daughter's. When neither shoe fell, she asked into the now useless receiver she still held in her hands. "And then what?"

"My landlady gave me till Friday to pay our rent…and, and…" More sobs, sniffling.

"Damn it, Chrissy, stop sniffling and tell me the bottom line before my heart stops beating."

"…and I don't have any money!"

There it was. The words *don't* and *money* in Chrissy's sentence always came stuck with a big emphasis, like Sid was stupid for ever asking.

"What about Maxx, isn't he helping you? I assume the baby's his."

"*Yes* it's *his*, and *thanks* for asking." Chrissy's clipped, overemphasized words made it clear Sid's question offended her. "I haven't told him yet."

"But, why Chrissy? You have to tell him!"

More sobbing. "He's out of town on a band trip. Took the kids to Spain, and won't be back for a couple of weeks." Sid held her breath, knowing what was coming before it got there. When she glanced at Annie, she could tell Annie knew too, and welcomed it.

"Can I come home for a few days, until I can talk to Maxx?"

Home, where the hell was that? Since her divorce from Sam, she didn't have one either. The brief stay in an apartment hadn't been long enough to feel like hers, and now, she lived with Annie. Think, Sid—

Before she could, Annie chimed in. "Of course you can, honey, you pack your bag and get yourself here. We can put you in one of the upstairs bedrooms. This house has a ton of them. Shoot, when the time's right, we can even turn one of the rooms into a nursery."

"Aunt Annie? Is that you? Where'd Mom go?"

"Oh she's over here shaking her head at me. I just put you on speaker phone."

"Speaker phone? You mean I've just broadcast that I'm pregnant and unmarried to the whole world?"

"Not the whole world baby, just your mom and me. We're here for you."

"Did you talk to your dad?" Sid asked, shushing Annie with a wave of her hand. "He's probably moved back into the parsonage by now, I'm sure he'd let you move back into your old room again, at least until Maxx gets back in town."

Chrissy brought her sobs under control, which slowed Sid's racing heart, but the next words jerked Sid right back into adrenalin overload.

"He and Mrs. Carpenter—I mean Mrs. Smart—aren't back from their *honeymoon* yet." Chrissy's mocking words reflected a deeper pain.

The room grew quiet. Sid looked at Annie and Annie looked at Sid.

Evidently a light bulb went off in Christine's head, and she added, "You knew Dad had gotten married didn't you?"

"First I've heard about it. Came up kind of sudden didn't it?"

"Yeah, last week, but she's been after Dad for a long time—even before you left. I knew she was into him—saw it in her eyes when they talked. She moved in for the kill while he was still vulnerable—before someone else got him. Mom, I tell you, she's eager to turn herself into the woman Dad needs—one who agrees with everything he says and does. She looks at him like he's God."

Chrissy stopped and took a deep breath, but Sid knew she wasn't done.

"So you see, I can't go there and live with them, much less tell him I'm pregnant. You know how he'd react. He'd make me feel like a woman caught in sin and ready for stoning. I couldn't stand that."

Good lord dog, Sid certainly knew what that felt like.

"You come on, sweetie," Annie filled in the silence. We'll have your room ready. Your mama is ignoring me these days, anyway. All she does is call contractors about her new *office*.

After Chrissy rang off, Annie huffed out the door, saying over her shoulder. "Won't it be fun to have a baby in the house?"

"You're getting a little ahead of yourself, Annie." A grandbaby might be fun, but where was the money coming from? And then there was Boo, upstairs.

To get her mind off the situation, Sid dialed the sheriff.

"Quade here," he answered in his usual, brusque but friendly manner.

"Good evening, friend. Thanks for fixing my flat."

"Hey, Sid, what's up? I heard you got Boo Murphy at your house. You sure are a softy. That woman is guilty as sin."

"Maybe she is, maybe she isn't. From what I've seen, your evidence looks circumstantial. Ever consider whodunit, instead of grabbing the first person without an alibi?"

"Dang, Sid, whatever happened to that nice, sweet little lady that first moved to Orange?" He laughed after his words, but even Sid realized that woman was long gone—thank goodness! They talked a few more minutes when Sid heard the familiar bleep of another call coming in. The caller ID showed it was Chrissy again.

"Oh God, don't tell me…"

"What? What's wrong?"

"It's my daughter calling on the other line. I just talked with her, and she's sick. I really need to take this."

"Bye," he said. "We'll catch up later. I still want to know how you plan to prove Boo innocent."

"I don't plan to prove it," she said, panic rising in her chest, but he'd already clicked off the line.

"Hi Mom, it's Chrissy again. I've got some good news."

Was this the same Chrissy she'd just talked to?

"Right after we talked, Maxx called. I told him about the baby, and he's so excited. He's cutting his trip short and he wants me to go stay at his mom and dad's here in town until he gets home next week. So I won't be coming there after all. Tell Aunt Annie thanks for me."

So Maxx stepped up to the plate, and Sid wouldn't have a cat, a dog, Annie, Boo, and pregnant Chrissy all in one house at the same time.

When the call ended, Sid headed upstairs and told Annie about Chrissy's change of plans and then peeked in Boo's room. She was fast asleep, her hair spread across the pillow like a gray halo. Sid knew better. No halo would ever fit this cantankerous, sharp-tongued old woman.

For that, Sid gave thanks!

She crawled in bed, eager for sleep, for respite from the exhausting day, but she ended up struggling with whether or not she should take Boo's case. Part of her said yes, the other part said no. Truth be known, she already had.

Slider apparently sensed her concern. Instead of lying on his back in his chair, his legs straight up in the air, and snoring, he crawled in bed with her and snuggled in close. He fell asleep before Sid, and for once, his snoring put her to sleep.

Thirteen

The morning sun shot through the window and hit Sid in the eye like the blade of a broadsword. "Damn, that's bright." She struggled up out of a dream so deep she felt like she'd entered another realm.

After she pulled on a pair of khaki shorts and a tee shirt and crammed her sockless feet into sneakers, she and Slider headed outside. The heat and humidity made her feel like she'd donned a plastic bag over her head.

By the time they'd rounded the corner and headed back toward the house and air conditioning, both she and Slider panted, his long tongue dangling out of his mouth dripping saliva. She chuckled. "Lucky duck, wish I could go around with my tongue hanging out. Maybe I'd be cooler." Slider pulled his tongue in and slurped then it dangled out the side of his mouth again.

Despite the weather, she dreaded going back inside. Dreaded listening to the two battleaxes argue over the tiniest thing. Yesterday, the topic had been the best way to cook chicken and dumplings. At one point Sid just knew the two nags were about to exchange blows, and then Boo just backed off. But Sid had seen the grin on Boo's face as she'd turned and nonchalantly strolled out of the kitchen, unaware that Annie stood behind her holding a large metal spoon in the air and steam coming out the top of her head.

Shaking off that memory, Sid picked up the newspaper from the front lawn and jogged around to the back of the house. Lifting the lid to the trash can she tossed in the Ziploc bag of Slider's business, and headed up the back steps and through the door.

Inside, the cool quiet—vacant!—kitchen welcomed her. Laying the newspaper on the table next to the sugar bowl, she hurried upstairs to shower and dress before Annie and Boo came downstairs and started another cat fight.

"I don't know how much longer I can put up with those two women in the same house," she confessed as she and Slider escaped to her office without getting caught.

Slider nudged her hand and she dug her fingers into his curly red mop. "Those two biddies are driving me crazy. I've got to get Boo back to her house pretty soon or…"

Slider sat back on his haunches and whined in sympathy.

"If I have to listen to those two arguing about who's the better cook one more time… Besides, Sasha says Boo hates to cook and doesn't if she can get someone else to do it for her, so why in hell does she argue with Annie?"

Desperate to get her mind on something else, she pulled out a pen and a tablet to list the few clues she knew about the case she hadn't admitted to anyone but herself that she'd accepted.

After several minutes sitting with a blank piece of paper, she tossed the pen on the desk. "Truth is, Slider I don't have a clue what's going on, and that's a problem. A non-existent pirate schooner, a dark-haired man who dresses like he lived in the 1800s, and a big-busted pirate queen not afraid to bare her breasts not only leaves me at a loss of how to get my hands around this case, but it also makes me fear for my sanity."

As if her words concocted a vision, the image of Andrine Gilbeaux formed in the middle of Sid's forehead right above her eyes, and she remembered she'd dreamed about the voodoo woman the night before, right before she'd awakened in the middle of a hot flash.

Andrine Gilbeaux was a dark-skinned woman who lived in a house on stilts out in the middle of the swamp. Just the word voodoo rattled Sid's cage. To intentionally go visit a voodoo priestess raised every warning flag in Sid's religious training not to trust her own sense of knowing, but rather the dogma handed down from patriarchs.

In her lifetime, when anyone thought Sid's opinion was wrong, she'd scurried back into her corner to hide, fearful of taking a stand on anything. But since she'd left Sam, she'd learned the difference between fear of everything outside that denominational norm, and trusting her own discernment between good and evil.

In the stillness of the moment between decision and indecision, Sid felt a quiver in her chest. Part of the quiver, she knew, stemmed from residual fear of the unknown, the other half, excitement over the same.

Once, Andrine had helped Sid make sense of things, maybe she could again. The choice made, Sid left a note telling Annie where she went and when she'd be back—by two p.m. at the latest.

"Sorry bub, I hate to leave you here to face those two by yourself, but I won't be long. Good luck." She hugged Slider and left.

Hoping against hope that she'd find Pirogue Pat, the same man who had taken her out to Andrine's before, she turned into the parking lot of Bluebird Fish Camp. Sure enough, there he sat mending fishing nets, dressed in a threadbare pair of striped overalls and a dingy white tee-shirt. If she didn't know better, she'd think he lived sitting at that very spot. As a matter of fact, she didn't know better. Maybe he did.

"Morning, Pat," she said, slamming her car door. "Got time to take me out to Andrine Gilbeaux's house again? You know, the one up on stilts?"

"Shore do, ma'am." A big toothless grin revealed pink gums surrounded by a gray scraggly beard and mustache. "I be glad to. Here, lemme put this stuff away."

When they climbed into the pirogue, she couldn't tell who smelled fishier, Pat or the handful of fish plopped in a bucket parked in the bottom of the boat.

Easing his long pole down into the murky water, he backed the aluminum, flat-bottomed boat away from shore and eased it out into the middle of the bayou and around the bends leading to Blue Elbow Swamp. The last time she'd been in this part of the swamp, she'd promised herself never again. The place gave her the willies. Maybe it was the play of dark and light on the water, maybe it was the quiet, or the critters. The bayou was beautiful, mystical even, but memories of what she'd seen the couple times she'd been in Blue Elbow overshadowed the beauty.

Hopefully it wouldn't always be so.

The alligators along the shore didn't seem as surreal as they had the first time she'd gone to Andrine's house, but they still reminded her of logs floating lazily downstream. Their appearance of passivity didn't fool her. One clamp of those jaws and the reptile had its dinner.

Mosquitoes dive-bombed. She slapped three of them off her forearm, and then had to clean off the resulting smear of blood. Served her right for not wearing a long-sleeved shirt—that and the big-brimmed straw hat that Annie wore when she trimmed the yellow rose bush near the back fence.

Beads of sweat popped out on her top lip. She wiped them off with her shirttail as she eagle-eyed a fat water moccasin gliding across the surface. Spanish moss dangled in her face when they passed underneath low hanging trees. She batted it away, wishing she could do the same to the chills coursing down her spine, on the one hand regretting her decision to go, and on the other, eager to get there.

But when Andrine's house, high on stilts, came into view, and the tall dark-haired, dark-skinned woman stood waiting on dock's edge, sunlight glistening off the mass of multi-colored beads around her neck, Sid knew why she'd come. Andrine knew, too, for before Pirogue Pat got the boat tied to the dock, Andrine reached in, grabbed Sid's hand and pulled her up and out of the boat.

Goose bumps popped up on Sid's arms. After both feet were

firmly planted on the creaky, dilapidated dock, she looked up into Andrine's face and received not a welcoming smile, nor a forbidding frown, but a mouth stretched into a thin tight line, and opaque black eyes that revealed nothing.

Andrine held Sid's hand tight, and in silence led her up the plank walkway to wide, rough-hewn steps, through a screened-in porch, and straight to a back room.

Of course Sid had a choice. She could break tail and run, but a powerful force inside her nudged one foot ahead of the other. Unable to stand the silence another minute, she blurted out, "You knew I was coming didn't you?"

Andrine headed to a table covered with the same crocheted, ecru-colored tablecloth and indicated Sid's chair, across from hers. With slow, deliberate movements that only heightened Sid's discomfort, Andrine struck a match and touched the flame to the wick of a thick white candle sitting in the center of the table.

Andrine reached across and clasped Sid's hands in hers, jangling the long beads on the edge of the table. "Yes, I knew you come 'cause I bid you."

"You bid me? How? What? I don't understand."

"I bid you from here—" Andrine placed the tips of her fingers on the middle of her dark-skinned forehead—"last night in you dream. I go to you and say come. I know you hear, 'cause I see you sit up and lie down both at the same time." She nodded. "Yes, I know you come. I know why you come."

"How do you know that?" Sid waved her hand. "Never mind, even if you told me, I doubt I'd understand."

"Sure you understand. You like me, you just don' know it yet. But you getting there, child."

"I don't want to take the case, Andrine, but I know I already have." Sid cried.

Andrine offered nothing, no words of encouragement, no sympathy, and no tissue to wipe her eyes and nose. Instead, she closed her eyes and grew quiet for longer than Sid could keep still. She fidgeted in her chair, scanned the room, looked out the open window while Andrine's eyes went blank, like she looked into the back of her head, or out into another world.

Trance-like, she spoke, but her words made no sense to Sid. "She don't smile, she don't frown, but she look bold ahead out to sea with her green eyes. She buxom, like," Andrine lifted her own pendulous breasts in demonstration. "Hmm, yeah, she nod yeah." Andrine turned to a shelf behind her and randomly picked a card from a Tarot deck. Sam preached that any type of divination was of the devil. But nothing in the room felt evil. Quite the contrary.

Andrine flipped the card face up on the table. "Queen of Swords."

"Okay."

"Not powerful card, like you might think from sword in her hand. See how she look? Chastened, sorrowful, embarrassed even?" Andrine stared through Sid. "You know female, name starts with M? Older, much older.

"No, not that I can think of."

"M, like Mary, Martha."

"Oh, yes, Martha, George's wife."

"She shake head, no, not Martha, shorter." Andrine corrected.

"Mary?"

"That it."

"But I don't know anyone named Mary."

"She relation to woman with ghost name."

"Ghost? Do you mean Boo?"

"She smile nod yes. She back to clear karma. Make amends, she say, help you find killer."

"Help? How in the world is she going to help me? I can't hear her, I can't see her, and I don't even know who she is."

"Listen, child, and breathe, breathe and listen."

"Listen? To what?"

"Listen to what you know be true for you. Stop taking everybody else word on what truth be. Listen deep inside. Close eyes, listen—listen. What you look for is right there, right beside what you not seeing."

Sid sat rigid, staring at her white-knuckled fists on the table in front of her. "That makes absolutely no sense to me," she said through clenched teeth. "And I don't know if there is any truth in divination—at least for me."

Andrine turned and pulled out another card and put it on the table in front of Sid. "Page of Swords."

"So?"

"Page passes over rugged land. Secret service, spying. Something going on deep, deep, deep. And when Andrine look at card, she see double. Maybe mean two spies. Listen."

The room grew quiet. Somewhere off in the corner a cricket chirped. A gull squawked outside the window. Swamp water lapped against the stilts. Breathe, she reminded herself, and blew out a long, heavy breath. Then, filling her lungs to capacity, she held it for a second and breathed in a subtle hint of burned sage she hadn't detected when she'd first come in. Her muscles softened. Tenseness flowed off her shoulders and her jaw went limp.

"Listen," Andrine whispered. "Listen to what you hear."

"But—"

"But nothing, just listen."

"But all I hear is the crickets and the—"

"Jus' practice, child. In time you will. You got truth inside you. Ain't nobody else can tell you what that truth is for you. You got answers, honey, trust me. Now go home and make them pickles."

Pickles? What did making pickles have to do with any of this? Frustrated at her inability to hear whatever in the world Andrine was talking about, Sid bid her goodbye, unsure whether or not she'd wasted her time coming out here. Actually, she felt more confused than ever. As if Durwood wasn't enough, she now had this buxom red-headed spirit named Mary telling her what to do, and some secret something going on—which could be related to George's recent involvement in illegal activities. One message she'd heard loud and clear. Don't fret over whether or not to take Boo's case. She'd already taken it on, and that fact was enough to make a more experienced detective shudder.

Back at Bluebird Fish camp, Sid thanked Pirogue Pat as she crammed a few bills in his hand. He gave a deep bow of thanks, climbed into a jalopy of a pickup and drove away, leaving her alone in a deserted parking lot backed up to the bayou.

She rounded the car and climbed behind the wheel, but just as she stuck the keys in the ignition, a movement from the back seat startled her. She jerked to look when large, hot hands locked around her throat. She slammed her hands to his, pulling, prying, fighting for air.

He loosened his grip enough for the descending blackness to lift, but his fingers still clenched her neck. She tried to fight him off, but every time she moved, he squeezed tighter.

"I'm warning you, lady," he hissed, "stay out of business what's not yours."

She slammed her eyes toward a movement on her right just as a large hulk of a figure in a black ski mask lunged inside the passenger door and fighting off her hands, crammed a small canvas bag over her head. The man behind her slowly released his hold while the other successfully tied the bag around her throat despite her effort to stop him.

Her breath came a little easier when he removed his hands from her throat. Desperate now, not knowing how long she had before he cut off her supply again, she inhaled a big gulp of air. When she did, the sour, foul-smelling sack over her head made her gag. Oh God, she couldn't throw up now, or…

Barely aware of hands rushing, pushing, pulling, shoving, soon they had her out of the car, hands tied behind her back. They shoved her forward.

My god, the bayou lay straight ahead. Ben flashed in her mind. She guessed he'd been right about her needing a less-risky job. And it galled her that he'd say so at her funeral.

They half-dragged her across the old wooden dock. One of

her sneakers came off, but the two maintained forward movement. Rough hands half lifted and half dragged her and dropped her down onto a firm, but rocking surface.

Pat's pirogue? He'd left it there when he'd driven off. Was that what she was in? It must be, for there hadn't been another boat in sight when she and Pat tied up.

Disoriented, when the men released her she toppled backwards, slamming her spine against the edge of the metal seat.

"You won't need these, little lady," one of them said, and jerked the pole and the paddle out from under her.

"We don't want to kill you bitch. We just want to get your attention." The other voice said. "Your ropes aren't too tight. You can get them free, but it'll take a little while. Have fun out there with the 'gators."

They shoved the boat away from the dock, laughing.

Sid scooted to what she hoped was the center of the boat, hoping to stop the sway.

"You take care, bitch, and keep your nose out of business that ain't fuckin' yours," one of them yelled.

Who's business, Boo's?

The boat floated away from shore. When an engine started and she heard a vehicle burning rubber, she relaxed a little, certain that being tied up and alone out in the middle of the swamp was better than being with the two who had just attacked her.

That didn't alter the fact that her hands were bound behind her, a stinky bag tied over her head, and she sat in the hull of an oarless flat-bottomed boat out in the middle of the swamp. If she caused the boat to tip over, she'd either drown before or after she became dinner for the alligators.

The pirogue continued its slow glide through the water, but how far she'd moved from where she'd started, she had no idea. It couldn't be far, she guessed, but without a paddle and unable to see, she might as well be in the middle of the equatorial doldrums.

Despite her attacker's claim, the ropes were so tight she couldn't move her wrists. Maybe she could work her arms under her butt and get them in front. At least then, perhaps she could get the bag off her head.

But all of that required movement—and with it, a rocking boat.

Steadying herself again, then, slow-like, she squirmed until she got her hands down to her rear and tried to ease them underneath. But it was no use. Her arms were too short and her butt too wide. All she accomplished was rocking the boat. If, by per chance, she ever got out of this mess, the first thing she'd do was go on a diet.

She yelled through the canvas bag until she grew hoarse, but when she stopped, all she heard were cicadas, tree frogs, buzzing mosquitoes, and an occasional splash in the water. Mosquitoes feasted on exposed skin, but all she could do was twitch in pain.

At length, she dozed, awoke, and dozed again. Once, when she'd awakened, she realized the day had grown cooler and realized sunset approached. Maybe in the morning a fisherman—maybe even Pirogue Pat—would find her. Just lie still and wait, she told herself. She could survive a night out in the swamp as long as the boat stayed afloat.

But, jinxed by that thought, a trickle of water puddled around her bottom.

Fourteen

"Sid? Sid, can you hear me? Is that you out there? Sid? Answer me, Sid, please answer…"

She twisted around toward the sound of Ben's voice, a voice coated in desperation and panic. "Ben? Is that you? I'm over here," she yelled through the bag, uncertain how far her muffled voice carried.

"How the hell did you get out there? Is that something over your head? Are you hurt?"

"I'm okay, but yes, it's a bag. I can't see you, and my hands are tied behind my back, and I don't have an oar."

"Hang on. I'm coming out to get you?"

"You have a boat?" she yelled.

Instead of an answer, she heard a splash. Was he swimming in this treacherous water? "No, Ben, don't swim out here. It's too dangerous. Just go get help. Call Quade or 911."

The thought of Ben in the water scared her more than her abandonment in a boat. She spun around listening for any sound that might be a threat to his safety. What in the world she'd do if she heard one she had no idea—other than scream, and a lot of help that would do. She'd screamed for hours.

Her ears attuned to the sounds of Ben's strong strokes, she peed her pants in relief and excitement—either that, or the water seeping into the bottom of the boat had gotten deeper.

"Ben, Ben, I'm over here. Can you see me?" She wanted to wave her arms so badly, and without thinking, tugged on the ropes, driving them deeper into her wrists.

Settle down, settle down, she told herself, when, in her excitement, she made the boat rock furiously. That's all Ben needed, her going overboard.

They'd never talked about swimming before, but even blindfolded, she could hear the power in his strokes. The words *my man* came to mind and she giggled like a middle-school girl. She hadn't felt that way since she'd been that age.

She felt him pull his forearms over the edge of the boat to support himself, dripping water all over her as he worked. He twisted her around, grappled with the rope until he got it untied, then slipped and fell back into the water.

"Ben, are you okay? What happened?" She grabbed her head and fought to get the bag off. Then he was back, wet and winded, reaching up through her frantic hands to untie the bag.

"Wait, here, I'll get it," he said.

The first thing she saw as her eyes adjusted to the light, was Ben shaking water off his face and out of his hair like Slider would have done.

"My god Sid, someone set you up for a slow death. Who did this?"

Without another word, he slid back down into the water, edged his way around the edge of the boat and started kicking and pushing.

He swam a few yards, stopped to catch his breath then started again. By the time they reached shore, the sun had set, and the only light in the area was one lone mercury vapor light high on a pole. Ben tied up the boat, got Sid out, and soon had her in his arms. Nothing had ever felt so good, even if both of them stank something awful.

After a time, her clothes now as wet as his, he leaned back and stared her in the eye. She wasn't sure which emotion looked the stronger, fear or anger.

"Now tell me who in hell did this to you." Panic smoldered in the demand. He held her at arm's length then snatched her close again, as if afraid to let her go.

"I don't know who they were, honest. They wore ski masks. But how did you know how to find me? How did you even know I was in trouble?"

"To tell you the truth, I'm not sure. I called you this morning, and Annie said you'd gone to see Andrine. She figured you would leave from Bluebird Fish Camp like you had before, but she wasn't sure. Said you'd be home by 2 at the latest and she'd have you call me."

"But I didn't call."

"No, you didn't. I hesitated to call back because… Well, because I know you don't like accounting for your whereabouts—especially to me." He looked at her sheepishly.

"And it damn near got me killed." Sid pulled away from Ben and flopped onto the weather-beaten bench where Pirogue Pat had mended his nets earlier that day. Had it just been that morning?

Staring at her raw wrists she said, "I can't believe how stupid I've been. How in hell did I think I could do a job like this? I'm just a naïve ex-wife of a preacher who has spent her whole damn life in a bubble, who knows nothing about the real world."

He sat beside her and put his arm around her shoulders. "It's okay, you deserve a few minutes to beat up on yourself, but you're carrying it way too far."

"Humph." Tears of relief started to flow, making her even madder at herself. She swiped her arm across her eyes.

"I'd give you my handkerchief, but it's soaking wet." Ben laughed. "Anyway, by seven o'clock, Annie was calling me, worried sick. Said you weren't even answering your cell phone—and she's called it *a hundred times*."

Sid laughed. "I'll just bet she has."

"I decided to risk you getting angry with me. I drove out here and found your car with its door hanging open and your bag in the passenger seat, untouched. That's when I panicked and started yelling for you. You know the rest."

When she didn't say anything, Ben took her chin in his hand and turned her face up to his. "I'm just so glad you told Annie where you were going. Otherwise, I don't know how long it would have been before we found you—days even—months." He shuddered.

Sid knew what he was about to say, she should give up the practice. Do something that didn't put her life at risk on a daily basis. Well, she couldn't argue against that anymore. "Okay, you win. I'll close the Third Eye."

"Close it? You mean let these guys win? Sid, they almost caused your death and you don't even know who they are or why. You can't just throw up your hands in defeat. That's not the woman I love and respect."

Sid stared at him, dumbfounded.

"What about the cases you're working on? You can't leave them high and dry."

"Well shit, Sam, that's what you've been wanting. I figure these guys played right into your hands. For all I know, maybe you hired them to scare the hell out of me."

Ben looked her in the eye. With solemnity in his voice he said, "I am not Sam. My name is Ben."

She hadn't even realized her slip of the tongue. "Whatever." Mixed emotions oozing out of every pore, she marched to her car, surprised he didn't try to stop her. She backed around and headed out, disappointment and heartache swelling into a giant lead ball plopped in the middle of her chest.

When she looked in her rear view mirror the reality of what she fled hit her. Ben, who had just saved her life, still sat on the bench, head down, shoulders slumped, his hands clasped between his knees, with the sound of sirens heading their way in the background.

That did it. She couldn't leave like that. She swung the vehicle around and headed back, feeling like a first-class jerk.

He stood and watched her come, his smile glistening in the pale light.

She screeched to a stop and, with the motor still running and the door wide open, she jogged around the front of the car and plunged into his arms. "I didn't even thank you," she said between sobs.

"Yes you did, Love. Not in words, but..." He ran a comforting hand up and down her back, sobbing himself. After both of them stopped laughing and crying and hugging, Ben said, "Okay, babe, we need to talk. We can do it here, soaking wet and half-starved, or we can get a good night's sleep and talk in the morning. I suggest the latter."

Sid nodded. "I'll give you a call tomorrow. Maybe we can meet for lunch. The Bread Box, okay?"

"Perfect. 11:30?"

"See you there." She blew him a kiss and returned to her car just as a police cruiser pulled into the lot. "Who called them?" She looked quizzically at Ben.

"I called 911 right before I jumped in the water."

"Hey, sweetheart, you're 911 all rolled into one." She squeezed his arm and watched as the policeman headed their way, reporting to dispatch through the radio phone on his shoulder.

After retelling her story while the officer took notes and another cruiser showed up, Sid promised to go by the police station the next day and submit a full report, and they all headed home.

Uneasy, she checked her rearview mirror and saw Ben's car following her, making sure she got home okay. This time, she didn't mind.

While she drove, she pushed speed dial one for Annie, remembering how scared she herself had been when Annie had disappeared last year. By now, Annie must be fit to be tied. She tried to hide the tears in her voice while she assured Annie she was okay, but knew Annie hadn't bought it.

As she expected, when she pulled into the driveway, Annie stood on the steps of the front porch wringing her hands. Slider stood at her side, looking as lost as he had the night Sid found him in an ice storm.

Ben tooted his horn and waved as he drove by, calling out as he passed, "See you noon tomorrow."

Bracing for an onslaught of hugs from Annie and slathering tongue-swipes from Slider, Sid exited the car and headed into Annie's open arms.

"Siddie, my poor darling," she squealed, rocking Sid from side to side.

Unstable enough by Annie's hugs, by the time Slider added his weight by leaping on her with his front legs, they all three tumbled to the grass. For a few seconds, arms and legs and tail all intertwined, the owner of the red hairy tail barking wildly, and then licking every square inch of bare skin he could find.

"Slider, enough! Hush!"

But Sid's words only made him bark louder.

Unable to hold back the laughter, first Sid and then Annie sat up, hugging their knees to their chests, and laughing. The more they laughed, the funnier it got. The giggles continued until the front door slammed and they looked up to see Boo heading their way.

"What in the world is so dang funny?"

Slider loped over to Boo and barked an explanation while Sid and Annie regained their composure.

Sid rose to her feet and stuck a hand out to Annie. "Here, let me help you up."

They all went inside and while Annie prepared hot tea, Sid ran upstairs, took a quick shower, dotted Calamine lotion over hundreds of insect bites that itched like hell, and slipped on her white terry cloth robe. Feeling halfway human again, she went down to the kitchen and inhaled the sandwich Annie had fixed for her, and recounted the day's events. But she stopped short of sharing the doubt she had felt about her ability to run a private detective business.

"Boo, I need to say this outright to you. I plan to do everything in my power to uncover the truth about Zeke's death."

Boo waved her hand at Sid. "Aw, pshaw, I knew that, everybody did."

The next morning when Sid and Slider walked into the kitchen after their morning stroll, Annie and Boo sat chatting over the remains of scrambled eggs and bacon. The air seemed, well, almost…friendly?

"Can you drive us to the beauty shop, Siddie? I got to get this woman's hair done. I can't stand it stringing down her back like that another day. My car's out of gas and we're running late. By the time I got Boo's clothes on over the cast, and we ate breakfast, we've run out of time."

Irritated by the delay this would cause, but even more, unstable over the new and almost unbelievable change of attitude between the two women, Sid looked over at Boo. "You okay with this?"

She nodded. "I figure it's time I spruce up a little, what with my picture being in the paper and all."

Sid figured it also had something to do with the way Durwood had been giving her the eye, but didn't dare say a word about that. "Okay, if we're going, let's load up. I have to go by the police station and sign a statement then I'm meeting Ben for lunch. I need to get you two back here by mid-morning." She hustled them out the front door.

Between the seatbelt and Boo's casted arm, getting her settled in the front seat was a bigger ordeal than Sid expected. Thank goodness Annie climbed in the back seat without making a fuss about getting booted out of the front. The passenger seat belt buckled around Boo, Sid buckled her own. "Okay, where to?"

"We're going to the Pamper Me Parlor. Its over behind Wal-Mart. Boo said she'd been there with Sasha one time."

All the way there Annie questioned Boo about the hairdresser. "How old is she? I hope she's not some scrawny-butt gal with tattoos and body piercings."

"Well, I'd hardly call her scrawny. She's more a broad-assed redhead."

That comment reminded Sid of the buxom redhead she'd seen—or thought she had—and the one Andrine talked about. Seems the area sported a lot of the fire-hair folks. All that Scots-Irish blood, she guessed.

"Hey, she sounds like me."Annie perked up.

"She's kin to me and Sasha somewhere down the line, but I ain't never been to her to get my hair washed. Heck, I wash it in the kitchen sink when it needs it. But not that Sasha, she throws away good money every week getting hers done." Boo pointed to a small white house with an attached carport between it and a room on the other side. "There it is, right there."

Annie leaned over the front seat and peered through the windshield, drowning Sid's olfactory senses in Tabu cologne. "You sure this is it? I don't see a sign or nothing."

"Oh, this is it all right. She don't advertise none, and she don't take new clients excepting what she calls *referrals*."

Sid parked in the driveway and unbuckled her own seat belt first, then reached over and unlatched Boo's. "Hang on a minute and I'll help you out."

"Never mind, I can get her from my side." Annie exited with a grunt and then assisted Boo. Sid walked behind the two as they headed up the driveway and into the shop. A perfect example of the blind leading the blind. Or better yet, the stubborn leading the stubborn.

Sure enough, a big, attractive red-head with dark intense eyes stood behind a chair combing out her last client. The shop's décor matched that of the owner—nothing shy or retiring about either of them. Purple and gold walls blended with green plastic chairs positioned in front of a big window. Bright sunlight filtered through white sheers. The warm temperature of the room matched the reception.

"Come in and have a seat," JoAnn said, not missing a beat

either combing or talking. They got in on the last of a conversation, and from the sound of it, Sid wished she'd heard the first.

"I told him to de-ass my shop." JoAnn waved the comb toward the door. "Ain't no man coming in here and telling me how to run my business—he may be the dictator at his house, but here, I'm queen-of-the-hill."

The woman under the comb egged JoAnn on. "Did he leave, then?"

"Well, he argued a little more, but I told him he'd had his last tra-la-la to town with me, and don't show his shiny ass round here no more."

When Sid looked over at Annie, she'd have sworn her ears stretched to the ceiling. Unable to resist the conversation any longer, Annie finally chimed in. "Sounds like he really pissed you off. Wha'd he do?"

"Bottom line, he'd been trying to get me to go out with him, said if I'd lose some weight he'd make it worth my while. Humph, worth my while my eye! Hell, I shop in the junior moose department, and I got to butter my ass to even get through that door. I ought to own Weight Watchers by this time—I've been in the program for 30-40 years. If I was meant to be some anorexic-looking thing, I'd be skinny by now. Hell, a girl who does look sexy is expected to pay for it with some silly old man out there dressed in his sex clothes. No sir, that ain't for me. I'm just fine the way I am."

The customer pointed to a hair out of place and JoAnn straightened it with her fingers.

She took the cape from around the woman, shook the hair to the floor and swept it into a dust pan. The customer waved over her shoulder as she left the shop. "See you next week JoAnn."

"We better get your hair done, Boo, before you collapse here on the floor and break another arm." Annie said, helping Boo over to the shampoo bowl.

JoAnn did hair as fast as she talked, and in no time Boo had been shampooed, trimmed, blow-dried and styled.

"You look like a million bucks, Boo. You should have gotten that long straggly hair cut years ago," Annie said.

Boo cut her eyes over at Sid and smiled. "Next thing you know, she's gonna be setting me up on a blind date."

"Hey, honey, you don't need a blind date. Hadn't you seen them eyes Durwood's been cutting over at you? If you hadn't, I sure have. He's got it bad." Annie took Boo by her good arm and marched her out the door and to the car while Boo protested about Durwood all the way.

By the time they got back to Annie's, Slider stood at the front door desperate for a potty walk. He squirmed and whined as Sid grabbed a couple of plastic sandwich bags and the two headed outside. Lacy patterns of afternoon shade dappled a sidewalk hot enough to scramble the proverbial egg, except this time Sid wasn't sure about the proverbial part.

As soon as they stepped back inside, she heard the phone ringing. She unleashed Slider and, still breathless, hurried to grab it before the caller hung up.

"Wow. How about that—I've taken your breath away!"

"Not really," she said, laughing at the male voice on the other end—evidently someone with a sense of humor. "I had to rush to get to the phone. Who is this?"

"Hoke Faulkner. Forgive my sick sense of humor. I called to see if I might come by and talk with your client, Boo Murphy, I understand she's the one that says she saw the schooner, and that she's staying at your house right now."

"That's correct, but she's not really up to questioning yet. She fell and has a compound fracture of the arm. Plus, she'll need to check with her lawyer first. After all, she's been arrested for murder."

"So I hear. When do you think she'll be up for it? I've got some questions for her."

"Like what?"

"Oh, just some details I need to tie up for the university.

They keep calling me asking for more and better description of what she saw."

"No one has even seen the ship but her, and I'm not even sure she did." In the back of Sid's mind niggled the thought that what Boo saw might well be the same thing Sid saw that day she went out with Shipwreck and the others to look for Boo's schooner. If so, there was no way in hell anyone could crawl up on a—a—ghost ship—or whatever the hell that was. "I don't think Boo climbed on anything, except maybe in her mind. What convinces you she did?"

"Well, she said she did. If she'd just talk with me, I think I'd know how to proceed, or even whether I should just forget the whole thing and go back home. As it is, I don't know which way to go."

The conversation grew quiet. Sid held the phone to her ear and listened to him breathe while she debated his request.

"I'm not going to get her in trouble, if that's what you're thinking. Actually I can probably help her, if she did indeed see the schooner and take something from it."

Take something?

"Well, if I can't talk with her, how about you? If you haven't had lunch, meet me over at the Bread Box—my treat."

"Sorry, I have lunch plans—can you hold on a second," she asked, as Annie stepped into the office and handed Sid a note.

It seems Ben had called on the other line. He was caught in court and couldn't make lunch. Could Sid save dinner for him that evening?

Back on with Hoke, Sid said, "My lunch date has had to cancel."

She agreed to meet with Hoke, but for some odd reason, before she left, she made sure the Glock was in her handbag, along with an extra round of bullets.

Fifteen

Quaint southern charm started at the door of the 50s style house which had been converted to the Bread Box restaurant, and continued to the small table for two, decorated with a small vase of fresh flowers in the middle of a table covered with a chintz tablecloth.

Sid saw Hoke Faulkner sitting at a table by the window sipping from a glass of tea. She headed that way without waiting for the hostess. He stood when he saw her, and by the time she reached the table, he'd pulled out her chair and held it for her.

"Thanks Sid, I appreciate you meeting me here. I also hope you don't mind that I ordered for both of us—kind of in a hurry myself. I've got an appointment this afternoon."

"No problem about the ordering. I just don't know if I can help you. I suppose you want information about the schooner, but you probably know more about it than I do. After all, you're the archaeologist."

"Business is not the only reason for our lunch meeting. Sid, you're a good looking woman. I enjoy your company." He winked then glanced down at the engagement ring on her finger. The one she'd purposely pulled out of her nightstand and put on before heading to lunch. She fingered it, turning it around two or three times, resisting the urge to tuck her hands in her lap.

Okay, time to change the subject from her, to her purpose for the meeting, and that was to get a better picture of this guy and what he wanted. Something about him still didn't sit right.

"I figured some of your graduate students would have arrived in town by now to help you look for the ship. The sheriff's cleared the area for further study. When do you think they'll be here?"

"As soon as I give the go-ahead, a carload of them should arrive within the next couple of days. We've had to get permission from the state and federal park services, since the schooner sits in the Intracoastal canal—or at least we think it does. That's why I wanted to talk to Boo. I need details from her before we start."

The server walked up with two small clear-glass bowls of white gazpacho soup.

Sid dipped her spoon into the bowl and tasted the cool, refreshing soup. "Mmm, delicious, try it."

She waited for Hoke to take a spoonful before she continued. "I don't understand what you think I can do for you, or how you think Boo can be helpful. She's not at liberty to say much of anything until the charges against her go away."

Hoke's next words surprised her. "I'm just interested in what she found when she climbed up on the bow."

What she found? Archaeologists were usually more interested in the schooner itself, rather than what a person might find when they climbed on board. "If you want my opinion, I'm not even sure she saw an actual ship."

Hoke looked up, questions in his eyes. "Why do you say that?"

Sid sat her glass down harder than she intended and splashed iced tea on her hands. She wiped it off with her napkin and returned the napkin to her lap. "I don't know, just a feeling. That and the fact no one else has seen the schooner." Not counting the ghost ship Sid had seen, of course.

"I can't let it go yet." He looked at her with eyes that pled his predicament.

"She's recovering from a broken arm, Hoke. Someone broke into her home and trashed the place. Any idea what they might be looking for?"

He shrugged. "Not a clue."

To Sid, he didn't sound or look surprised.

"I won't stay long. Just a couple of questions are all I need to ask her. Sure would appreciate it."

They each took their last spoonful of soup. The server replaced the bowls with sampler plates of sandwiches and refilled tea glasses.

Sid picked up half of an egg salad sandwich. "Okay, tell you what. Let me check with her lawyer first. We don't want to get her into more trouble than she is already. If he says okay, I'll ask Boo. But if she says no, you're out of luck."

"That's a deal." The man looked relieved and settled down to finish his lunch.

Afterwards, they headed separate ways, Sid promising to get in touch with him after she talked first to Marv, and if he approved, with Boo.

Sid headed to Marv's office to ask him about Boo talking with Hoke, but halfway there, got a hair up her butt about something else. She'd never really talked with Sasha. Hoke could wait, and if she stalled long enough, he might go away.

It took a good fifteen minutes to get there, but when she pulled into the dirt driveway between the two houses, she saw Sasha in the yard picking up trash. Dog trailed along behind her sniffing at the ground. Soon as she saw Sid, she hurried up the steps, went inside and slammed the screen door. And in about the time it took to walk from the door to the window, a hand pulled the curtains aside for someone to peek out.

Dog acknowledged her presence with a couple of monotone barks, tucked his head and tail in surrender and sniffed the smell of Slider on her pants leg.

She held her hand down for him to smell. "See? I'm friendly and so is Slider. The two of you would get along great."

Dog looked up and wagged his tail, inviting personal contact. She squatted down to his level and rubbed his head back and forth with both hands. "Hey, boy, think we might be able to convince Sasha I'm not a witch?" She looked back up at the window to see Sasha still watching her. Okay, Ms. Sasha, it's time for us to talk. Sid headed across the yard, up the steps, and knocked on the screen door. "Sasha, it's Sid Smart. I'd like to talk to you for a few minutes. May I come in?" She waited for any sound from inside, for Sasha's footsteps heading to the door.

Nothing.

"Listen, I know you're upset. You've lost your husband and you feel betrayed by Boo. That's okay. You're entitled. I just want to hear your side of the story, that's all. I'm not trying to get Boo off if she killed Zeke. I just want the truth. Okay?"

Sid was about ready to turn around and walk off when the sound of soft soled feet shuffling across the floor gave her hope. She waited another couple minutes.

Sasha eased around the open wooden door and faced Sid on the other side of the screen, defiance in her eyes.

"Shall I come in, or would you rather us talk out here on the porch?" Sid indicated two weather-worn rockers with faded-blue seat cushions. She stepped back as Sasha opened the screen and, without a word, led them to the chairs.

For a couple of minutes, they both sat and rocked, neither of them saying anything. Sid waited, hoping for Sasha to start. When she didn't, Sid did. "I'm sorry for your loss."

"No you're not." Her ruby red lips tightened into a stubborn line. "You're just being polite." She reached up and tucked a wandering strand of hair back into a silver bun.

"Sorry you feel that way. That's not the truth."

"Boo didn't like Zeke. She never gave him half a chance. It didn't matter what he said or did, she always put him down for something or the other. I seen the way she always looked at him—like she wished for a chance to get a rope around his neck and pull." She spat out the last couple of words.

"I know his death came as a shock, and what an awful way to find him."

"Me and Zeke was married close to seven years. Before that, I was an old maid, just like Boo. She's never forgiven me for marrying first." Sasha sat and stared at her hands folded in her lap. It hit Sid, how little she knew about Boo. "So Boo never married—I suppose she doesn't have children either."

Sasha shook her head.

"So, it's been just the three of you living out here next door to each other all these years, huh?"

"That's about it."

"Boo should be coming home soon. I guess you've seen the detective watching her house huh? Did you know someone broke in and trashed it?"

"I seen the ambulance come get her." Sasha looked up, concern clouding her eyes.

Sid explained the event and the fact that Boo was at Annie's house.

Sasha shook her head. "I can't believe she didn't let me know where she went. All this time I could've been looking out after her instead of sitting here twiddling my thumbs and thinking…"

Sid reached over and placed a gentle hand on Sasha's shoulder. "I think she felt like you hated her, after your dear husband's death and all."

Sasha's chair rocked faster. "Death maybe…yeah, I could see that, but he never was a dear."

"I don't understand. What do you mean?"

"Zeke was a bastard—a mean, hard-headed, self-centered, pig-headed, secrets-keeping bastard. I'm a good Christian or I'd give you a string of real ugly names for him. Names that would make your toenails blush, Missy." She glanced down at Sid's feet.

Without intending to, Sid wiggled her toes.

"Most folks might not've seen it, but I lived with it. Boo knows—she seen it. And if you ever tell anyone, even Boo, that I said what I said, I'll say you lied."

Sid had never heard of an Indy 500 for rocking chairs, but if there were one, Sasha's would win hands down. And at the moment, Sid's would come in second. She gouged her thumbnail into her index finger to suppress a snicker. Why she found it funny, she wasn't sure. It wasn't funny. It was sad—heartbreaking. Maybe Sasha's story hit too close to home, too close to the subterfuge she herself had lived with for so many years. She suddenly felt a kinship with this woman, unlike her in so many ways, so alike in others.

"Why is it you don't want anyone to know what kind of man he was?" Sid nudged, fearful Sasha, whose body had grown tense and rigid-looking, was about to rock up on her feet, head inside and lock the door.

Instead of getting up, however, Sasha tightened her jaw and spoke through clenched teeth. "Because I won't have those biddies down at the church talking about me behind their hands, snickering, acting like their husbands are *God's gift to mankind*, when I know all the while most of them are bastards too, because in private, the biddies tell me they are. Treat women like their only place here on this earth is to wait on men hand and foot. I know all men ain't like that, but those at that church dang sure are. They act like they're the almighty himself, telling women what they can and can't do. How women are supposed to be submissive, obey the husband and all that shit! Zeke's dead, so I'm not a deacon's wife anymore. I won't never set foot in that place again."

Okay... Sid rocked faster, afraid to say anything, uncertain what to say even if she could get words out of her mouth.

By the time Sasha wound down, their dueling rocking chairs had almost walked off the porch. Sid went inside and got Sasha a glass of cold water and waited while she emptied the glass. She pulled out a business card and put it in Sasha's lap. "Are you going to be okay?"

"I am. I don't think I've ever felt better in my life. Would you please tell Boo I'm taking good care of Dog?"

"I certainly will. And my phone number is on the card. If you need me, or want to talk again, give me a call."

Sid got in her vehicle, her head reeling over what she'd learned about Zeke. She'd been so busy feeling sorry for Sasha, then cheering her on, that the idea that perhaps Sasha had been the one to kill her husband didn't hit Sid until she'd gotten out on the highway. She headed to the law office of Marv Bledsoe, Boo's court-appointed lawyer, hoping he could advise her about the wisdom of Boo talking to Hoke.

When she arrived, she learned Marv was in court. She told his secretary, Evelyn, what she needed to know and Evelyn sent him a text message. He replied immediately and saw no problem in Boo talking to Hoke. He'd be in touch with Sid soon.

Yeah, right. He saw no problem because he didn't care enough about Boo. What was it about some lawyers who only focused on the outcome of a case, winning, instead of working with an impeccable intent, focusing on the process with a high degree of integrity? She wondered if Marv only did that in high profile cases of wealthy clients.

Since his law office sat just a block away from the original Third Eye office, the burned-out office, Sid took advantage and stopped off to talk to the contractor she'd hired for the rebuild before she headed home. After they finished talking, Sid stood outside her car, called Hoke and gave him the okay to talk to Boo.

"Can I come by now?" He wanted to know.

"Sure, I'm headed that way. I've got one more stop to make. Meet me out front in an hour. I'd like to check it out with Boo before you barge in."

"I'll wait out in front of your house until I hear from you," he said. "See you then."

Just as she punched the off button, Quade drove up in his patrol car and stuck his head out the window and called out. "Hey Sid, I hear you have my suspect at your house."

"Damn it, Quade, you know she didn't kill Zeke. What reason would she have?"

Quade gave a belly laugh. "Greed, Sid, greed! G R E E D. Ever hear of it?"

"That woman doesn't have a greedy bone in her body. Ornery bones maybe, but not greedy ones. Have you learned what Zeke was doing out in the swamp?"

Quade got out of his vehicle and leaned against the car door. "Well, yes and no. That's what I called to tell you—that is if you're working this case—which, remember, I advised against."

"And I still don't understand why you're against it."

"The plot thickens, as the melodramatics say." Quade made his own melodramatic pause. "I'm not sure about all the details of this. I'm still looking into it, but it looks like Zeke Harris was also known as Dexter Sweeney. It seems he got in trouble with the law, paid his debt to society, and then moved here calling himself Zeke Harris. It wasn't long afterward that he married Sasha."

"What kind of trouble?"

"Smuggling. It seems he was from a family of smugglers."

"I thought you said the plot thickened. This one just got thicker than gumbo. How'd you find out all this?"

"And that's not all. It seems there's a family connection somewhere down the line to Boo and Sasha."

Sid's heart skipped a beat. "Boo? What kind of connection?"

"Boo's mother's maiden name was Radcliff. That name may mean nothing to you, but it goes all the way back to the eighteenth and nineteenth century pirates who were active in the Atlantic and along the Gulf of Mexico and the Caribbean."

"Oh good lord dog, don't tell me they're kin, that would likely mean he was kin to Sasha, too, besides being married to her. Both women had to know that. You can't marry someone you're kin to and not know it! I might just be the biggest fool in town, believing whatever Boo and Sasha told me. All this time they might well have been in cahoots with Zeke."

By the time Sid finished the last sentence her voice reached fever pitch.

"I told you not to get involved in that case." Quade sucked through his teeth. 'If you'd only listened to me, I could have saved you all this grief.'

"Oh shut up, Quade. I'm dealing with enough right now, I certainly don't need to hear your 'I told you so'."

He grinned like a kid handed a bright red lollipop.

She spun on her heels and stalked to her car. She raced home, tore into the driveway, got out and slammed shut the car door. By the time she'd marched across the yard and into the kitchen, her anger had subsided not one iota. "Where's Boo?" she asked, heat singeing her words.

"She went up to her room to rest. That beauty shop trip played her out." Annie folded the last piece of laundry and packed them in a basket for easy transport upstairs.

"I'll *play her out*," Sid muttered as she turned and stomped out of the room. She'd thought about getting Boo and Sasha together so they could talk about this whole situation with Zeke, but betrayal rose inside her chest with every step up the stairs. By the time she reached the top landing, the anger felt like a solidified ball of rage churning in her gut.

Boo lay on the guest room bed, eyes closed and a slight smile stretched across her lips. Any other time, Sid would have quietly backed out of the room and eased the door shut. This time, she stood with her hands balled into fists so she wouldn't hit the woman. No need to get arrested for elder abuse.

"Why didn't you tell me you were kin to Zeke? And I don't mean through his marriage to Sasha."

Sixteen

Boo's eyes popped open. "What?"

"Oh, you heard me all right. I've been played as the biggest fool in town and you're the maestro with her hands on the Stradivarius—acting so damn innocent."

Boo bolted upright. "What the heck you talking about?"

Sid hadn't heard Annie charge in the room behind her until Annie spoke. "You mean to tell me Zeke was her blood kin?" She stared from Boo to Sid and then back at Boo. "We've been on your side all along, and you keep something like this from us? How could you not tell us that?"

Sid tapped her own forehead. "Easy, she found a couple of dunces. As it turns out, Zeke Harris was an alias. His real name was Sweeney, Dexter Sweeney."

Confusion floated across Boo's face, and a deep crease burrowed an already lined forehead "Dexter? I don't know anybody by that name. Honest, Sid. I wouldn't lie to you. Ain't no Cormac ever been kin to a Sweeney."

"Cormac? Who's a Cormac?" Annie stepped further into the room.

"That's a good question, Annie, one I'd like answered." Sid crossed her arms over her chest and locked her knees in a no-nonsense stance.

"Cormac was my ma's ancestors. Ever hear of Anne Bonny?" Boo swung her legs off the side of the bed and, using her good arm for support, eased her feet to the floor.

The image of Sid sitting on her father's lap and listening while he read a pirate tale of two female pirates flashed in her memory. "She and Mary Reed rode with the pirate, Calico Jack Rackam."

Boo scratched her head. "Dangdest girl pirates you ever did hear. That Anne was wild, beautiful and strong-headed, my grandma always said." Pride glistened around the bottom lids of Boo's eyes, almost ready to spill over and run down her cheeks. She stuck out her chest and said, "Well, Anne Bonny is my ancestor."

"I don't mean to burst your bubble, but okay, so she's you ancestor. What does that have to do with Zeke, or his death?"

"Don't right know that it has anything to do with Zeke's death, but it has everything to do with the feud between the Cormacs and Sweeneys in County Cork, Ireland. You see, Anne's father was a Cormac and his wife's maiden name was Sweeney. The problem is, Anne's ma was one of his household servants. That started a feud between the two families, setting the whole town in a riot. Later, Daddy took the servant Peg, and their baby Anne, and they fled for their lives, settling in Charleston, South Carolina."

Slider crept into the room. He ducked his head, tucked his tail between his legs and eased over to Boo. She patted his head absently while staring at Sid and Annie. "What I don't understand is why Zeke, or Dexter, would come to town and pass his self off as somebody he ain't? I don't get it."

The room grew silent.

Dawn broke across Boo's face. "Sasha will just die of shame when she hears she was blood kin to her own husband. But what I don't understand is why'd he go out in the swamp that day and look for the schooner? You think he believed there was gold on board like other folks in this town think?"

"Could be," Sid said then held back. Boo's innocent expression had fooled her once before.

"Maybe he thought you'd gone out there?" Annie piped in.

Boo scratched her head again. "Yeah, but that don't make no

sense. Why would me being out there have anything to do with what he did?"

"It would make sense if the two of you were in cahoots." Annie stepped over closer to Sid.

That remark turned Boo's face crimson. "I'll take one of them lie detector tests, I swear I will! I ain't never seen that man before in my *life* until he married Sasha. And I dang sure didn't do nothing with him, except maybe tolerate him for Sasha's sake."

Sid turned her back on the others so she could think straight. It didn't help. "There's something else I haven't mentioned. It seems this Dexter Sweeney served prison time for smuggling."

"Smuggling? Well, that makes more sense than anything else I heard. Our ancestors were into smuggling—but as far as I know that ended when Jean Lafitte and his gang were put out of business."

Jean Lafitte? Everywhere she turned she met someone fascinated by the guy, but what could he possibly have to do with any of this? Sid's anger settled down to a sputtering glow. She paced the large bedroom, feeling the eyes of the two women and the dog following her every step. Andrine said the Queen of Swords indicated she should take Boo's case, but she didn't claim Boo's innocence. Who the hell was Queen of Swords?

"Okay, I don't know what is going on, but for some reason, I believe you."

"I am, Siddie, I swear to you."

"Oh no you don't—don't call me Siddie. Call me Sid, or Sidra, but not Siddie."

"But Annie calls you that, why can't—"

"Annie's different."

"Okay, I got you—Sid."

"On my way home I called a cleaning service to go out and put your house back in order. They should be done later today. And since we don't know what the intruders were looking for, I'll call the sheriff and convince him to have officers check on you on a regular basis. It won't be easy, since he thinks you're lying to us—which you better not be."

"I ain't, Sid. I'm telling you the truth."

Sid remembered her conversation with Hoke and looked out the window. His car sat at the curb.

"Hoke Faulkner is out front," Sid explained. "He's the professor from A & M and wants to talk to you about the schooner. He's called several times and I've kept putting him off until you were strong enough."

"Out yonder?" She pointed to the front of the house.

"Yes, he's out there waiting for me to tell him if he can come in or not."

Boo got up and the two of them peeked out the window, but as soon as Boo saw Hoke pacing in the front yard smoking a cigarette, she half-turned to Sid. "I'll tell you one thing, that guy ain't no Faulkner."

"Then who is he?"

"Don't rightly know—but I can tell you he's a Sweeney if I ever seen one."

Sid's words bristled up and out. "I thought you said you didn't *know* any Sweeneys."

"I never said I didn't *know* any. Sure I do. They're kin. Just on the other side of the family. What I said was I didn't know a *Dexter* Sweeney. But that guy's got Sweeney blood running through his veins."

"How can you tell from this far?" Sid glanced back out at Hoke while Boo looked over her shoulder. "He's a professor at A & M."

"Ain't neither—ain't a one of them ever went to school."

"Maybe he just looks like a Sweeney."

"See that nose—that's a Sweeney nose—no mistaking. You heard of the feuds between Scottish clans? Well, that's us. The Sweeneys and the Cormacs been feuding for generations."

When Boo looked back at Sid, a new day had dawned in her eyes. "Oh good lord, how could I have missed it all these years?"

"Missed what?"

"Zeke's nose looked just like that. I was so busy disliking the guy, it never dawned on me that he had the Sweeney nose." Boo stared back out the window at Hoke, shaking her head. "Like I said, ain't no way I'm gonna talk to that *professor guy*."

"Hey, no skin off my nose."

Boo grimaced.

"Sorry for the pun," Sid said, smiling. "You don't want to talk to him, and I don't care. I'll tell him…"

"If'n I was you, I wouldn't tell him what I said."

"I'll just say you're not feeling up to it. I told him I doubt that you did anyway."

Sid headed out front and gave Hoke the message. He wasn't happy about the situation, but the longer he stood and argued with Sid the larger the hump on his nose grew. She couldn't help but think of Pinocchio. Finally, she just walked off and left him standing there. Eventually he got in his car and drove away.

Despite her calm-down, Sid figured it best to go ahead and get Boo back home. So after a quick phone call to the sheriff's office, and some arm-twisting to get an extra deputy to keep an eye out, Sid went to the grocery, picked up the essentials Boo would need for a day or so, and the three headed to Boo's house.

Sid wondered if she'd see Sasha, or if the woman would be too embarrassed that she'd revealed her soul to Sid.

The cleaning team drove off as they pulled into the yard. Dog met them with a light-hearted bark and a serious tail wagging. Annie helped Boo out and in, while Sid gathered Boo's belongings and the few groceries she'd bought—bread, milk, cereal.

Sasha stood on her front porch and watched them go up the front steps of the house that looked like a fishing cabin. Sid looked over at Sasha and wondered if she would come over.

She didn't have long to wait, for just as they got inside, Sasha came hustling in.

"Can I talk to you, Boo?" Sasha asked, stepping inside without waiting to be invited.

Sid stole a quick glance at Boo, waiting for her response.

"Sure, Sasha, come in. You know you're always welcome. And honey, I ain't killed Zeke, although sometimes I'd a liked to." The two women fell into each other's arms.

"I'm so sorry. I don't know why I said what I did. The police just came and started asking me questions so fast I didn't know which end was up." Sasha patted Boo on the back. "And whatever you did to your hair, it sure looks pretty."

"Thanks, I went over to the same woman what does yours. Durwood likes it, too." She ducked her chin and gave a sheepish grin before changing the subject.

"And I know what you mean about all them questions. Sometimes I wondered if the deputies talked to my ass or to my face. Come on and sit down. I'd like for you to talk to Sid, she's one of them private eyes, and she's going to find out who done it, so I can go free."

Sid and Sasha shook hands. "Nice to meet you," they both said in unison, neither of them revealing their earlier conversation.

Annie had already put on the tea kettle and now ushered everyone to take a seat and she'd serve tea. When each held a cup of the steaming liquid, Sid broached the subject of the first day Boo went out and saw the ship. "Take us through it again, Boo. Start at the beginning and tell us anything you remember.

Boo set her cup on a side table, spread her legs wide, tucking the long skirt down between her knees, and stared at the floor. "Well, let's see. First thing I remember was seeing this big brass bow sticking up out of the water."

Sasha reached over and laid her hand on Boo's cast. "Now Boo, I don't mean to interrupt, but are you sure it was a bow, and not some piece of drift wood? I've heard tell of those things being seen out in the swamps, but I've never known anyone who saw one."

"Well, you have now." Boo finished her tale, concluding with the part Sid hadn't heard before. The part about Boo imagining she sailed with Jean Lafitte.

"You mean your ancestor was Laffite? The pirate?"

"No, no. I was kin to Mary Anne Radcliff, not Lafitte. Mary Anne just sailed with him. She was the granddaughter of the infamous Anne Bonny, but Mary Anne ended up infamous in her own right."

Sid's mind reeled. "Mary? Mary, did you say? Your ancestor was named Mary?" Sid's heart stopped its beat and a whoosh of air moved in and surrounded her. She shivered even in the heat and humidity.

"History don't show it, but she started out as Lafitte's cabin boy, worked alongside Charles Cronea, a man from High Island, which is down the coast. 'Cepting no one knew she was Mary. Jean was the only one that knew she was a girl, and he wouldn't tell no one, 'cause it was seen as bad luck to have a woman on board. Hear tell, she was a spitin' image of her grandma and had to strap herself down so the men on board wouldn't know she was female. Story goes she was a hell cat, fought like the best of them. Even lived in Lafitte's settlement near Galveston for awhile—till he burned it down before the feds came to take it over. No one knows what happened to her after that. Some say she went down to Central America and lived out her days as a madam. You know, one of them houses of ill repute."

"Good lord dog. So that's the Mary."

"The what?"

"Never mind." She didn't want to go into her meeting with Andrine, but now the whole thing was starting to make sense—and there was the smuggling connection. "No wonder you were excited about the schooner. But who do you think murdered Zeke?"

"Lots of folks around here believe there's buried treasure, even sunken treasure in them pirate ships. Rumors done gone around for years about these three shell middens that make a triangle. You know—those piles of shells left behind by the Atakapa Indians?"

"Yes, I know what you're talking about."

Boo shaped a triangle with her thumbs and index fingers. "Well, right there inside that triangle, hear tell, is where the treasure is supposed to be. One man's found two of the middens, but no one's found the third yet. You can't triangulate till you have three."

"Still…" Sid couldn't believe someone would murder Zeke based on long-hoped-for buried treasure. Zeke wasn't the easiest guy to love, but murder?

"Anything else? What about the day before you and Sasha went out and found Zeke—anything unusual that day?"

"Well, let's see, as I told you, I bathed Dog and… Wait, yeah, I almost forgot, there was these two Mexican-looking men who took off in a boat just up the way. They had something in the boat, looked like it was wrapped in a tarp or something. I figured they'd caught a big turtle or something they was taking back out in the water. That or one of them big alligators."

"That's the most promising information I've heard." Sid made a note and stuck it in her pocket. Leaving the two women to renew a friendship broken by a husband, she left and headed to Ben's office on the second floor of the courthouse.

The dark paneling in his office had recently been replaced with a coat of soft, toasted almond and a border added with artistic pictures of books and gavels. A shiny mahogany desk now replaced the old oak one, but it still held piles of papers stacked helter-skelter. But she knew Ben. The careless-looking stacks didn't reveal that he had everything catalogued and easy to find—at least for him.

He'd stepped out for the moment, so she took a chair and waited.

When he walked in a couple of minutes later, his mouth broke into a big smile. "Hey, babe, what's going on? How's the new cases?"

She smiled, stepped on her tiptoes, and kissed him square on the mouth. Hopefully, his excited-sounding voice reflected how he really felt about her new case, even if it was pro bono.

Well I'll be...that was the first time she'd ever thought of Boo's case as hers.

"That's why I'm here. I wanted to talk to you about it."

"Not the pirate ship I hope. I've heard those stories of buried treasure all my life. No way am I going to believe there is—or was—a resurrected ship out in the swamp, much less that the woman climbed up on it."

That comment cinched Sid's decision not to reveal that she'd actually seen the ship out in the middle of the swamp, and that it disappeared in front of her eyes.

Ben gave her another hug then indicated a chair. "Have a seat. I haven't talked with Quade about the Murphy case yet. Figured I'd wait till he makes an arrest and then get all the info. That way I'm not prejudiced ahead of time. So, what can I help you with?"

"Well, after that declaration about not believing there was a ship out there, I'm not sure you can." She pulled herself loose and walked over to the window that now sported white plantation shutters. "Looks like the county came into some money. I like your new digs." She opened one of the shutters and glanced down at her car parked across the street. A man with a hood over his head stood behind it writing something.

Her license plate number?

She opened her mouth to mention it to Ben, but thought better of it. Instead, she tried to memorize his looks, as much as she could tell from that far away, before he jumped into an old industrial-gray van and drove off.

Ben walked up behind her and sniffed her hair. "Mmm, you smell so good. Say, when can we get together again? Come over this weekend?"

"Sounds good. I just moved Boo back into her house, so maybe things will settle down a little. Annie and Boo are a handful by themselves, but together? Geesh! Changing the subject, but do you know anything about the Mexican cartel running smuggling operations off the Texas coast?"

Ben released her and strolled over to his desk. "I've heard rumors, but we haven't had such a case in Orange County since I've been D.A. That's been ten years or more. From what I've read, the cartels from South American countries, and some from Central America, are edging their way in, running everything from stolen humans to priceless artifacts."

Stunned, Sid sat in a chair across from the new desk. "Wow. My life inside the ivory walls of a parsonage sure never exposed me to this."

"And that world is one you've not shared with me. I'd like to know what it was like to *live in a fishbowl*, as you call it."

"That's off topic, Ben. Can we save that until this weekend?"

He shrugged as he pulled a chair next to her. "Putting me off a little longer, huh? Okay, well, I can wait until this weekend. So—for sure Saturday night?"

"You cooking?" She inspected miniscule flecks of dirt underneath her fingernails.

"Sure, I'll cook," he chuckled, "if you'll tell me about your fishbowl life while I do so. Six o'clock?"

"Works for me. I'll bring my sexy sleep shirt." She smacked him on the lips and headed towards the door.

"You mean the one that says *Don't touch me when I'm sleeping!*"

"That'd be it." She smiled and waved goodbye over her shoulder.

By the time she reached her car, she remembered the guy she saw writing down her license tag. Had he known the car was hers? Had he seen her getting out? Had he followed her?

Seventeen

From Ben's office, Sid headed across the back parking lot to the Sheriff's Office. She found Sheriff Quade Burns outside surrounded by reporters questioning him about the murder, the schooner, Boo, and about what buried treasure might still be hidden in the area.

Listening, she learned more of the local history and folklore about sightings of sunken ships sticking up out of the water, and time after time, how the whole investigation of such had been shut down by federal authorities. Why would the authorities care? Perhaps they feared widespread panic, another *War of the Worlds*.

Certainly folks should have opportunity to see examples from the past, perhaps even the chance of treasure. After all, wasn't that searching the same that had set folks on a quest to California in the 1800s?

Settling into the new job of sheriff, Quade handled himself well before the throng of inquisitive women and men hot on the trail for news. Then again, before appointment to the vacated Sheriff's position, he'd been the police chief, so the new job wasn't that different.

One man, full of himself, stepped forward and ordered Quade to reveal details of what the crew had found when they went down into the belly of the vessel.

"And what newspaper are you from?" Quade demanded, holding his own through the melee.

"*The Inquirer*," the man said, belligerence in his voice. "We have a right to know what was found on the ship."

"Well, not that I owe you that information, Mr. Inquirer, but we didn't even find the ship, much less go down in it. And if we had, all we'd have seen would have been a pile of rotten timbers and mud."

"You didn't find a safe or anything like that in the Captain's Cabin?"

"We didn't find the Captain's Cabin."

"What do you mean, you didn't find it?"

Despite the red that crept down his neck, Quade made up-and-down motions with his hands and continued. "As I've explained, we went out to where the ship was reported to have been seen, and we found nothing there except an old rusted cannon and a couple of cannon balls."

"You mean you found nothing in the pirate schooner? Not even a single coin, or a…"

"You know what? This news conference is over. If you have any more questions, you'll have to save them for later. Right now, I'm busy."

"You really think the old woman killed that man?" A small, inconspicuous-looking woman pushed her way to the front of the throng, and asked.

"If I didn't have evidence to that effect, I wouldn't have arrested her. Now if you'll excuse me." Quade turned and walked back into headquarters. Sid followed.

He turned just as he stepped into his office and almost tripped over her. "Oh, sorry Sid, I didn't know you were following me. You need something? I'm not in the best of moods, I can promise you that."

"I was wondering if you could give me the names of any relatives listed on the death report of Zeke Harris—other than Sasha, of course."

"Yeah, I think I have that, here, let me see." He scrambled through his inbox until he found the report, flipped through a page or two, and then looked up at Sid. "Seems he has a relative by the name of Vi Sweeney from Port Arthur—Pleasure Island, actually. Fifty-eight years old. We haven't learned how she's kin to Zeke Harris, but we're working on it."

"You have an address?"

"Yeah, it's…here let me write it down for you." He grabbed a scratch pad and wrote. "One of my deputies went over and talked with her, but didn't get much information. Puzzling thing is this Mrs. Sweeny says she doesn't have a relative named Zeke Harris."

"What about a Dexter Sweeney?"

"Vague answer, says there's lots of Sweeneys in the area. Swears she's not kin to any of them."

Sid stared at Quade while she tried to put the pieces together in her head. After he finished, she said, "Well, I think I'm going to take a ride out there and pay Vi Sweeney a visit."

"Keep me posted on how it goes," he said, winking at her. "Maybe you'll find evidence to help me get a conviction on your client."

"Yeah, right, I'll do just that."

On the way back to her car she remembered her suspicions about Hoke Faulkner. Something about the guy just didn't ring true. Maybe the department head could shed some light on their interest in the schooner—or more importantly, on Hoke's.

After a call to Information Assistance, she dialed the number and asked for the department head.

"I'm sorry, ma'am, but Dr. Castigliano is out of the country, and will be until the fall semester."

"What about Professor Hoke Faulkner? Might I speak with him?"

"Excuse me?"

Sid repeated the name.

"Sorry, ma'am, we don't have anyone by that name here on staff."

"What about in another department?"

"Hold on, let me check the directory."

Sid heard clicks on a keyboard then quiet.

"No ma'am. And I don't even see a student here by that name."

She thanked the receptionist, disconnected the call, and using her caller ID to locate Hoke's number, punched it in.

When he answered, she started in without greeting or preamble. "This must be your cell phone number. It sure as hell isn't your office at the university."

"Sid? Is that you?"

"At least you know who I am. Ever get confused when you look in a mirror?"

"What do you mean?" Hoke sounded innocent.

"You told us you were a professor of marine archeology from A & M. The problem is, I called them and they've never heard of you. So what's your real name and why are you here?"

"I'm sorry you found that out, Sid. Now, I'll have to kill you."

"What?"

"Just kidding. But I can't tell you who I am, or why I'm here. Just call me a treasure-seeker trying to get his hands on something before someone else."

"Get your hands on what? Before whom?"

"I can't talk about it. I just hope you'll trust me enough to keep me posted if you see the pirate schooner. Others are looking for it, too, but you don't really want them to find it."

It didn't take her long to end that call, but afterwards she sat with her head in a brain fog. What in the world was the man talking about? What possibly could be on board a sunken pirate schooner that would make her care one way or the other who got their hands on it? And why would it be of such interest to the fellow named Rodriguez? And why would a man who lied to her think she would ever trust him?

The next morning broke hot and sticky, but regardless of the storm clouds looming off in the distance, Sid headed to the small coastal area called Pleasure Island in search of Vi Sweeney. Quade said the woman denied knowing Zeke Harris or a Dexter Sweeney. Sid intended to put a little more pressure on the woman, jog her memory maybe.

Following a map she'd printed earlier, she soon spotted the unpainted house built atop tall stilts. The front of the building faced the water and the back faced the coastal wetlands. In the front yard five Rhode Island Reds clucked, scratched and pecked at the ground. A heap of old cars lay piled over on the side of the house, half-covered in waist-high weeds. Another car squatted underneath the house as though in fear it too might soon find itself atop the pile of junk. Keeping the cars company, a couple of bicycles, an old refrigerator, and odd pieces of furniture sat waiting for either rust or mildew to put them out of their misery.

Sid parked and headed up a set of weather-worn stairs leading to the front door. After she'd knocked three of four times, the sound of approaching footsteps gave her hope she hadn't made the trip for nothing. The sound grew louder until a grizzled man dressed in a filthy undershirt and over-sized denim jeans stuck his head around the edge of the screen door. His left eye twitched when he spied Sid. "Yeah? What'cha want?"

"Good morning, Sir, I'm Sid Smart." She almost stuck out her hand, but pulled it back at the last minute, not sure what germs she might touch and take home with her.

"Do I know you?" The man pushed the screen door open and stepped outside.

"No, you don't. I'm kind of new to the area."

"Then what you want?"

The man's blunt manner surprised Sid. "I-I'm a detective, and I'm—"

"You're a *copper*?"

She smiled at the slang term, but quickly corrected the missimpression she'd given him. "No, no, I'm a private detective," she said, emphasizing the word *private*.

"Well, don't know if I've ever met one of your kind before, ma'am." He gave a brown-toothed grin. "Folks call me Winker. My name's really William, but folks always call me Winker, 'cause of this tick, you know?"

"Okay, Winker, pleased to meet you. I wanted to talk to Vi Sweeney, is she your wife? Are you Mr. Sweeney?"

"Uh, well, what about?"

"I hear you lost a family member recently, a Zeke Harris, or maybe you knew him as Dexter Sweeney."

"We ain't got much family left—family that we claim, if you catch my drift." He snickered, his shoulders hunching up around his neck.

"Is Ms. Sweeney here?"

"Not right now, she ain't."

"Well, would you mind coming out here so we can talk?" Sid motioned to the small stoop on which she stood. She definitely knew she didn't want to go inside with the man.

"Guess I can, what do you want?" He stepped around the door. Only then did Sid notice his bony bare feet and yellowed, uncut toenails.

Lovely.

She explained the nature of her visit once again, that she wanted to talk to Vi about a relative of hers who had recently been found dead. "The man's name was Zeke Harris, but may have been known as Dexter Sweeney. I've heard that Vi Sweeney was the man's sister. Have you heard of the man?"

Winker shook his head. "Nah, Vi lived here with my brother, but Vi said he died not long ago. When Ma died, Vi brung me here to live with her and my brother. She took care of me like a mama would. But the other day, she packed a bag and just took off."

The more they talked, the more Sid realized the man wasn't quite all there—simple-minded—maybe with a borderline IQ. "So, who's taking care of you now?"

"Well, I got some other relatives, I reckon they'll come."

"You know their names?"

"Yeah, I know one of them. Do you?"

"No, I'm afraid I don't. I'd like to though, would you tell me?"

"One time I heard Vi and my brother talk about this woman named Sasha," he explained. "When I asked them who she was, they said she was my aunt."

Odd that Sasha had not mentioned that connection.

"Does your Aunt Sasha know you're here by yourself? Has she come by since your brother died?"

"Yeah, she come out here after Vi left. Went through Vi's things, said she was looking for keepsakes, but she ended up taking nothing but a few pieces of paper. I don't know what she wanted with 'em. Vi's pretty pin is still here. I asked Aunt Sasha if I could keep it and she said yeah, she didn't want it. She didn't even look at it."

"May I see it?"

"Sure, come on in." He stepped aside and held the door open.

"Could you bring it out here?"

"Nah, Vi would be mad at me if I took it outside. She always made me promise not to take it outside—afraid I'd lose it, I guess—but I wouldn't."

Sid felt a little creepy going inside the man's house, and thought of Ben—who'd have a fit if he knew. But with that image, she pushed her shoulders back and walked inside, ill-prepared for the sight that greeted her—a fancy living room packed full of high-end antique furniture and collectibles, each polished to a high shine.

Sid knew little about antiques, but she had a good eye for authenticity. Her intuition-alarm screamed these were the real thing. From the looks of the house from the outside, she certainly hadn't expected this. The place looked like a mansion—except for the occasional vacant spot where a piece had sat.

"Nicely decorated, Winker. Vi had good taste, it seems."

"Yeah," he nodded, swiped his hand under his nose, sniffled, then yanked up his pants. "Broke her heart when my brother died. Said she didn't have the heart for the business after that."

The business? What business?

Again, his left eyelid closed, adding a touch of humor to his comment, whether intended or not. He headed off to the bedroom. Sid followed, but with an uneasy gut.

The room held a massive four-poster bed and a chifforobe that looked a good two hundred years old. Winker opened the double doors of the cabinet and slid open a tiny drawer. With reverence, he reached in and pulled out a piece of white linen. Like a priest unwrapping something most holy, Winker pulled back the layers of cloth until he'd revealed a diamond-encrusted silver alligator pin, its tail curled up behind. With the index finger of his other hand, he caressed the glistening jewelry. "This is Vi's favorite piece. My brother give it to her."

"Oh, it's gorgeous. May I hold it?" Tentative, unsure how he would react, Sid put her hand out to him.

He looked at her with hesitation, then, "I guess I'll let you hold it if you promise to be careful and not drop it."

"Oh, I'll be very careful."

Winker placed the pin in her open hand like he'd just entrusted to her the kings' ransom.

Sid watched sunlight sparkle off of the beveled edges of the crystal-clear stones. "Did the sheriff's deputy see the pin when he came?" They hadn't talked about the deputy's visit, so she didn't know how Winker would respond to her bringing the topic into the conversation.

He answered without hesitation. "No, he just asked if I knowed where she'd gone. When I told him no, he just left."

She handed the pin back to Winker with the same care he'd used in passing it to her. "It is beautiful. I know Vi must love it a lot. Does she wear it very often?"

Winker chuckled. "That's the thing, my brother said why'd she want something like that if'n she never wore it nowhere. But that's Vi. She goes in every day and checks on it, makes sure it's still there. She really loves it. But what I can't figure is where she went so sudden like and why she left the pin here. Now me, I can take care of myself, but…" He folded the linen back over the pin and returned it to the drawer. One push and the drawer squeaked shut.

"You mentioned their business, what kind of business was it?"

He didn't answer at first. Instead, he shuffled over to the window and peeked out through white lace curtains fluttering in the warm breeze coming off the water. "They called it import export," he said, still looking outside.

He turned and looked at Sid. "That's how he got all this stuff, but after he died, some men came and took a few pieces. After that, Vi took off."

"I see." So that was the reason for the vacant spots in the room's arrangement. "You sure you'll be okay here by yourself, with Vi gone?"

He nodded, leading her back toward the front of the house. "Yeah, as I said, I can take care of myself okay, even though Vi never thought I could." When he passed a large bedroom with a king size bed, he pointed. "This here is Vi's room. Brother slept in here with her when he was here, but he worked out of town a lot."

Okay, so Vi must have been intimate with Winker's brother.

A look of grief crossed his face, along with the closing of the eyelid. "It don't take much for me to live, I can sell a piece of this stuff and make money to last me a while. Besides, I done yard work all my life. Got my mowers and edgers out there in the shed. I got me a few customers, and they usually feed me lunch when I'm there. I'll be fine. Besides, my Uncle Pete, he'll probably come out and check on me."

"Uncle Pete?" The only Pete she knew was Pete Baxter, the volunteer archaeologist that drove the boat the day she'd gone out with Shipwreck to find the schooner. She made a mental note to check with him and see what he knew. "Vi used to keep some of his stuff for him 'til he was ready for it, then he'd come and pick it up."

That seemed odd. Surely it must not be the same Pete. Sid moved toward the screen door.

"Thank you for showing me the pin and all."

"One thing I don't figure though," Winker said, coming up behind her, "is where did Vi go, and why ain't she come back?"

"I'd like to know that myself, Winker. It may take some time, but hopefully we'll get down to the bottom of it."

"My mama would be mad if she knew they'd left me here like this."

"Your brother died, though. I'm sure he wouldn't have left you alone."

"Probably would. He stayed gone most of the time anyway." Winker stared at his bony feet. "They never told me nothing. Didn't think I could understand—but they was wrong. I understand a lot more than most folks think I do."

"Like what?"

The question seemed to agitate Winker, for he glanced down at the floor, fidgeted, and after a couple seconds, spun on his heel. "Like knowing Nathalee's disappeared. They made excuses for her being gone, but I knowed," he mumbled, shuffling out the screen door with a gait characteristic of a limited IQ. A more pronounced gait, she noticed, than the one he'd come in with.

"Who's Nathalee?"

"She's my niece. Vi and my brother's daughter. She left awhile ago and never come home. Vi said she figured she'd run away, but I don't think so."

"Why is that?"

"Ma'am, I might not be the smartest man in town, but I do know when you put on jogging clothes, you probably going jogging."

She thought about questioning him more on the topic, but

decided she'd pushed her luck far enough. Just as she excused herself, she realized she'd never learned the name of Winker's brother. She turned and headed halfway back up the outside steps. Winker leaned over the banister and watched her. "Did you forget something, lady?"

"I did." She smiled. "I forgot to ask your brother's name. Would you mind telling me?"

"His name was Brother."

"Okay, but what did Vi call him? She didn't call him Brother, did she?"

"Nah, she always called him Dexter."

Eighteen

Sid tapped her fingers on the steering wheel as she headed back up the coast towards Orange, the water lapping against the side of the road. Dressed in loose fitting, casual clothes, men and women stood along the river bank casting their lines out into the middle of Sabine Lake, minnow buckets on the ground beside them.

Okay, Dexter Sweeney had changed his name to Zeke Harris after he got out of jail on a smuggling charge. And until his recent death, the same man had lived, at least part time, with Vi Sweeney.

Dexter Sweeney and Zeke Harris—both the same man—had an intimate relationship with two women at the same time. Dexter lived with Vi, albeit infrequently, and Zeke lived with Sasha. Was Vi his mistress or his wife? And which of these roles fit Sasha?

Odd set of circumstances, she thought. Too odd, really—all these folks, if not related, connected in some way. Sasha, Boo, and now, Vi and Dexter—or Zeke. Odd that Sasha hadn't mentioned any of this although she'd gone out there, and looked through Vi's things. And who was the Pete guy? What connection did he have with any of this?

She headed straight to Durwood's house that sat alongside the Neches River. The Neches, the Sabine, Adams Bayou, Cow Bayou, Blue Elbow Swamp, how in the world did anyone ever know where one started and the other ended?

Nothing had changed at Durwood's. The old, flat-bottom

boat still leaned against the side of the house like it had the first time she'd come. Durwood wasn't in the yard. Evidently the heat and humidity had driven him inside.

It took a few minutes for him to get to the door after she'd knocked. When he saw her, he pushed the screen door open wide. "Hi, Sid, honey, come on in, that is if you can stand my fishy smell. I've been out in the boat drowning a few worms. If you'll pardon me, I'll go change outta these stinky clothes."

The stretched-cowhide chair in the corner of the living room looked and felt just as uncomfortable as it had the first time she'd sat there. Whiz, Durwood's retired bloodhound, lay flattened to the floor in his usual manner beside Durwood's rocking chair and nearby spit can. His long, dangly ears lay spread out to either side. A fly still buzzed at the window. Sid felt like she was in a time warp from her first visit to the house. Kate's picture still sat on the sideboard. This time, without hesitation, she looked over at the woman in the tin-type photo, and gave her a colluding smile.

Soon, Durwood came back into the room carrying a pot of coffee and two mugs. "I'd just put the coffee on right before you got here, how about that, I must've felt you coming." He gave her a sideways grin as he set the tray on the sideboard and poured. Grabbing both mugs by their handles, he handed Sid hers and eased himself down into his rocker. Whiz didn't bat an eyelash. "What brings you out today? I can tell you got something on your mind."

"Do you know a Vi Sweeney?"

"Name sounds familiar. Why? What's on your mind?"

"I went out to her house and talked with—I guess, her nephew, a simple-minded man named Winker. Know him?"

"Ain't he the one what does yard work for folks?"

Sid nodded.

"Then yeah, I know him, leastwise I know *of* him. Seen him around town, that sort of thing. I heared people talking about Winker—that he's a little *tached* in the head, don't you know."

"That's the one. According to him, and he seems to know what he's talking about, Sasha is connected to them some way—maybe kin. Do you know anything about that?"

"Vi and Sasha ain't kin, but they shared a husband as I recollect."

"Shared a husband?" Sid leapt to her feet. "What the hell are you talking about, Durwood, and why haven't you told me this before?"

"Like when?"

"Like when you talked me into taking Boo's case, for chrissake." She forced her voice down an octave. "Does Boo know about this?"

"I doubt it. And I never figured it to be my place to tell her. She hated the man enough as it was."

"But Sasha knew about Vi, plus, she put up with it? Why?"

"Nah, she didn't know nothing about it till just a few days ago."

"How did she find out about his double life, and just how do you know this?"

Durwood ducked his head. "I was out there the day Vi came by. It was during the time that Boo was in jail. I'd gone out to check on Dog, be sure he had food and all—you know. Well, this Vi—Sasha's wife-in-law, I guess you could call her—came over and demanded to know what Zeke did with any treasure he found out there at the pirate ship, 'cepting she called him Dexter. That's when Sasha learned she'd been wife number two for years. The two women got into a heated argument out in the front yard. I could hear 'em all the way over to Boo's. That's when I went over to try to keep the women out of a fist fight. Now the why of this, I ain't got no idea."

"And you haven't told Boo. Don't you think she should know since she's accused of his murder?"

"To tell you the truth, I hated to rile the woman up. You know how she gets. She ain't never had much use for the man anyway, and I didn't think it had anything to do with the murder."

"It may not, but it may have—and that isn't up to you to decide, Durwood. You need to tell me any and everything. Let me make the decision about what's relevant and what's not."

"Yes'm." He stalled long enough to finish his coffee and set the cup on the floor beside the rocker. "I reckon then, I ought to tell you about this kid that I caught nosing around Boo's place that same day Vi showed up."

Sid almost swallowed her tongue. "I reckon you should. Hell, Durwood, I assumed that fact was understood."

Whiz looked up. When he saw no danger coming his way, he flopped his head back down on his forelegs.

"Sorry, Sid, I just didn't think one had anything to do with the other. Anyway, the kid said his name was Dutch. Looked like some weird gang member or something, with tattoos all down his neck and arms. I scuffed him up a little, but still didn't get nothing out of him. Just said he'd lost his dog and thought he might've wandered into the yard."

"What else did you find out about him?"

Durwood looked up through thin, white eyelashes and grinned. "He dropped his wallet in the yard while we were scuffling. I didn't see it till after he'd skedaddled." Durwood limped over to the sideboard, opened a drawer and pulled out a blue fabric wallet. He stuck it out at Sid. "Seems he lives out in Deweyville off of Highway 12."

"Mind if I return it to him? It'll be a good excuse for me to go out there and question him."

"Sure, glad to get rid of the thing."

Sid took the wallet from Durwood and tucked it in her pocket. "Winker said Sasha huffed by his house earlier this week and went through all of Vi's things, but all she took was a few papers. You know what that was about?"

He rubbed his chin. A sandpaper sound filled the quiet room. "No, but I sure wonder about it."

God, this man could be so infuriating! "I'm suspecting that the lot of them have been involved in some kind of theft ring."

"Sasha?"

"No, I haven't figured out how Sasha figures into all of this, and I'm not sure she does, other than being married to Zeke, or Dexter, or whoever the hell the man was. Winker showed me this expensive jewel encrusted pin Sasha didn't even touch. I'm no diamond expert, but it looked like the real thing to me."

Durwood rubbed his scratchy chin again. "That don't make much sense to me, that's for sure."

"How long have you known Boo and Sasha?"

"Well now, I met Sasha first time when she moved into that house next door to Boo. Me and Boo go all the way back to Tilley Elementary School. We was much older than most kids what went there in those years, but my ma insisted her boy weren't fighting the war till he finished his education. Boo said her ma put her in school to try to keep her away from some of the riffraff who came to town during that time. You see, she was a beauty even then."

His eyes sparkled just talking about the woman.

"Tilley? Where's that, I haven't heard of that school."

"No wonder you ain't. It's long gone. You know out Simmons Drive? Highway 90 it is. Like you go down Green as far as you can go and then it turns left and heads over towards I-10?"

Sid nodded.

"Well, during the war they had all these people flooding in to work at the shipyard building destroyers and the like. Weren't near enough places to live, so they pumped in sand from the river bottom and, while it was still wet, built thousands of these duplexes for people to live in over on the right side of Simmons. Called it Riverside, but heck, when it rained, the river ran smack down the middle of the streets. Cars drove with their right wheels up on the curb to keep from drowning out their motors!" He laughed, remembering. "We kids had a ball playing in the muddy water that stayed there for days."

"So Tilley Elementary School was out in that subdivision?"

"Sub-division? Riverside ain't never had no fancy name like subdivision—we just called it Riverside Addition. Anyways, yeah, they had two-three elementary schools for all the kids. Named the schools after local boys killed in the war. They're all torn down now. Supposed to have lasted twenty years, but people lived in them dang things near forty years or more. Some of 'em still around, moved out on private lots."

Durwood's faced glowed with fond memories, but Sid ached to get him back on track.

"Okay, so you went to school with Boo. Did you know her family—any of her relatives?"

"Well, yeah I knew her relatives all right, but one thing I remember is that she hated any kid with the last name of Sweeney. I never figured that one out." He blew on his coffee, cooling it enough to drink more comfortably. "Seems I heard tell her folks been in this area long time—years. Back 17… 1800s maybe. Some of 'em was smugglers all along the coastal area, from New Orleans all the way past here, and down to Galveston. Boo's always been 'shamed 'bout it. Never wanted no one to know her family smuggled."

"Well, that's all fine and good, but it doesn't help me figure out where Vi went, what Sasha took from Vi's house and why, and who killed Zeke."

"You never can tell, Sid. You just never can tell."

Nineteen

Sid left Durwood's, and as she drove alongside the Neches River, she toyed with the idea of whether or not to go find this guy called Dutch. The one Durwood had seen messing around at Boo and Sasha's place. Feeling like a little think time might do her good, she found a good place to pull over and park. She caught herself watching the river carry a broken tree branch along in its current and wondered how that must feel, to not resist, to allow yourself to flow.

She found a shady spot, sat on the grass and stared, mesmerized by the fast-flowing current.

Danger is a part of life, Sidra Smart. Face it head on, stare it down.

Sid turned and, there, in the shadow of a giant pine tree sat a young woman with a head full of long auburn curls and emerald green eyes. Dressed in a pair of striped sailor breeches from another century, she sat with her black-booted feet flat on the ground, arms resting on her knees. Her long-sleeve white blouson shirt, open at the neck, revealed a cleavage to die for.

Sid almost asked the woman who she was, and what she meant by that comment, since Sid had obviously put her life in danger quite a lot lately, but when she realized she could see the tree trunk through the body of the young woman, she got to her feet, raced to her car and took off.

Her other world, the *preacher's wife* world, had always been so predictable, but a ghost ship and now this?

Rattled, she made a quick calculation of distance and time and headed home to pick up Slider. He wasn't much good as a watch dog, but maybe this Dutch guy wouldn't know that. Besides, she'd feel better having the dog along. Indeed, danger was a part of life, but so was a beating heart.

After a quick check of the house, she saw Slider in the backyard with Annie, who was taking her crisp, white sheets off the clothesline.

"I'm heading back out, sweetheart, and I'm taking Slider with me. We won't be gone more than a couple of hours, but don't wait dinner. Come on boy," she called. The dog bounded up on the porch, thrilled she'd come home.

Annie picked up the basket of bed linens and headed up to the house. "You keep your cell phone in your pocket, you hear? Call me if you get into any kind of trouble."

"I will, sweetheart," she called out, hustling Slider through the back door.

Slider liked his walks, but Sid learned the day she found him in a driving ice storm, that the dog did not like cars. Not only car and car rides bothered him, but looking out the front and back windows bothered the hell out him. Passenger window? Okay, he tolerated that, but just barely.

She latched the red, grosgrain leash to his collar and led him, happy and content, out the front door, to the front yard. But as soon as he saw her heading to the car, he locked his legs and planted all four feet firmly on the driveway.

"Aw, come on, Slider, riding in a car is not nearly as bad as you make it out to be."

Evidently it was. His knees stayed locked and his feet stayed planted. She dragged him and he slid, the whole way to the car. Wrapping the leash around her hand, she picked up his front paws, put them on the back seat, and then shoved from the rear.

Finally, she got him fully inside the vehicle and slammed the door closed.

Great idea, Sid, she told herself. If anyone were intent on

doing her harm, she'd first have to protect the dog.

She climbed into the driver's seat and closed the door. "See, it's not that big a deal," she said, glancing around to the back seat, but Slider had stuck his head in the gap between the two front seats. "Give me a break, Slider. You have to carry your weight around here. I need you. Besides, this won't take long. You'll survive riding in a car."

As they headed out Highway 87, Sid turned into the parking lot of The Jumping Bean, a quaint coffee shop with a pretty blue awning over the front plate glass window. Deciding the drive-in window would be the safest, she drove around the building, pulled up to the window and ordered a cup of Chai tea for herself, and a macadamia nut biscotti for Slider. That settled him down to no end, but he sure made a mess on her black leather upholstery.

By the time they hit Highway 12, they'd both finished their refreshment and Slider had climbed into the front seat and alternately looked from Sid to the passenger window, refusing to acknowledge that the car had a front windshield.

"What is it with you and front windshields? All it does is show you where you're heading. You aren't any less likely to get hit just because you see what's coming."

He whined and screwed around on the seat, forcing his eyes to the front, then hastily brought them back to focus on her, a look of pride on his face, a look that said, *see, smarty pants!*?

"Well, that's a start, I guess. Keep that up, and you'll soon be cured of your phobia."

Uncertain as to why she felt so nervous, she decided talking to the dog about it might relieve some of her fear. "We're going to see this guy—I'm not real sure about him—he sounds kind of loopy, maybe on drugs. I don't know what we're going to find when we get to his house, but I need you to be on guard. Make a distraction, commotion, anything like that if I get into trouble, okay?"

Slider kept his vigil looking out the passenger window.

"Okay?"

He swung his head around and gave her a look that called her sanity into question.

"Just do the best you can, okay?"

He chuffed, but kept his focus out the side window.

By the time she'd located the address, she realized her northward trek had led her to the banks of Sabine River. Two or three small houses on stilts sat back away from the shore. Although a couple of cars and trucks were parked in each driveway, the place looked deserted. "Okay, Slider, you stay in the car, but I'm leaving the window down just in case. If I need you, you come. Okay?"

She rolled down the driver's window, turned off the motor, and got out just as two men in dark suits and ties hustled out, letting the screen door slam behind them. They jogged down the stairs, an air of elevated power on their shoulders and an aura of darkness surrounding them. They passed Sid without a word.

She watched as they climbed into a waiting vehicle, slammed the doors shut and soon the non-descript vehicle spun gravel as it turned around and drove off. Sid looked to catch the license plate, but mud coated the numbers.

Behind her, the screen door squeaked open. She swung around to see a man, maybe twenty, with a blonde Mohawk, body rings, and a heavy conviction regarding his own self-worth. He took a swig from a Shiner Bock bottle as he walked out and onto the porch. "Whacha want?" His expression said get the hell out of here.

"Hi, I'm looking for a man called Dutch."

"You're lookin' at 'im. Who are you and whaddaya want? I got things to do."

"My name is Sid Smart." She headed up the stairs towards the impudent young man, her eyes never leaving his. "You dropped this wallet when you were snooping around Boo Murphy's house."

He snatched the billfold out of her hand and looked at her like he was God and she was trespassing through the pearly gates uninvited. The closer she got, the more piercings she saw—in his eyebrows, lower lip and nose, and barrel-looking pegs in both earlobes. A black muscle-shirt bore the faded logo of AFI, a hardcore punk band from the early 90s. The shirt looked like it had been one of the first printed and sold, and the last to ever be discarded. The band had been her son Chad's favorite, and her then-preacher-husband Sam's mortification which, of course, made young Chad love the band even more.

"Are you of legal drinking age?" She had to ask. Kids besotting their brains with alcohol irritated the hell out of her. Adults providing it for them really pissed her off.

He threw his hands up in the gesture of disgust, turned and headed back up the steps. "I'm going back inside where it's cooler. If you have any more stupid ass questions to ask, you'll have to do it in the house."

Sid hastened her step and slipped through the screen door right behind him. The living room looked like a disaster had struck it some time ago and no one bothered to clean up the mess. She stumbled over a coffee table laden with empty beer bottles, over-flowing ashtrays, and the ubiquitous empty pizza container. A thick, legal-size envelope lay on the corner of the table, its loosened flap revealing a stack of bills.

Dutch caught her looking at the envelope, snatched it up and stuck it in the back pocket of his jeans.

She knew she should act like she hadn't seen it, but the words shot out of her mouth before she could bite her tongue. "Come into some money recently?"

"That's none of your fuckin' *beeswax*, bitch. Now get outta here before I make you sorry you stuck your nose into my shit." He took threatening steps her way.

"Who were those men? Did they give you that money?"

He snatched her by the arm and started for the door. His strength was such that her feet skimmed the floor as he stalked. Over the sound of the blood-rush in her ears, she heard herself push him a little more. "What did you do for them?"

"I said *enough!*" He charged through the screen door and down the outside stairs, half-dragging Sid behind him. She yanked and tried to pull away from his grasp, but still he hung on.

Vaguely aware of a growl heading their way, she didn't see the large airborne ball of curly red fur until it knocked both of them off their feet and sent her handbag flying. Intertwined arms and legs tumbled down the last few steps, along with what she now realized was a raging bull named Slider. As she struggled to her feet, she felt the sting of gravel and wood splinters driven into bare skin.

The impudent young man lay sprawled on his back, arms flung out to the side, his fingernails digging tiny rivers of sand into the earth. Without moving a single muscle not required, he spoke through clenched teeth. "Get the damn dog off of me."

Slider stood stiff-legged, a deep growl emanating from low in his gut, his jaws clamped around Dutch's throat. Sid got her handbag, pulled out her gun, and pointed it at Dutch. "Okay, I'll make a deal with you. We'll call a truce for now. You leave me alone, and I'll call off my dog."

"Ma'am, what the hell you doing pointing a gun at my boy, and why's that dog got him by the jugular?"

Sid whirled around and there, not ten feet from her, stood a man who looked identical to the picture she'd seen of Sasha's late husband—Zeke Harris.

Twenty

"Zeke? I thought you were dead."

The man looked down at himself, shook first one leg and then the other. "No'm, it don't look like it, and I sure ain't Zeke Harris. The name's Sonny Sweeney. Now, I'm goin' to ask you again real nice. What the *hell* you doing with a gun pointed at my boy?"

Swallowing that bit of information to chew on later, Sid sucked in a deep breath and gathered her courage. "Pardon me for saying so, Sir, but you sure didn't teach your son any manners."

The man shook his head and sucked through his teeth. "Dutch, Dutch, Dutch, what'd you do now? Didn't I tell you to mind your manners around city women?"

Slider growled, cut his eyes up at Sid, begging permission to proceed.

Sid lowered her gun, but remained wary. "It's okay, Slider. You can let go." When he did, Dutch scrambled to his feet, gravel flying, and stomped back up the steps and through the screen door, letting it slam behind him.

Sonny Sweeney took a few steps toward Sid. "Pardon my son's behavior. I done taught him better than that." The words were right, even if the grammar was off, but the sound of them wasn't. Not a drop of sincerity in a single word.

"Okay, Mr. Sweeney, tell me, were you related to a Dexter Sweeney?"

"Reckon I am. Most of us are kin one way or the other—if you catch my drift." He gave her an obscene smirk. "You can be kin to me, too, if you like."

"Come on, Slider, we've worn out our welcome." She opened the car door and Slider jumped in. As she punched the button to raise the window, she noticed a few red hairs caught along the edge where Slider had exited. Pride swelled in her chest.

Pulling out of the driveway, she looked over at the still-panting mutt, now staring out the front window like he owned the road. When he realized Sid looked at him, he cut his eyes over to her as if aware of the significance of the moment.

"You did good, boy, real good. But it's okay if you're not fully over your phobia."

Slider chuffed in agreement, but he stretched himself what looked to be a foot taller.

"What say we stop off and get you a treat?"

Slider wagged his tail and grinned.

"Maybe a frozen yogurt?"

His tail now in overdrive, the dog clambered over the console and into Sid's lap, ready to be petted.

"Watch, it, Slider, you're going to get us both killed!" She laughed at the silly grin on his face, then turned on her blinker and pulled into a convenience store, hoping they sold frozen yogurt.

Slider waited in the car while she went in and purchased each of them a cone, but as soon as she stepped outside into the heat, the white, creamy tower began to melt and run down on her fingers. She pulled first one cone and then another up to her mouth and licked the drips while contemplating the two look-alike men, one with an alias—the dead one. Glancing across the street as she headed to her car, she noticed a man sitting in an old gray van, watching her. Although the top half of his face was in the shade of a baseball cap, something about him looked familiar. When he saw her looking, he took off. She wasn't positive, but it sure looked like the same van and the same man who had checked out her car in front of Ben's office.

She pitched the cones of yogurt into a nearby trash can while

Slider barked at her through the window. "Sorry, babe, I'll get us another one soon as I find out who this guy is watching us." She jumped in the car, backed out and took off in the same direction as the gray van. Once again, she regretted her choice in vehicle color and felt herself slump down as if that would lower the height of the taxicab-yellow Xterra.

At the last minute, the gray van lurched across the freeway and took the immediate exit to the feeder road. Sid threw a quick glance in her rearview mirror and yanked the steering wheel. With her tires skidding across the freeway, she rounded safety barrels separating her car from a concrete barrier, while she cringed, expecting the screech of wheels behind her and the resulting crash. "I'm sorry, I'm sorry," she whispered to anyone who happened to be in the blind spot on her right, but without time to double check.

The van driver sped up, winding around cars like a half-starved bat exiting a deep, dark cave. The sun reflected off the van's rear window, blinding Sid. She swerved into the path of an unsuspecting driver. Correcting, she regained control, as the van exited and headed off another direction. Slider skated back and forth on the passenger seat, barking his head off, demanding she slow down.

When she realized the driver headed to Bridge City she felt better. The police there were tough on speeders. But when she got there, she didn't see a single one, which was probably good. With her luck, the cop would stop her, and not the van. They sped over the Rainbow Bridge and on beyond Port Arthur, until at last the van driver slowed and made a right turn onto a narrow, paved road. The sign read, *Boondocks*. If ever Sid felt like she'd entered the boondocks, this was it. And what was that roar in her ears?

The driver ahead made several turns down unpaved side roads, her right behind, until they came into a clearing near what looked to be a long-abandoned restaurant. A sign propped alongside the front announced *Boondocks Restaurant*. Beside it, another sign warned, *Feed alligators at your own risk*. A wrap-around porch surrounded the building, and in the rear, she saw a swamp-like lake, which indeed looked infested with the reptiles.

Her mind was so focused on the possibility of alligators that she missed seeing the van driver's brake lights until his vehicle swerved sideways.

Sid slammed on the brakes, admonishing herself for letting Slider ride unrestrained. He toppled head first to the floor, but quickly scratched and clawed his way back up on the seat. Fully engaged in the chase by now, he put his front paws on the dash and barked at the van.

"Slider, Slider, quiet, boy!" He cut his eyes over at her and whined, his front paws now doing a dance on the dashboard.

Once Slider quieted down, she realized the roar in her ears wasn't her imagination. Something flew over her head. She leaned forward and peered out the windshield to see a fairly large black helicopter glistening in the sun. It had a gold stripe around its middle and wide, wraparound windows, with "R-44 Clipper II" painted on its side.

Mesmerized by the giant, metamorphic mosquito out of some global warming-Al Gore movie, she knew she had set her own trap and driven right into it. But who in the hell were these men, and what itch had she scratched? It couldn't simply be that of a dead man. Something larger—much larger, or maybe it was some*one*—someone much more powerful than local treasure seekers.

The pilot steadied the craft over a makeshift parking lot helipad. Inside, sat two men in dark suits and sunshades, staring at her; the same two men who had been leaving Dutch's house as she arrived. Evidently the same two men who had left an envelope full of cash on his coffee table. She thought about George Léger, and wondered if these men were possibly the same ones who had bought him, as well.

Flashbacks of movies with men dressed and looking exactly like that came to mind, but her pounding heart and the sweat on her top lip told her this was no movie.

The van driver leapt out, motioning the pilot to follow him toward Sid.

Desperate for a way out, she noticed a small trail opening between high weeds and swamp and, making a decision born more out of survival instinct than detective work, she jerked the steering wheel to the right and headed into the cane breaks.

Slider's pant sounded a lot like, *its get-even time, buster.*

The road she'd taken led nowhere, no houses, not even a small, occupied shack where she might stop for help, or long enough to make a cell phone call. Bumping through potholes filled with muddy water, soon the sound of the whirling blades returned. At least this road wasn't wide enough for the bird to land. Neither did it lead anywhere. Without warning, she ran out of road.

At times, she couldn't tell which sound grew louder, the helicopter or her heart. She tried to convince herself it was her heart, and that no helicopter chased her, and that this impossible set of circumstances didn't exist. But when she stole a quick glance over at Slider and barely recognized the animal, any and all doubt evaporated.

A few feet away, a small, dilapidated dock stood alongside a marshy swamp. Low-hanging branches and moss dangled just above the dock's wooden planks, and nearby, a small abandoned boat bobbed in the water.

"Come on Slider, I reckon that boat's our only choice out of this mess." She slammed on the brakes, grabbed her handbag, with her gun and cell phone inside, and jumped out.

Slider, still panting *get-even-time*, bounded out behind her while the big black *bird* hovered overhead. Sid expected gunfire to rain down on her as she darted toward the boat—after all, that's what happened in make-believe television, but for some reason, the guns hadn't yet fired.

As she approached the boat, she realized Slider wasn't with her. A quick glance behind her and she saw him crouching in the cane, watching back down the road. It looked as though he anticipated the arrival of the gray van.

She sprinted to the dock, untied the frayed rope and gave a quick scan of the anything-but-water-proof vessel. Water puddled in the bottom, but Sid wasn't sure if its source came from the recent rain, or from holes in the craft. An oar gave her hope she could navigate the thing. Holding onto the side of the dock to steady herself, she tossed her bag onto the seat and crawled in, the boat rocking against her weight. Once seated, she screamed above the roar of the blades.

"Slider, come on boy, what're you doing?" A quick glance back confirmed her fear when the gray van plowed into the opening, stopped, and the man leapt out. Over a sudden hail of bullets, rotating blades, and her pounding heart, she heard screams that could only come from someone attacked by one hell-of-an-angry dog. She plunged the paddle into the water, shoving every other thought aside but getting underneath the low-hanging branches just upriver.

Just as she did, a barrage of bullets hit the water all around her. "I'm leaving, Slider, but I'll come back for you. Hang on boy!" She knew he wasn't listening, and at the moment, evidently didn't care. A more primal instinct had taken control.

Figuring the men expected her to continue fleeing from the direction she'd come, instead she scudded back underneath the first of the low-hanging branches and pulled in the paddle. The boat sat as still as if it were in the doldrums.

The bird hovered momentarily and then continued on ahead. With a moment's break, she scratched in her bag, pulled out her gun and put it in her lap. Without a clear shot into the cockpit, the only option available was to empty the nine millimeter into the helicopter's thin skin and hope she hit something vital enough to bring it down. But if she didn't, the unloaded gun would be useless until she had time to reload, and she just might not have that much time or ammunition. The best bet was to lie low and hope the thick overhanging trees hid her from view. She sat motionless, barely breathing, while the chopper hovered back and forth, spraying a wide area ahead of her with automatic gun fire.

Good, they thought she'd headed farther up the coastline—but for how long? She didn't have long to wonder, for after a couple of minutes, the *whoop whoop whoop* grew stronger. Wanting nothing more than to squeeze her eyes shut and wait for oblivion, or whatever came after this life, she forced herself to squint up through the treetops. Perspiration ran down her forehead and into her eyes, the salt stinging like fire. Stagnant water now seeped in around her ankles, insects buzzed her face, but survival instinct forced a bare, shallow breath.

She waited, afraid to trust that the men and the helicopter were not coming back, that instead they were simply biding their time—like the deacon board had at the church in west Florida when a campaign of disgruntlement brought Sam's leadership under fire. Within weeks they were *out on the street*, or would have been if Sam had not *followed God's will* by getting *called* to another church. The life of a preachers' wife, compared to what she now experienced seemed at such odds. But come to think about it, there were indeed similarities—even the threat of death. The comparison lightened her spirit, for she realized she'd take this very world, right here and now, in a heartbeat.

The whoop of blades heading her way brought her back to the now. The sound grew closer until they were again nearby. She hunkered down, stilling her breath with slow, deep inhales and exhales. But wishing didn't work any better than prayer. For once again, a spray of bullets peppered along the edge of the canal for a quarter mile or more then disappeared again.

Her hearing numbed by the rotary motors, even the sound of water lapping against the sides of the fast-sinking boat sounded far off, muted. She yanked out her cell phone to call for help, but zero bars displayed at the top. She'd entered a dead zone, in more ways than one.

She crammed the phone back down in her pocket and clawed at the welts on her arms, realizing if she intended to keep living in this area she needed to start spraying herself with Deet every morning, instead of perfume.

Breathing a little easier, her thoughts went back to the dog. Poor Slider—what had happened to him? And what had turned the placid dog into a fighting machine?

She lifted first one foot and then the other from the bottom of the boat and propped them on the seat in front of her, for the water now reached her ankles. Next, she put her Glock on safety, tucked it in the waist of her pants, grabbed an extended tree branch and pulled the boat closer to shore. She scrambled out and into the cold, shallow water.

Once ashore, she released the safety on the gun and tromped through underbrush in the direction she hoped she'd come, stepping over fallen, rotting trees, and making a wide path around wild dewberry bushes laden with thick, full berries.

Breathless, stinky, skin coated in sweat and insect bites that itched like hell, she plodded through scrub oak that clawed at her skin. Feeling like she moved in slow motion, senses on alert, she listened and watched for the men and her dog. After several minutes, she caught sight of the yellow vehicle through the bushes and breathed a sigh of relief. At least she had her orientation correct.

But when she stepped into the opening where she'd abandoned her SUV, the place looked downright eerie. Thick, dark puddles seeped into the dirt. Patches of reddish brown dog hair, along with what looked like pieces of raw flesh lay strewn on the ground.

What had happened? None of it made sense. Had the man and Slider fought? Had Slider been killed? Or had Slider... The thought of a man-eating dog scared her more than the men in the helicopter. What kind of animal had been sleeping with her?

She inspected the area closer and noticed drag marks in the dirt—drag marks leading to the water. Alongside, and in front of the drag marks, were deep indentations looking almost like a man's hand with... Four fingers and webbing?

So it wasn't Slider that had turned man-eater. It was an alligator, and from the looks of it, a huge one. The bullet-riddled ground showed that the helicopter had come back and taken the man out of his misery before the alligator dragged him into the water.

But had Slider been so lucky? Grief rammed its fist in her gut. Nausea welled up in her throat. Damn it, she should never have brought him out her with her.

One thing brought her comfort. At least, before his death, he'd found his voice again. What was it about the man that had set the dog into such frenzy? Had he reminded Slider of someone who'd abused him? She'd never seen him act like he had today, both at Dutch's house and now soon as he saw this man. Evidently the old woman who had Slider had not been the original owner—not that anyone ever *owns* a dog. Actually, it felt the other way around. Slider owned Sid.

She turned away from the canal and stumbled back over to the SUV. She'd fled so quickly she'd left the motor running and her front door open. She climbed in and pulled the door shut behind her then put her head on the steering wheel and the tears flowed unquenched. A lump formed in her throat she couldn't get down. Then a creeping numbness filled her chest. She swiped her runny nose on her shirt sleeve and then brushed the wetness off on her pants leg, trying her best to stall thoughts of Slider at the bottom of the canal being consumed by an alligator.

Twenty-One

Heartbroken over the tragic loss of her dog, Sid shifted into reverse just as a soft chuff emanated from the back seat. She turned toward the sound. There lay Slider sprawled on the rear seat, his paws over his eyes. Apparently he sensed Sid looking at him, for he peeked up and his tail started pounding the seat.

"Slider! I just knew the alligator got you, too!" She slammed the gear back into park, half-clambered over the back seat and hugged the still-shaking dog to her chest. Or was she the one shaking? After a couple minutes of being slathered with a long, wet tongue, Sid straightened in her seat, threw the car into gear and spun out. "Let's get out of here before that helicopter decides to come back."

She alternately watched the road and glanced at Slider, still prone in the back seat. "What happened back there?" She asked. "That man brought something out in you, reminded you of someone, or maybe…?"

Slider pulled up on all fours, tottered as she made a turn and accelerated, then slowly put one foot in front of the other until he'd joined her in the front seat. He sat up on his hind legs and chuffed.

"What is it, boy? Something or someone did something to you before we found each other, didn't they? But what does that have to do with these guys today?" Slider whined, inched around on the seat while looking out the passenger window. The more she thought about it, the more sense it made. She rather suspected it wasn't the old woman Sid had found dead in her chair all those months ago when Slider first came into her life.

But what did any of this have to do with Zeke's death and the men who just tried to kill her? And why were they even after her in the first place? She checked her cell phone. When two bars came up, she punched in Quade's number. When he answered, she launched into a long diatribe about what she'd just been through and asked what the hell was going on.

After he asked a hundred and one questions about whether or not she was okay, was she sure the bad guys were gone, and exactly where was she, he asked her to go back to the site and wait. He'd be there as soon as he contacted the sheriff in that neighboring county, certain the guy would want to join him and investigate the scene.

Three hours later, the authorities completed the investigation and dismissed Sid, who left the Boondocks hoping it was the last time in her life to ever be there.

"Slider, think you can handle another trip out to the old woman's house?" She glanced over at him, turned the car around and headed out Highway 90. "Someone in the neighborhood must know something." Slider cut his eyes at her. "You're not too sure about this, are you?"

He looked at the road, and then back at her, chuffing softly.

"You need to do this, boy. I need to do this. Otherwise…"

His wagging tail pounded against the back of the seat.

She wasn't too sure about her ability to recognize the house where the old woman lived, but she knew without a doubt she'd recognize the barn out back, especially if it still had turquoise balls painted on the sides.

By the time she found the house back off the main highway, and confirmed her guess by spotting the barn with the balls painted on the side, it was supper time and they hadn't eaten since breakfast. Scrounging in the console between them, she pulled out a protein bar, took off the wrapping and divided the bar in half. She tossed one piece to Slider, he gobbled his portion before Sid got hers halfway to her mouth. With one ear up and the other down, the dog slowly inched toward her.

"Don't you even think about snatching my food!" She warned. "This half is *mine*! You gobbled yours down like a pig!" The dog ducked his head in shame, but still kept one eye on her while she crammed her piece in her mouth.

She opened the car door to go explore the barn, but before she could exit, Slider bounded over her lap and charged up the driveway. He slid to a stop and looked back, grief filling his eyes.

"She's still gone, boy. Sorry."

The house looked abandoned, but numerous deep tracks led back to the barn. She checked the front door of the house and found it locked, along with the back door, and every window in the place. Whoever inherited the house after the old woman's death still hadn't put it on the market and it didn't look like anyone had moved in. She headed out to the barn while Slider stayed rooted on the front porch, evidently not wanting to leave the last place he remembered the old woman being alive. Numerous tire tracks led from the front drive up to the barn door. Whatever the use of the barn, the frequency of travel along the path indicated frequent trips there and back to the highway. Perhaps a neighbor leased out the barn for hay storage, or…

The turquoise balls painted on the barn's side still glistened in the late evening light. The latch on the barn door held a shiny, oversized padlock locked tight.

She headed back to the porch where she called for Slider to follow her. "I saw a house a half mile back," she explained. "Let's see if we can find out who owns this place." They got back in the car, turned around and drove away. A soft whine emanated from the dog sitting across from her.

When she pulled into the driveway of the neighboring house, two young girls and an even younger boy sat on the ground playing in moist sand. Scooped up mounds of sand had been patted into side-by-side rows, effectively creating their own super-highway. The children putt-putted whittled sticks down the narrow roads. So absorbed in play, they ignored her as she parked near them and lowered her car window.

"Plack you're my wife, and I just came home drunk," the small boy said, kneeling in the dirt, making engine noises as he pushed his car down the road, weaving it back and forth.

It took a minute before Sid realized *plack* melded two words—play like—into one, and as so often happens, their play imitated their life.

"Yeah, and I'm mad 'cause I already cooked your supper, and it's cold now," the girl replied.

"Slider, I think it might be better if you waited in the car. I'll leave the window down, but don't get out, okay?"

He looked at her with eyes that pled his desire to get out and play with the children. But he sat back on his haunches—at least for the moment.

Sid got out and headed around the children toward the front porch. When she got closer, she realized a fight brewed inside.

"Not that one, Earlie, that's the best I got!" A woman yelled out over the sounds of crashing dishes.

"Hush up, woman, you ain't got the right to tell me what I can and can't do!"

Sid stopped mid-stride, wondering if she should just leave, but what if the woman and children were in physical danger?

When Sid knocked, the voices inside grew quiet. A couple minutes later a young woman came to the door holding her belly swollen with another child. Sid's heart went out to the woman when she stepped out, one hand holding her back and the other shielding her eyes from the late evening sun now hanging low in the sky. Her long, mouse-brown hair was pulled back and banded at the neck. Shorter, limp strands curled around her face. She wore not a speck of make-up. "Can I help you?" the woman asked.

Sid held her ID and badge open for the woman to see. "I'm trying to find out something about the previous owner of that dog there in my car." She pointed as she spoke. "He used to belong to the old woman in the next house up the road. I took him home with me after she died. Did you know her, or where she got this dog?"

Sid's gaze followed the woman's as her eyes moved from Sid to the children. They still ignored the adults, all except the oldest girl. She watched Sid, wary, protective of her mom. The mother cut her eyes from side to side, nervous, like she'd get in trouble if someone saw her talking to Sid. "I'm afraid I can't help you," she said.

"But did you know the woman?"

"Not really. I got my hands full here with…"

"Maybe your husband knew her?"

The woman stuck her head back inside the house and called out, "Earlie, this woman is asking about the dog what belonged to old Mrs. What's-her-name, the one what lived up the road yonder before she died?"

A shuffle came from inside and an unshaven man with a beer belly came to the door. He wore faded jeans and a tee-shirt as yellow as his teeth. His hands clutched what Sid swore looked like a white sheet with two holes cut out for the eyes.

"Whatcha looking for?" he gruffed.

"I'm trying to learn who owned the dog that's out there in my car." She pointed to Slider, his head hanging out of the window watching the children. Occasionally he yapped at them, asking if he could play.

"It seems he lived there with your neighbor up the road before she died. I'm just trying to find out who owned him before her?"

"Whacha wanna know that for? Seems that's none of your business."

Sid hadn't expected the sharpness in his voice. She took a step back before answering. "Sir, if you don't know, or don't want to tell, that's quite all right, but there's no need for rudeness. I asked you politely, and I expect politeness in return." She turned on her heels and headed to her vehicle, a sudden chill making her wish for a sweater in the 100 degree heat. For some unexplained reason, she half expected a gunshot to her back. When it didn't come, she opened the car door, moved Slider over and got behind the wheel.

"You better leave well enough alone, woman. Let bygones be bygones—all I got to say. Mind your own business," she heard Earlie yell as she headed out the drive.

Since that effort was a wipe-out, she decided to check with the man at the truck stop where she'd first found the frozen dog that icy night. She pulled into the almost empty parking lot. "Stay here, boy, I'll bring you something to eat."

The man behind the counter wore a spotless white apron, and a white cook's cap, and made busy work out of wiping down the already-spotless counter. Chrome chairs with red plastic seats and backs sat pushed under chrome tables with red laminate tops. Reminiscent of a 50s diner, Sid figured the place wasn't a replica, rather the original. A poster of a young Elvis Presley hung on the wall alongside one of Marilyn Monroe standing over a street vent, holding down her white dress. A silent juke box over in the corner waited for someone's quarter, while the empty dining room waited for the supper rush. Sid chose a stool at the counter.

"Coffee please, and maybe a piece of that apple pie. And if I could have a hamburger patty to go."

"Sure, ma'am, but just a patty? No bread or anything?" The man, Tab, his name badge claimed, glanced at her as he spoke. If there was any recognition from the ice-night, he gave not a clue.

"Just the meat, but make that a couple of hamburger patties." If she knew Slider, he could eat a dozen of them.

"You got it." He set a quick cup and saucer before her, turned around to the coffee decanter and soon had her cup filled to the top. As Sid added sweetener, Tab got a small plate from a stack behind him, opened the cover and cut her a big slice of pie.

Poor Slider waited outside.

After collecting a napkin and fork, he set them in front of

her, still with little eye contact.

Sid forked off a bite of pie. "You may not remember me, but a few months ago during that freak ice storm, I came inside to see if you knew who owned the dog shivering outside in the cold."

The man stopped his wiping and sized her up like he would a future waitress. "Oh yeah, I remember. You're the one who ended up finding the house where he lived, and the owner inside, dead. I read about it in the paper."

Sid smiled. "Yep, that's the same dog. Thanks for the tip on the house. It took me a while to find it, but I was glad I did. I ended up taking the dog home with me."

"Read that in the paper, too. Thought about what a nice thing that was you did. How's he doing?"

"Oh, he's well. Still has a trust issue, that's why I'm here. I tried talking to the old woman's neighbor, asking if he knew anything about the dog."

"My guess is he wasn't too polite."

Sid laughed. "That's an understatement. Actually, he was downright rude."

"Well, best I can recollect, he does."

"Knows something about the dog?"

"Yeah, after the story came out in the paper telling how the old woman died and how the dog let people know about it, that jerk came in here bragging about how he'd been the one to give the dog to the woman in the first place. Claimed someone dumped the red mutt off out on the road in front of his house," Tab stopped long enough to give an aside about the man. "He hates dogs, cats—even his own kids… Anyway, he claimed he gave the dog to the old woman—said it like he'd done her a favor."

"Then why didn't he just tell me that?"

Tab shrugged his shoulders. "Because it was a lie. He didn't give her that dog. He never gave anyone anything, except more babies for his poor wife. All he does is drink and hang out with men just as mean as he is."

"Is there anyone around here that might know a little more about the dog?"

Tab scratched his stubbly chin. "The best I recollect, it was old lady Marsh that came in here talking about it afterwards—lives in that trailer court at the edge of town." He pointed south, and added, "Hers is the first one inside the gate. You can't miss it."

"Thanks much, yes, I passed it coming in." She finished her pie and coffee, collected the hamburger patties. Settling her bill she went back to where Slider impatiently awaited the food she'd promised. While he gobbled it down, she sat wondering why she'd come out here in the first place. Certainly she had other things she should be doing, like helping Quade find out who had just tried to kill her.

She may be going down the wrong road, or barking up the wrong tree, but when she looked at Slider, with his head hanging over the front seat, licking the last hint of hamburger from the hairs around his mouth, she knew there must be some connection to his hang-ups, and his attack on the man at the Boondocks.

Old lady Marsh, as Tab called her, was hoeing in a tiny weed garden as Sid walked up and introduced herself, explaining she needed information on Slider's background.

"Yeah, yeah, I remember that dog. That old woman that took him in was senile, but she sure loved that dog." The old woman stopped short, hacked up phlegm and spit in the dirt before she continued. "But her son what lived with her used to beat the poor dog till he bled. Best I recollect the son wanted to make him a guard dog that would attack anyone that came near that barn. Said they wanted him to sniff out authorities or some such." Ms. Marsh snorted.

"Do you know the son's name?"

"Sure do. She called him Sonny, Sonny Sweeney, and his tattooed, pierced son she called Dutch."

Twenty-Two

A good night's sleep did little to relieve the confusion cluttering Sid's thoughts. She felt blown away by the idea of yet another connection to the Sweeneys. All of whom seemed to tie, one way or the other, to Slider's previous owners, her own kidnapping and abandonment in the swamp, and without a doubt, the men in the helicopter. But what about Zeke's death? How much of all this was coincidence, and how much was not?

There are no coincidences, Sid. The certainty of the young woman's voice pounded in Sid's head. Without knowing why or how, the image of the auburn-haired beauty Sid saw sitting under the pine tree accompanied the unspoken words. Regardless, the only thing Sid knew to do was keep walking behind that plow, hoping, one of these days, to reach the end of a row—and be alive to tell about it.

"You talking to yourself, Sid?" Annie walked into the office with a plate of oatmeal raisin cookies and a glass of milk. "You skipped breakfast. I thought you might need a snack."

"Thanks, I need something to take my mind off of that woman." She took a swig of milk.

"What woman? Don't tell me you're thinking about giving Ben up for some woman."

Sid laughed. "No, no, that woman pirate that Boo keeps talking about, and who keeps talking to me."

"What in heaven's name are you talking about Sid? What pirate?"

"Never mind, the whole thing is too crazy-making to try to explain. You know, I think I'll go back out to the area where Boo says she saw that pirate ship, and where they found Zeke." And where Sid had seen what looked to be a ghost ship, but she certainly didn't claim that to anyone, otherwise, she'd be the one Quade locked up.

Sid shut down the computer and headed upstairs to change into something more substantial, while Annie headed to the kitchen. Roused from a nap, Slider followed Sid, and watched as she stepped out of her black slacks and pulled on a pair of blue jeans and a long sleeve shirt. Fiddling with the last couple of stubborn buttons, she stared into the dog's eyes. They'd had a deep bond before the encounter with the men in the helicopter and the bad-man-eating alligator, but that bond seemed light now, compared to how she felt about her *partner*. "I think you better go with me again, Slider. No telling what we may get involved in again."

He sat on his haunches and barked up at her.

"I know, last time got kind of hairy, but this time, we'll be more careful now that we know we've got really bad guys watching us."

Downstairs, she gathered up bottles of water, a pair of binoculars, and a compass. Annie charged into the kitchen decked out in putter pants, a long sleeve denim shirt, with a floppy straw hat plopped on her head. Extra rouge colored her cheeks a bright orange. "Now, Ms Siddie, don't think I'm gonna get left behind this time. If you'd had me with you yesterday we'd have been better able to…"

"Sweetheart—really? You sure you want to mix it up with the bad guys again? After last time—"

Annie flapped her wrist at Sid. "Ah shaw, that was then, this is now. I'm getting bored here at the house cooking and cleaning. Let's me, you and Slider go figure out this mess."

"But you don't even know where we're going…"

"Do too."

"Where?"

"Don't matter none. What matters is you're not leaving without me. I'm in this up to my neck, remember?"

"I'm going to Boo's house and ask to borrow her boat. Thought I'd take a trip back out there to the swamp and see what I might have missed earlier. And that boat isn't big enough for all us."

"Well... I need to check on my patient."

Giving up the battle for lost causes, Sid shrugged. "Okay, grab another bottle of water and come on. You can visit with Boo while Slider and I go out in the swamp."

Annie held up a lunch pack. "Already got it. But you think you should take him?" She gave Slider a condescending look. "After what happened yesterday..."

"If Slider doesn't go, I don't." Sid dug in her heels.

The three of them piled in the car, loaded down with hats, boots, her gun—just in case—and they drove out to Boo Murphy's house.

They found her in the kitchen, frustrated at attempting to duplicate Annie's chicken and dumplings recipe—which thrilled Annie to no end.

"I need to borrow your boat," Sid explained.

"Sure you can, come on. I'll go out there and get you set up."

"That's okay. I was in one the other day. Don't leave your chicken boiling, you and Annie stay where you are, I saw where it's tied."

"You sure? I'd go with you but..." She held up the arm still in a cast.

"I'll be okay, I just need to go out and look around."

Sid headed out to the dock, Slider trailing along behind.

"Go ahead, jump in, boy," she motioned to Slider.

He sat on his haunches and whined.

"It's okay. I'm coming in right after you. Get in."

Still on his haunches, the dog slid backwards, away from the dock.

"I can't believe this! You afraid I'll cast you afloat on your own?"

He turned his head and looked the other way. A stubborn grunt emanated from the back of his throat.

"You have to get over your trust issues, young man." Sid held onto the dock post and stepped inside, and after steadying herself, tried one more time. "Are you going with me, or aren't you? If you don't get in, I'm taking off, and you will have to wait here with Annie, Boo, and Dog."

With care and caution, he walked over to the edge of dock, bent over and sniffed the boat.

Her patience with the animal had run out of road. "Yes, it smells fishy, what did you expect? Are you getting in or not?"

He cast his big brown eyes at her.

"Okay, I'm out of here. Do what you want." She shoved off, confident if Boo and Pirogue Pat could handle one of these things, with a little practice, she could too.

Without warning and with the boat a good three feet from shore, Slider took a flying leap from the dock and plopped into the boat atop Sid's lap, all four legs scrambling to catch his footing while she scrambled to catch her balance before the boat tipped over.

"You crazy critter! And here I thought I had a difficult time making up my mind. You're worse than me!" She laughed at him.

This was the first time she'd been out in the swamp by herself, except the kidnapping, which didn't count. She laughed when her mother's voice sounded in her head. "Sidra, you're going to get yourself lost out in that swamp and nobody will ever find you."

Maybe so, but something had to make sense soon. She didn't know if the damn schooner had been the Hot Spur, or some other pirate vessel, but its resurrection had brought a boatload of problems, including a murder, and now connections to a smuggling ring, which involved her most trusted friend. It was time to make some sense out of this whole mess.

Everyone was fighting over the rights to a schooner once believed to be dead and buried. Reminded her of the tale of Lazarus, and how he'd been supposedly risen from the grave after three days. She'd always thought dead was dead, but now she wasn't so sure.

She paddled through the swamp wondering if Mr. Jean Lafitte or Mary Anne Radcliff would dare show their faces again. These days, she wasn't sure if she was going crazy, or had ever been saner. After a couple of hours, and getting lost several times, she finally poled the pirogue around the bend and recognized it as the one where she had come with Shipwreck.

Pulling out the binoculars, she peered through them for the longest, without a single clue to jump out at her, until way over in the Y of two tree limbs, she caught a glimpse of something that looked out of the ordinary. She poled over, reached up, and pulled down, of all things, a Brownie box camera. Someone had mentioned a camera. Sid replayed her first discussion with Boo until she reached the sentence for which she searched.

Me and Sasha and my Brownie box camera headed out the next morning.

How in the world had she overlooked that piece of information?

Beating up on herself for her ineptness, she tucked the camera in her bag, her heart pounding so fast sweat popped out on her top lip. Maybe this was it. Maybe this would confirm that Boo had really seen a pirate ship—if in fact she had. Sid still wasn't convinced, and neither was anyone else.

Not ready to concede she'd found all there was out here to find, she poled along, alert for any visible sign of something out of the ordinary, stopping every few minutes to peer through the glasses. Eventually she sighted a piece of fabric on a high branch. Sid poled over, yanked until she got the branch low enough to reach and snatched the cloth from the branch and tucked it in her pocket, sweat now coating her clothes.

When the air turned cooler in the middle of the day, Sid

feared a storm brewed. Instead, a slow-moving fog rolled in on a cool breeze and lay just above the surface. The misty patch covered just the area in front of her, nowhere else. Odd, she thought, maybe it was just building, but this seemed an odd time of the day for fog to roll in, even over swamp water. Mesmerized, she stopped the boat and stared at the fog, convinced if she entered it, she'd enter a time warp or a dead zone.

The breeze rustled the leaves. A critter scampered out of sight. A chill coursed through her veins. And then she saw it—the schooner—with its bow stuck up out of the water in the mud. "There it is again, Slider," she whispered, her voice hoarse, strained.

Slider understood every word, or sensed whatever she saw—for his hackles rose. He worked around until he stood with all four feet on the seat in front of Sid. A low growl emanated from his throat—a watchdog type of growl. A growl Sid had only recently heard for the first time.

She pulled the pole up out of the water and laid it across her lap. The water lapped softly against the sides of the pirogue while she sat, contemplating the big brassy ship.

But then, the same young woman she'd seen under the pine tree appeared at the ship's bow, auburn curls blowing in a nonexistent wind. Startled, Sid wondered what she was doing on the boat, and how the hell she'd gotten there. The voluptuous beauty stood tall, confident, defiant, with a cameo profile, and with curves to die for. "Holy shit, Slider, it's Mary Anne Radcliff, in the flesh. Impossible!" she whispered.

The young woman held a cutlass in her left hand and a flintlock pistol in her right. She stepped back from the bow and moved with the grace of a dancer as she swooped around the deck, brandishing weapons as though she fought the duel of her life. Sid paddled closer, reached out to touch the shiny bow, but her hand went right through it as if she'd tried to grab a handful of air.

Mary Anne Radcliff smiled and winked, as though they shared a secret and Mary Anne asked Sid's compliance to tell no one. Then, as quickly as it had come, the fog, the schooner and the woman sailed around the next bend in the river and were gone.

Sid sat with her mouth open. "What the hell was that all about Slider? First, it was Jean Lafitte and now, who, Mary Anne Radcliff? No, that's impossible," she said, stewing over the encounter. "Boo said she climbed up on the vessel. That doesn't make sense. Makes me wonder if she thought she climbed up on it—imagined it. That would make sense, especially for someone her age. But if that's the case, why would she kill Zeke? And if she didn't kill him, who did, and why, and did it have anything to do with the ship? And what does all of that have to do with the men after me?"

More confused than ever, Sid found her way back to shore. Annie and Boo stood on the dock peering out over the swamp as Sid poled around the last bend, heading towards shore. Boo spoke first. "Lord a mercy, I was about to call in the sheriff, what took you so long, child? You had me worried sick thinking I never should've let you go out there by yourself."

Slider jumped out of the boat as soon as it got close enough to the dock, while Boo grabbed the guide rope and pulled it over to a post so Sid could exit. Annie stood with her hands on her hips. "Well, did you find what you went looking for?"

Sid decided to keep the ship and the pirate to herself less someone think she was as crazy as folks were beginning to believe about Boo. Instead, she asked, "Boo, didn't you say you climbed up on the schooner? Stood on it for awhile?"

"I dang sure did, and nobody can convince me I ain't."

"Well, I certainly can't say you didn't. But look what I found up in a tree." Sid pulled the camera out of her bag.

"Lord a mercy." Boo clasped her hands over her heart. "I took that out with me the next day when Sasha and me went out to see if we could find the schooner. I forgot all about it."

"Did you take any pictures with it?"

"I took a couple when we first got there, but when Sasha fell face first in the water, I stuck it up in a tree so's I could go help her up before she drowned. I must've forgot all about it after we found it was Zeke what tripped her."

"Mind if I take it to the store and get the pictures developed just to see what we have?"

"Sure, go ahead."

Sid rewound the film, took it out and tucked the roll in her pocket, giving the old camera back to Boo. "I still have a couple of things I need to ask you about. Why don't we go back inside where we can sit and talk?" Boo agreed and the three women headed that way while Slider ran off to play with Dog.

After Boo had settled in an old rocking chair, Sid dug a little deeper. "Was there anything else that happened that morning that you haven't told us about?"

"No, not that I can think of—unless… Well, when I pulled up to the dock and saw Zeke out in his garden, I hurried over to tell him what I'd seen, but now… it seems… yes, there was these two fishermen pulling in and tying up behind Zeke's house. I started to yell at them about the schooner, but they were busy unloading something off their boat. So I just paid them no nevermind."

"Could you tell what it was?"

Boo glanced up at the ceiling, thinking. "Some kind of packages. At the time, I thought maybe Zeke had just come from talking to them 'cause he sure was all out of breath. They sure skedaddled after they heard the gunshot."

Sid made a mental note of the new tidbit of information. "Okay, tell me more about the Sweeny's. Do you know a Sonny Sweeny? Has a son named Dutch?"

Boo leaned forward in the rocker and rested both her arms on the chair arms. "Heard of 'em, yeah."

"Heard what?"

"Heard they're smugglers. Don't have any proof, but I hear tell that rumor's been going around since even before I was born,

"Smugglers? Of what?"

"Most anything worth money."

Sid reached in her pocket and pulled out the piece of fabric she'd found stuck on a tree branch. "Recognize this?"

"I dang sure do! It's a piece of my shirt—the same shirt they found around Zeke's neck."

"Do you have any idea how this piece got up in a tree?"

"Last I seen it, that is before it wound up around Zeke's neck, was the day before when I was paddling underneath these low-hanging branches. A twig snatched the muckle-dun shirt out of my lap and took it high up in the tree. I just let it stay there. Sasha hated the shirt anyway. Said it reminded her of those filthy mud pies kids used to make. Well, I ain't like my persnickety cousin. I ain't got no argument with dirt, and for the life of me, can't figure out why some folks think so little of it."

Twenty-Three

After Sid dropped Annie and Slider back home, she headed to the store and dropped off the film for development. It was so old and damp, the woman said, she wasn't sure anything would show up on the negatives, but they would try. Of course it had to be sent off for development and it might take a couple of weeks before they got it back.

Sid crossed all her fingers and toes, hoping when the pictures came back, she'd have a definitive answer about something or someone out there the same day Boo and Sasha were out there looking for the schooner. But do ghost ships show up in photographs?

From there, she headed to the library. Intrigued to no end by the pirate queen she'd seen in the swamp, she *had* to learn something about the woman. Of course, she might be in the Lafitte book in Durwood's truck. She could borrow it, but by the time she cleaned the crud off of every page, she doubted there'd be any ink left.

After she'd searched for what seemed an hour or more, she went to the reference desk and asked for help. The heavyset masculine-looking brunette young woman led her to the reserved section, reached up on a high shelf and pulled out a book with a blood-red cover. "*Lafitte's Pirate Queen,*" she read the cover to Sid. This should be what you're looking for. It's been out of print for years. You can check it out, but only overnight."

Sid checked it out, agreeing to return it before the library closed the next day, and headed home, eager to relax and dig into the story. She waltzed in the front door and tossed her handbag and the book on the sofa, calling out, "Annie, you here?"

Slider loped downstairs and Chesterfield sauntered in from the kitchen. They both *ruffled their feathers* when they saw each other.

"Evening, you two, I see you still get along like cats and dogs. So Annie went out, huh? Well, come on, I'll get you both something to eat." She headed to the kitchen and hurriedly fed the dynamic duo. After Slider woofed down his yogurt-coated dog nuggets, she let him out in the backyard, and headed upstairs to change, leaving meticulous Chesterfield to eat his dinner without getting a single whisker dirty.

Dressed in a comfy pair of shorts and tee shirt, she settled on the sofa with a glass of red wine and let the first smooth sip slide down her throat. "Okay, finally."

The delay heightened her eagerness to learn more about Mary Anne Radcliff and Jean Lafitte, pirates, or privateers, as they preferred to be called. She still couldn't believe what had happened when she'd rowed up alongside the resurrected schooner in the swamp, how the sexy pirate queen stood at the bow, waving and winking at Sid, who blinked a few times until, at last, the young woman disappeared.

Sliding back, she leaned against the cushion and stared at the cover of the book. Superimposed on the red cover, lusty beauty Mary Anne Radcliff stood alongside debonair Jean Lafitte, who wore a black hat, long, black curly hair, handlebar moustache, and a black suit. Only a hint of a white shirt showed at his neck. His arms were crossed in concentration over his thick chest, and in his left hand he held a spy glass, as if he tracked a ship offshore. White ruffles peaked from underneath the long-sleeved coat, softening his looks.

Mary Anne wore a black hat atop long, windswept curls, and a black, off-the shoulders blouse, and a long black skirt tied around the waist with a blood-red sash. She held a pistol in one and a cutlass in the other. The hostile look on Mary Anne's face defied anyone who might dare approach.

Sid's eyes followed the curve of the imposing figures, and then landed back on their faces. The stern expressions of both, more than likely scared away many an enemy. But Sid couldn't help but remember the wink and the sideways grin Mary Anne had given her earlier when she'd stared at the ghostly figure with shock and awe. For the life of her, Sid found herself unable to move beyond the cover to the inside of the book until she'd memorized every element in the picture, their broad-brimmed hats that sat on their heads with a cockiness that defied anyone's attempt to remove them, the self-assuredness surrounding them like the aura of a divine spirit.

Dammit, as everyone else in this area, she too had fallen in love with 19th century outlaws. No sooner had Sid opened the cover to learn more about this strange couple than Annie hustled in the back door, whistling and plopping bags of groceries on the table. A second later, she stood in the doorway of the living room, dressed in a big, floppy-brimmed hat and earrings that dangled alongside her turkey-waddle neck. "I hope you found something to eat, Siddie, I didn't cook anything fresh. We had leftovers in the fridge. I wasn't sure what time you'd be home."

"Um hmm."

"What'cha reading?"

Sid held up the book. "Look what I found at the library. The book tells about the legendary Jean Lafitte and Boo's ancestor, Mary Anne Radcliff, who rode with him. Seems she took after her grandmother, the infamous Anne Cormac Bonny, who rode with Calico Jack Rackam. Oh, and I fed Chesterfield and Slider. They both acted half starved to death, so I assumed they hadn't eaten yet."

"Thanks. My shopping took longer than I expected, and I took a few things back out to Boo's house. I noticed she was a little low on some staples like bread, milk, eggs. She's still not driving, you know."

"That was nice. How'd her dumplings turn out?"

"Well, I hate to admit it, but they were good. I sat and ate with her. As far as how she's doing, she's just as ornery as before."

Eager to get back to her book, Sid didn't encourage further conversation, and Annie turned and headed back to the kitchen to put away the groceries. She'd barely read a couple pages when Slider sauntered in. Head down, he sneaked over to her and sat back on his haunches, waiting. She looked up. "Hey boy, heading to bed?" She gave the top of his head a good scratch, which served as her customary goodnight kiss, and he headed upstairs. "I'll be up after awhile," she called out, knowing with his head start her chance of getting to sleep lessened.

A few minutes later Aunt Annie came in and rattled on about her day then she and Chesterfield headed up to bed. By then, it was after ten o'clock and Sid's own eyelids felt thick. But fascinated by the family history of the two lusty female pirates with more guts and determination than Sid carried in her little finger, she forced her eyes open and read further.

She learned that Mary Anne Radcliff's grandmother, Anne, had been conceived in the midst of an illicit affair between Anne's womanizing father, John Cormac, and his wife's housemaid, Peg. The guy wasn't too bright, for when his wife announced she was with child, his immediate response had been, "Not another one!" That slip of the tongue set off a typical Scottish clan war between John Cormac's family, and that of his wife's—the Sweeney's. John fled to Charleston, South Carolina with the housemaid and their infant daughter, Anne.

Years later, Anne, now a rebellious teenager, married a no-good named James Bonny, and together they set sail for New Providence, later known as the Bahamas, and took up with pirates. Anne was arrested and sentenced to die for piracy on the high seas, but escaped the hangman's noose by *claiming her belly*. Soon afterwards, she married a man named Michael Radcliff and disappeared into the frontier. Mary Anne Radcliff came along a generation or so later, having inherited the same rebellious nature of her ancestor, Anne Bonny Radcliff. Women definitely ahead of their times.

The air conditioner turned on and a sudden coldness filled the room. She pulled an afghan over her legs and that helped for a few minutes, but when the cold grew deeper, she adjusted the rheostat and cracked a window to keep the room from getting stuffy. When she turned around, a crystal covered dish with *Texas* engraved on it floated across her retinas. Above the word, there was an engraved picture of an old mission, with a soldier standing in front of it, musket in hand. Underneath the mission, were the words, "Remember the Alamo."

When the door bell rang, she jumped, and looked over at the grandfather clock. Unexpected callers never came this time of night. She turned on the porch light and peeked out the front window. Hoke Faulkner, dressed in dark slacks, a white dress shirt unbuttoned at the collar, and shaved head glistening in the porch light, shuffled his feet and glanced around the neighborhood. He must have laid low since Sid had confronted him about his identity, for she had not seen or heard from him since then. Now, he stood on her porch.

She opened the door and peeked around the edge. "What do you want, Hoke, it's late."

"Pardon me, Sid, for not calling."

"No problem, how can I help you?"

"Since I haven't been able to talk to Boo yet, and my boss is pushing me to…for…for information. I just wanted to chat with you a few minutes. Besides, I wanted to tell you something."

"Who's your boss, and what kind of information is he wanting?"

"May I come in?"

Sid glanced over her shoulder. "I guess so. It is rather late, though, so… You haven't come to kill me, have you?"

"No," he laughed, "and I promise I won't stay long."

"Okay, a few minutes." She unlatched the screen door and he stepped inside. She led him into the living room where he glanced around the room, looking awkward. "You have a dog?"

"A dog? Yes, I do. He's around somewhere. Why?"

"I didn't want to startle him. I know it's late, and I'm a stranger to him. I've got a couple of them myself, and I know how they can be." He nodded at the empty glass of wine on the coffee table. "I wonder if I might have a glass of what you had."

"All right." She turned and headed to the kitchen.

Hoke followed. "I wanted to ask you if Boo said anything more about what she found on the schooner."

"Not really." She took the bottle of wine off the shelf, grabbed a glass from the cabinet and poured, aware of a vague discomfort creeping through her gut. Boo had said he was a Sweeney and not to trust him, so she remained wary when she handed him only a half-full glass and headed back to the living room. "How long have you been working for whoever it is looking for this secret something?" she asked over her shoulder.

"Excuse me?"

"The time I confronted you on the phone about your not being a professor, you said you were looking for something. I assume someone hired you. So how long have you been their employee?"

"Oh, yes, well, yes, a long time."

"I see." Sid turned and headed back to the living room. "Since you are being so *open* about everything, would you like to sit a minute?"

"Sure, but not long." He sat on the edge of the sofa, spotting the book she'd been reading. He picked it up from the coffee table. "Lafitte's an American hero, you know. Looks like you're doing your homework. Distinctive looking guy wasn't he? And who wouldn't want a beauty like that to sail with you."

Sid took the book out of his hand and held it behind her. "Excuse me, I'm afraid you'll lose my place, I didn't mark it." She laid the book on an end table, her discomfort growing stronger.

He drained the half glass of wine and asked, "Might I have a little more? Merlot isn't it? Robert Mondavi? Can't get the year, maybe…"

"Actually it's a Cab, and no, it isn't Mondavi, and I'm afraid the bar is closed for the night. I've had a full day and I'm ready for bed."

Hoke stood. "First, I have something I want to tell you, but I'm taking a risk taking you in my confidence. More than that, I'm putting you in danger. But you can't tell anyone. Not yet."

He stuck his hand in his pocket, pulled something out and handed it to her, and then he crashed to the floor in a heap, taking with him the empty wine glasses and her book.

First she thought it was a joke, or a part of some stupid plan of manipulation, until a thick wine-colored liquid oozed out from a small hole in the center of his chest and she remembered he'd drained the wineglass earlier.

She jumped like she'd been the one shot when Annie rushed up behind her.

"Was that a gunshot, Siddie? Who's that guy, and why's he on the floor?"

Twenty-Four

"All I know is, one minute Hoke Faulkner was standing there talking about his favorite Merlot, the next minute he's on the floor in a pool of blood." Sid explained to the super tall police detective for the umpteenth time. Meanwhile, another detective inspected Hoke's body still sprawled on the floor.

Detective Kitchens arrived looking like he knew what the hell he was doing. There wasn't the cocky arrogance about him she saw in some detectives. Instead he appeared a self-confident, knowledgeable veteran.

The first officers on the scene had cleared the house and then given Aunt Annie the okay to put on a pot of coffee. Now, as Sid and the detective talked, the sound of rattling dishes and running water from the kitchen gave some sense of normalcy to the scene. Hopefully the smell of coffee would offset the odor of blood and death.

"So, as I understand it, you and Mr. Falkner were having a glass of wine when he suddenly collapsed on the floor…"

"That's correct."

"Please tell me the topic of your conversation."

The detective sounded friendly and down home, but something about his manner and approach told her he expected an honest answer. His quick eyes assessed her demeanor, body language, mannerisms, and of course for signs of deception. She even caught him staring at the bruises around her wrists from when she'd been tied and left in the boat, and the ten million mosquito bites on her arms, and wondered if he suspected the physical damage might have been inflicted by Hoke, causing her to kill him.

She hoped it was evident that she didn't belong to the Bandito motorcycle gang, and that the detective realized the Joe Friday approach wasn't necessary. Even her state of shock wouldn't prevent her from snickering if he said, *just the facts, ma'am.*

"But surely you heard something before the gun went off, Ms. Smart." He stared at the lifeless form of Hoke Faulkner, still dressed in dark slacks and a white—now blood-stained—shirt. "I'm confused. But maybe I'm just missing something here." He innocently rubbed his chin. "Maybe you can help me understand how this happened. How someone came in here and shot your guest while you stood right beside him, and how you didn't see or hear a thing. Ma'am, you think you might have seen something you've forgotten?"

Boy, this guy was skilled at his job. This comfortable, reassuring approach had a deeper design at its depth.

Another detective walked in, interrupting the *pleasant* conversation. In her hand lay a gun atop a white handkerchief. "I found this out in the bushes near the front porch. Have you ever seen it before, ma'am?"

"I have one just like it—here in my handbag, and yes, I do have a license to carry it." Sid snatched her handbag from the sofa and scrambled through it for a gun that wasn't there.

Detective Kitchens' mouth pulled into a grim line. "I'm sorry ma'am, I know you're a private detective, but I'm going to have to swab your hands for gunshot residue, and then I need you to go upstairs with Detective Mitchell, here." He pointed at the detective standing at his side. "She'll get you to change into something else." He indicated what she wore. "We'll need to take those clothes in with us, the gun, too, of course. And a word of caution, flight would be interpreted in a negative way. It would probably cause us to seek a warrant for your arrest. So you may want to stay in town for now."

The only thought that went through her brain was, *shit fire and save matches!*

By the time Sid climbed the stairs to bed it was almost daybreak. Slider had settled down after his initial panic over the gunshot, and now lay sprawled in his chair, all four legs in the air, snoring like a freight train rumbling down the tracks—headed straight for her. Shivering despite the warm evening, she eased out of her clothes, slid a nightshirt over her head and slipped between the covers.

Confused, the detective had said. Good grief, he couldn't be more confused than she was. How in the world did someone get inside, get her gun—or even know where to look for a gun—before she, and Hoke, returned from the kitchen?

She reached over to the bedside table and picked up the item Hoke had taken out of his pocket—the item she'd tucked in her bra before the police arrived, and the item she'd concealed there when the detective had gone upstairs with her when she'd changed her clothes.

She'd almost given it to the police, but Hoke's warning to tell no one had stopped her. Evidently he had good reason to keep it a secret. She rubbed her fingers over the soft black leather and flipped it open. The ID inside the small leather case gave her a whole new impression of Agent Hoke Faulkner, Homeland Security.

She climbed in bed and turned out the light. Mary Anne Radcliff's voice pounded words against the inside of Sid's skull.

Sidra Smart, don't waste time thinking you can't do this, for you have a leader's gift to declare war on the whole world. You have a brain for battle and you relish the fight. You know your limitations. Devise a shrewd plan for the most effective attack.

Something shoved on the bed, rousing her from a deep, dark nothingness. She rose on her elbow to see what Annie wanted. But except for Slider, the room sat empty and quiet. She lay down again and pulled the covers under her chin as fog rolled over conscious thought.

You're lost as a goose, aren't you Sis?

You can say that again.

Got no idea who attacked you, the familiar, strange voice said. It sounded like humor danced in back of his words—like he knew something she didn't. She squinted, trying to see his face, but he stepped back into the shadows.

Not a clue, she admitted. *And that's the scary part.*

What's this deal you got going with that pirate woman?

You mean Mary Anne Radcliff?

I mean you've got to get your head out of the clouds and focus on the bad guys. This pirate gal, she's got lots of bad karma she's trying to clear out, but if you're not careful, she'll get you sidetracked.

What do you mean? What kind of bad karma? Boo thinks she was a goddess.

She was a hellcat, Sis, just like her mama. According to one of her crew members, she apprenticed with the worst of them. Jean Lafitte finally got rid of her because she tried to take over his command. She even wanted him to side with the British during the War of 1812. She's trouble, I tell you, Sis. If you're not careful you'll miss the clues of the case.

Clues? What clues?

Clues strewn all over the place, clues like...

A shrill sound off in the distance drowned out the voice of Warren, her dead brother, who'd been playing around in her head. Sid strained, tried to hold on, but the high-pitched "Siddie, Siddie, you okay?" startled her awake.

A click, and then the bright light from the bedside lamp, and there Annie stood over her, concern deepening the already existing lines on her face. "You must've being talking in your sleep, sweetheart. I could hear you clear down the hall. You okay?"

Sid sat straight up in bed and clutched the bedcovers to her chest. "Yeah, I'm okay. I must have been dreaming."

Slider, awake now himself, came over and climbed up in the bed with her. Annie kissed the top of Sid's head, switched off the light and returned to her room.

Sid's senses on full alert now, she rolled over towards Slider and he cradled his head on her arm. "Did you hear anything, boy?"

Slider grunted.

"I must have been dreaming about Warren," she said, digging her fingers into Slider's red, curly fur.

"He talked about clues," she recalled, still half asleep.

Later that morning Sid's cell rang so loud she almost fell off the bed when she tried to answer before the ringing woke Slider. She was not ready to take him outside, but once he awoke, his bladder demanded full attention.

She squinted at the display, but without reading glasses, couldn't make out the caller ID.

"Hello?" She spoke softly into the phone, looking over at Slider to see if he'd moved.

"Morning, Love, am I calling too early?"

The sound of Ben's voice made her pulse beat faster, and she quickly shoved back the covers and sat up. They hadn't talked in a couple of days. "Oh, hi Ben, you're up early." She ran her fingers through her hair.

"And from the sound of your voice—you're not. You sound tired. Have a rough night?"

She laughed. "Rough dreams! All kinds of people showed up." No way was she going to admit she'd talked to dead people.

"I've missed you something terrible. Think we might do something tonight?"

"I'm pretty busy..." Who was she kidding? She knew she'd clear her calendar for an evening with the guy.

"Maybe dinner and Willie Nelson. He's performing at the Lutcher Theatre, thought if I could get tickets we might take in the show."

"Sounds nice. Actually, maybe just dinner and back to your place."

"Really? Yes—yes, that'd be great." The words didn't hide the thrill of passion evident in the tone of his voice. "I've got a full day in court, what say we just meet somewhere."

"That'll work. How about your place? Sixish?"

"Perfect. And how about a sleep over?" Ben sounded eager.

"Sounds good. Since you haven't mentioned it, I guess you haven't heard the latest." Sid got out of the bed and headed over to the window seat.

"I guess not. What's up?"

"Hoke Faulkner, the guy who lied about being a professor at Texas A & M, came by my house late last night and while he stood in the middle of the living room, someone shot him with my gun and—"

"Shot him? In your living room? With your gun, did you say? My God, Sid, are you okay?"

"I'm fine, but I think the police may think I did the shooting—since they found my recently-fired gun right outside the open window." She went on to explain the details and gained reassurance from Ben that the police wouldn't think she killed anyone.

After a quick shower, Sid dressed and headed outside with Slider. But as they walked, her dream from the night before crept back inside her consciousness. Bits and pieces of Warren mixed in with Jean Lafitte and Mary Anne Radcliff. Warren had warned her against them. She laughed out loud, wondering what kind of threat a dead man from the 1700s could possibly be. Then her brother had said there were clues lying all around. What clues? And where?

Wondering what in the world Hoke was involved in, and what that had to do with the schooner, and what, in turn, that had to do with homeland security, Sid headed back out to check on Boo. When she turned into the drive between the two houses, she noticed a big Dodge Ram pick-up parked in front of Sasha's house. She'd recognize that truck anywhere.

It belonged to her friend and mentor, George Léger.

Uneasy, feeling like something wasn't right she exited her car just as George burst out of Sasha's house. When he saw Sid, he looked as guilty as sin.

"George, what in the world are you doing here?"

"Hey, Sha, I could ask you the same thing."

"Sasha's cousin Boo is my client. I'm trying to find out who killed Sasha's husband so I can get Boo off the charge—why am I explaining that to you—you know the way this works."

"Oh, you told me you wouldn't take her case."

"I figured I might as well go ahead, since I kept getting pulled into it anyway."

"I asked you not to." Affront was written all over his face. Or was it fear?

She stuttered, hesitating, and then wondered why in the world she let herself feel guilty. "I can take any case I want to. I don't mean to sound ungrateful or childish, but I no longer need your approval. Nor do I understand your reluctance for me to get involved with this particular case."

Sasha overheard the conversation and came to the door. "What's the matter?" She looked from Sid to George.

"Nothing," George said, and stomped over to his truck, but he turned and looked back at Sid. "You watch your back, Sha."

"What do you know that I don't?" She called out to his retreating back. She almost told him about Hoke being with Homeland Security, but something wasn't right, and she didn't know what that something was. Until then, she wasn't telling anyone. These guys knew the business much better than she did, they could figure it out for themselves.

Twenty-Five

Sid got home just as Annie climbed out of her car loaded down with packages. "Hey, Siddie, I bought some pretties for you to wear tonight."

"What? You bought what?"

"Come on inside, I'll show you."

Sid followed her up the steps of the wide front porch and through the front door. An ill feeling sat on Sid's shoulders. What was Annie talking about? She hadn't told her anything about the evening with Ben.

Inside, Annie dropped the packages on the living room sofa and pulled out a box from a Beaumont mall. "Here, let me show you this…" She flipped the lid off of the box and separated the tissue paper. "You look better in a darker red, a red with a little purple in it—not that orange-red outfit you wear all the time."

Sid closed her mouth before a bug flew inside.

"Look, ain't this pretty?" Out slid a filmy red dress with a handkerchief hem and a plunging neckline with sequins scattered around the top.

Sid's mouth dropped open again.

"I saw it in the window and I just couldn't resist buying it."

"Annie, I couldn't wear anything that low cut!" She almost said Sam would never approve of her wearing such a sexy-looking outfit out in public. In their own bedroom, yes, for he expected her to dress like a harlot there and like a puritan everywhere else.

But then she remembered—it didn't matter whether he approved or not. They were divorced and Sam had no say whatsoever about anything she said or did.

"Besides, I'm just going to Ben's house—and how'd you know I had a date with him?"

Annie looked at Sid without raising her head. "I was walking down the hall this morning and overheard you on the phone. And look, I bought these too." She pulled out a red bra and matching panties. "Just in case—you know…"

"In case what? I get in a car accident on the way over? Jesus, Annie…"

But her heart skipped a beat just thinking about the possibilities inherent in the evening. It had been a while since she and Ben had made love. Maybe tonight.

"But I can't wear that dress to his house."

"Sure you can. Do it, see how he reacts."

Annie finally left the room and Sid headed to the bathroom. Standing before the mirror, she grabbed the black-handled pinking shears and snipped a couple of places on her short hairdo then put the shears back in the drawer. Still standing in front of the mirror, she untied her robe and let it drop to the floor.

Hmm, well, not bad for her age. Maybe she *would* wear the red dress—see how Ben reacted when he saw her standing at his door, and maybe she should take an overnight bag.

⚓

"Oh my god, Sid, whatever you're trying to do to me, it is working." Ben looked down at himself and laughed. "It's definitely working! My god, Sid, you look gorgeous! Where'd you get that dress?" He swung the door wide and let Sid stroll past, taking every ounce of resistance he had left not to grab her and carry her off to his lair—or try to anyway. He had to get back to the gym and work on those muscles—those that were soft that is. He chuckled under his breath. Don't call him an old man, not with this kind of reaction.

Sid headed to the bar and poured herself a glass of red wine from a bottle already open. "If you must know, Annie came home with this today."

"Annie?"

"Seems she overheard our phone conversation this morning and took it upon herself to buy me a new outfit. I take it you like?" She walked over and looked him in the eyes.

"That word doesn't come close. Just looking at you makes me horny as hell. Come here, you." He took the glass out of her hand and sat it on the table then pulled her close.

"Since you like the dress, you might also like…" She pulled up the bottom of her skirt to reveal the new red panties.

"I'm coming Elizabeth," he mocked, holding his hand to his chest. "Careful, Sid, I can only hold back so long."

"Who asked you to hold back?" Sid closed her eyes and moved into him.

He brought her hand in and tucked it beneath his chin, pulling her closer, tighter, willing her body into his. He groaned in her hair, hair that smelled of lavender-scented shampoo.

She sighed when he brought his lips to hers and dipped his tongue into her mouth, tentative at first, tender, soft, exploring. When he opened his eyes and looked into hers, a shining hunger reflected back his own. Somewhere in the back of his mind he heard the admonition to slow down, to not push her this fast, but she lifted her lips to his and invited him back inside.

He went.

Afterwards, they lay naked, her head resting on his arm, the beautiful red dress and sexy undergarments tossed hurriedly onto the overstuffed chair in the corner.

"You tasted marvelous," he said, running his fingers down her stomach, over her belly button.

"Umm," she smiled, her eyes still closed. "You know just where to touch, and how."

"Just doing what comes naturally." He sighed and let his head rest on the pillow, staring over at her as she slipped into a light, peaceful sleep.

She'd needed this as much as he had.

She moved her hand to her stomach. The engagement ring he'd given her weeks ago—months ago now—glistened in the candlelight. Seems she left it in her drawer more times than she wore it. He'd been surprised she'd had the thing on when she'd arrived last evening. Maybe that was a good sign.

Ben drifted off to sleep.

When a giant orange ball of sun shot through the window, Ben stirred, and looked over at Sid, thankful she still lay beside him. She stretched like a lazy cat, opened her eyes and smiled. He reached his hand over and pushed a sprig of white hair off her face. "Good morning merry sunshine, how did you wake so soon?"

"What time is it?" She smiled back.

"Still early. Looks like we both got a good night's sleep."

"Oh man, did I ever!"

"I don't know about you, but I'm starving. We never did get dinner last night. Well, we ate, but it wasn't food."

"Hmm, I'm hungry, too." She snuggled deeper into the covers.

"Tell you what. I'm going to jump in the shower right quick while you take an extra snooze. I'll rouse you when I get dressed then you can shower while I cook us a hearty breakfast."

"Sounds perfect," she said dozing off again.

Ignoring one hunger to feed another, Ben stepped into a cool shower and let the water bring him down. No sense in wearing out the blessed act. After he finished the shower and dried off, he pulled on a pair of brown shorts and a tee shirt, stepped into a pair of sandals and leaned over the sleeping beauty. "It's time sweetheart. I'm heading to the kitchen. Eggs Benedict sound good?"

"Hmm," she rolled over and opened her eyes. "Sounds perfect. I'm up." She threw back the covers and scooted to the bathroom, exposing a beautiful round bottom.

Now he needed another cold shower. Instead, he headed to the kitchen and got busy preparing breakfast. He sipped on a cup of coffee while toasting English muffins when she sneaked up behind him and kissed his shoulder. "Hey, babe, I didn't hear you come in. Feel better?"

"Sure do. Coffee's ready I see, and it smells scrumptious."

"Here, have a seat at the counter and keep me company. I'll pour you a cup."

"Nice night, Ben. It sure felt good—back in your arms. Why have we waited so long?"

He sat the white mug of steaming coffee in front of her.

"'Cause I've acted like a jerk."

"True." She sipped her coffee, looking up at him through her eyelashes.

"You don't have to be so blunt!"

"Men are always the ones that are wrong. Don't you know that?"

"Since when?"

"Since Adam and Eve. The story just got twisted around because men wrote the story. If Eve's version of the event would have been the one that made it into the canon, the story would have been way different."

"Is that so?" He chuckled as he assembled the benedicts and sat their plates on the counter in front of her.

"Sure it's so. Ask any woman!"

"Okay Ms. Right, let's eat."

Both ravenous by now, they picked up their forks and dove in. After the hunger pains ceased and the eating slowed, Ben decided now was the time to demonstrate his change of heart.

"How's your case going?"

"Puzzling as hell. The more I uncover, the less it all makes sense."

"I heard you're cleared on the Faulkner shooting. No evidence of gun powder on you or your clothes"

"Who told you that? I haven't heard it myself?"

"I ran into Quade yesterday having lunch at The Bread Box. We ended up sitting together and eating. We got to talking about this and that..." He left the sentence dangling, knowing how sensitive she was to being the topic of anyone's conversation.

"The Eggs Benedict are delicious. What's your secret?"

"It's all in the sauce."

"Delicious, I'll have to tell Annie, and she'll want your recipe."

"I never give away my recipes," he said, smiling.

"What do you know about homeland security?"

"Why? You uncovering leads related to terrorists?" Oh God, not that. And he was trying so hard to not be afraid for her.

"Leads, but none that make sense."

"How so?" He reached for the coffee decanter and poured them a fresh cup.

"Okay, I don't know how this conflict of interest thing works, but I need to knock something around with you."

Ben put his fork down and looked her in the eye, hoping his lips weren't quivering. This was going to be harder than he'd thought.

When she explained what Boo had said about Hoke Faulkner, that he was without a doubt a Sweeney, and how that family had been involved in smuggling for a couple hundred years, and how she'd found out Faulkner was with Homeland Security, and how she hadn't told the police detective that came and investigated his murder, and how Zeke Harris also was known as Dexter Sweeney, and Dexter Sweeney had another wife, and how Sid had escaped the men in the helicopter, and how funny George was acting these days, and how...

His heart flipped over two dozen times. He caught her looking at him, but no way in hell was she going to see him sweat. Instead, he sat up straighter and assumed the professional role of inquiry.

"You think the other wife is involved? Or maybe dead, too? What about George? Sasha?"

"Could be any of the above."

Ben fiddled his fork on the counter top. "George is the one

who throws me. I've never known him to be anything but straight arrow."

She swallowed a mouthful then cut off another forkful of Benedict. "Regardless of what Sasha told the authorities, she knows Boo didn't kill Zeke. She told me so."

"Then I'm surprised Quade hasn't dropped the charges."

Sid shrugged. "Sasha hasn't told Quade that. Just me, as far as I know."

"Think Quade may have charged her, hoping to flush out someone else?"

"Now that's a thought—why didn't I think of it?" She laughed. "Wonder who he might have in mind—and if so, why didn't he tell me?"

"Quade's got his own way of doing things. It sounds to me like you've got your own way, too. You'll figure it out. If you need someone to knock it around with let me know."

She stood and picked up her cup. "Thanks, that means a lot to me. I've missed that part of our relationship."

"Me too, we did good on that first case didn't we? Worked like synchronicity in motion. Then I start acting like a jerk." He kissed the top of her head. "Just ignore me when I act like that. You're doing a fantastic job with the Third Eye. Warren would be so proud of you. Evidently he knew you had it in you. You think he really expected you to run the business, or just hoped you could get some money out it."

"Oh, he expected me to run the business. I don't have a doubt in my mind about that."

"Really, how so?" He turned on the faucet and let warm water run in the sink while he rinsed the dishes and loaded the dishwasher.

She picked up a clean dishtowel and started drying the ones he'd hand washed. "You'll think I'm crazy…"

"Crazy?"

"I feel like Warren's helping me."

"What? Warren's dead, how can…"

"I'm doing some crazy dreaming. Warren showed up and gave me some sort of clue, or he left me with a sense of a clue, something, somewhere, but when I awakened I couldn't hang onto it."

"So you and he are doing some dream-walking huh?" Ben picked up their empty plates and walked around the counter to the kitchen sink. Sid followed.

"Is that what you call it?"

"That's what Warren called it!"

"I don't understand."

"Warren used to tell me about what he called dream-walking. Now that I recall, he even mentioned something once about a sister—must have been you. There weren't any other siblings where there?"

"No, just the two of us. What'd he say? You've tickled my curiosity."

"It's been a while." He handed her a plate he'd rinsed and she tucked it into the dishwasher. "Something about his sister drowning, she'd been drowning a long time, and then something about him grabbing her hand and pulling her up out of the thick, dark mire—almost like a quicksand."

"He must have been talking about me before the divorce—I sure felt like I was drowning in a lake of quicksand." She shut the dishwasher. "Now his reason for leaving me the detective agency all makes sense."

"What about the dream you had the other night? What was he saying, doing?"

"That's the thing—now I can't remember, and it's frustrating!"

Her cell phone vibrated on the table, and before she could get it, the tune *I Fought the La*w started playing. "Oh, that's Quade."

"Quade?" You got a song by the Crickets as Quade's ring tone?"

"Yep, sure do, thought it fit." She punched on the phone.

When her face turned white, he knew whatever Quade had to tell her wasn't what she'd expected. He waited until she said, "I'll be right there," and punched off the phone.

"Got to go. Call you later." Sid smacked Ben on the lips and headed out.

No sooner had she left, than Ben's phone buzzed with a text message. He read it, grabbed his suit coat, and headed out right behind Sid.

Twenty-Six

Out of breath by the time she parked in front of the Sheriff's office and rushed inside, she found her friend, Sheriff Quade Burns, discussing the situation with others. The air in the room felt electric. When he saw her, he beckoned her forward. "Come on in, Sid, have a seat. Have you met Investigators, Alex Hebert and Ralph Fontenot from our CID unit?"

Alex Hebert, who looked to be in her late 30s, stood less than five feet tall, and might have been just as wide. She wore a maroon, short-sleeved shirt made out of some type of heavy cotton blend. The left shirt pocket had a golden-yellow badge embroidered on it, and on the right pocket, her name. Ralph Fontenot's shirt was similar in style, but dark green in color. They both wore pistols strapped around their waists and an extra magazine on each belt.

"No, we haven't met." Sid shook hands with both of them. Ralph Fontenot stood a good six feet tall, but Alex, although much shorter, carried the status of senior officer. Her bearing manifested an air of intelligence and sharp-thinking, complimented by green eyes and brown hair worn in a short, no-nonsense style.

Ralph looked to be around 30. Sid laid odds with herself that he'd graduated from college with a criminal justice degree. He looked the studious type with acute attention to detail. His spotless uniform included crisp creases down both sleeves and pants legs.

"Looks like you're hitting this case pretty hard," she said.

"This isn't the half of it." Quade stood and headed around the desk. "I just sent a page out to select a team of investigators to report here. In just a few minutes you'll meet a whole team of folks. Orange County has what's called a Homicide Investigative Team, or H.I.T, as we call it. This team is used primarily for homicide investigations, but we utilize it on any major crime such as this. When a crime like this occurs, a group page or text is sent out to select investigators from every law enforcement agency in the County as well as the District Attorney's investigators, the Texas Rangers, and the FBI. Only the best investigators are assigned to this team. The new police chief will be in on it, too. He's on his way here."

At that moment, Ben walked in the room. Startled to see him, Sid looked from him to Quade and back again. "Don't tell me Ben's the new police chief!"

Quade grinned at Sid. "No, not the police chief, but he is one of our team members."

Maintaining a professional demeanor, Ben gave her a quick smile and shook hands with the others in the room.

"Ben, I was just explaining H.I.T. to Sid. This is her first time to be included in something such as this." He turned and looked back at Sid. "As I was saying, when the call goes out all who are available report where the message instructs. Within fifteen minutes we normally have 20 of the best investigators around on the scene."

Quade looked at his watch. "A supervisor from the lead agency, which in this case is the Sheriff's Department, assigns the various investigators to tasks such as taking witness statements, going door to door. Going wherever and following whatever leads that may come up, or in assisting in the processing of the crime scene."

Sid closed her mouth, wondering if the same team worked on Hoke Faulkner's death. She'd ask later.

"It's proven to be very effective," Quade said. "We have inquires from all over the country asking for advice on how to recreate this in other jurisdictions."

Alex chimed in. "Every investigator has to check his or her ego at the door, because we may get the best assignment. Or we may be digging through a septic tank looking for something thrown in there."

"That certainly can happen." Quade paced the floor now, anxious for the rest of his team to assemble. "There can't be any ownership from heads of the various agencies. They have to stand back and let this team work. When investigators from the Orange Police Department go out into the county to assist, I never interfere, and I never fuss about the overtime being expended. Some agencies originally had a problem with paying overtime on cases that had nothing to do with their jurisdictions, but when they had cases such as this, they realized it all balances out."

"But I'm not a member of either one of those agencies you mentioned, yet you summoned me. Why is that?" Sid asked.

"As I said, we assemble a complete team. You've been working on this case on behalf of your client, Boo Murphy. No way could I shut you out. You realize, of course, you're expected to abide by the same laws and guidelines as we do."

Sid nodded. "I'm impressed. Now, what's this all about?"

"Alex just got word from an informant that the Mexican cartel has infiltrated and are fighting for control of a local group of smugglers. Things have heated up considerably. We already have a dead body—"

"Who?" Sid held her breath, wondering who'd been next.

"Vi Sweeny, the woman who lived over on Pleasure Island, kin to Zeke Harris in some way or the other. Some fisherman found her body washed ashore over on the Galveston Peninsular. She'd been bound, gagged, and beat up pretty badly before they put a bullet in her head."

"Quade, wait—" Sid stood and walked over to the window. In the space between the silence, she felt the eyes of everyone in the room focused on her. "Zeke Harris—or Dexter Sweeny, whatever his name was—he married both Vi and Sasha."

"Did Sasha or your client, Boo Murphy, know that?"

"Boo didn't know. Sasha found out after Zeke's death, when Vi Sweeny showed up on her doorstep looking for whatever Zeke supposedly found in the swamp."

"Okay, that's another piece of the puzzle." Quade wrote that info on the white board behind him, along with other clues already added before she'd arrive.

He turned back to the group. "A big heist is in the works—some local artifacts, special collections, and something about a document they suspect was on the schooner, a priceless historical document of some kind."

Alex raised her hand to speak. "But Sheriff, I can understand the heist, but, but…what schooner? I hate to mention it, but no one has seen a schooner but Ms. Murphy, or at least she says she saw it."

"I'm the messenger here, Alex, so don't shoot me. But I hear what you're saying. My concern is the local involvement, not so much about the schooner and what they think might be on board. But the thing is, if they think something valuable was on it, might'en that lead them to commit murder?" Quade paced the room.

"Sid?" Ben smiled, urging her on. She opened her pocketbook and pulled out Hoke's ID. "I found this between the cushions on my sofa. It must have fallen out of his pocket when…"

Okay, it wasn't exactly the truth, but it was close.

"Well, I'll be damned. Homeland Security." Quade shook his head. "That's scary as hell. That means most likely the agency heard about the cartel working in this area much earlier than we did—which means this may be more serious than a simple smuggling of artifacts."

"What are you saying, Quade?" Ben asked.

"I'm saying they may expect arms movement—or are trying to stop it before it gets started." Quade wrote the new information on the board.

"Quade?"

"What is it Sid?" He answered without turning around.

"I...I have reason to be suspicious of George Léger."

The muscles in Quade's back stiffened through his shirt. "George? I thought he was your mentor?"

"He is—was—and this is difficult for me, but this is getting way too serious for me not to..."

She shared what she'd seen and heard.

"I hope your suspicions are wrong there, Sid, I always saw George as one of the good guys." He recorded the notes on the board then turned back to the group. "Greed or need can tempt any one of us. Don't forget that, and keep your guard up. Okay, where were we?" He pointed to Alex and Sid. "You two get over to Galveston and see if you can find out anything further on the Vi Sweeney death. If there is any clue left unturned, I figure you two will turn it over and see what stinks underneath. Alex, wear a jacket or a windbreaker over your shirt. Let's keep it a secret that you're the cops for now. If you need her to, Sid's good at breaking and entering. And somehow she always seems to get away with it."

Sid laughed. "You keep telling me not to, Quade, now you're telling me to do it—which order shall I go by?"

"Only if you have to, sweet cheeks, only if you have to!" He winked at her.

"Guess we better take my Xterra then. We don't want to advertise with a sheriff's car."

"Hell, Sid, your car advertises itself. Alex, check out an unmarked car."

After the meeting dismissed, Alex pulled the dark blue unmarked car out of the lot and she and Sid headed to the ferry that would take them to Galveston, maybe an hour's drive away.

On the way out of town, Alex asked, "I heard you were Warren Chadwick's sister. Is that right?" She glanced over at Sid and then back to the approaching traffic.

"Oh, you knew Warren—yes he was my brother."

"So you hadn't done detective work before he left you the Third Eye?"

Sid choked. "That's an understatement"

"Sounds like I hit a chord."

"I was a preacher's wife for thirty years. I did detective work all right, trying to figure out the best way to get people to come to church."

"Successful?"

"I guess you could call it that, yeah. How about you? Been in the sheriff's department long?"

"Ten years now."

"I could tell you had experience under your belt. You from this area?"

"Born and raised. Orange has its own gravity that keeps you there unless you get out early. I did leave for a few years but am happy to be back. How long have you been with the Sheriff's office?"

"It's a long story—he and I worked in the same police department." Alex's fingers drummed the steering wheel.

"You and Quade?"

Alex laughed and looked over at Sid. "No, not Quade. I make it a habit to never say my ex's name."

"Your fingers are beating a hole in the steering wheel. Must be some history there."

Alex slid her hands down to the bottom of the wheel and held it lightly. "I left him, took my kids and high-tailed it back to Orange while I could still walk."

"Oh, oh. That doesn't sound good. Everything okay now? He leave you alone?"

"Yep, sure does. He got killed by some guy he was beating up. The guy pulled a knife and stuck it in his belly and ran. I wanted to do that so many times—let me tell you." Pain from the past rolled out the corner of Alex's eyes and dripped off her chin.

"Sorry to bring up such bad memories."

"S'okay. I need to be reminded every now and then. Helps me improve my choices in men." She cast a look over at Sid and then put her eyes back on the task at hand, driving off the ferry and onto the highway. "I've gotten lots more particular, I can tell you that."

"I'll bet you have."

"What about you?"

"Abuse of a different kind. I didn't have access to my own opinion."

"I can imagine. Being married to preacher probably gives you your opinion, huh?"

"Well put." Weary of talking about her past with Sam, she changed the subject to the case at hand—and her pirate mentor. "Ever heard of a female pirate known as Mary Anne Radcliff?"

"Yeah, she used to operate out of this area. Why?"

"There's just a missing link to something I'm working on."

"What do you mean?"

"Well, you've heard of everything coming up roses, it seems everywhere I turn, everything's coming up pirates."

"You mean the schooner? Oh, by the way, I heard no one has seen the ship."

"No one except my client."

"Yeah, so I hear. I don't know—could be an old woman's ploy."

"Boo? I really don't see her doing something like that."

"It might surprise you. I've seen worse than that." Alex shook her head.

"Then where does this Hoke Faulkner fit in, and why would someone kill him, you think?"

"Only thing I can figure," Alex offered, "is he was getting too close to something he wasn't supposed to."

"My client told me Hoke wasn't a Faulkner, but a Sweeney."

Alex chuckled. "Well, I guess a Sweeny can work in Homeland Security, as well as another can be a smuggler. Hell, maybe he was both. Maybe he worked with Boo and Sasha. Maybe both of them are involved in smuggling too, and got together and committed the murders."

"What?" Sid felt like she'd stuck her finger in a socket.

"If you think pirates are the only ones who smuggle, think again."

"What do you mean?"

"We live near the coast. Coastguards can't watch it all. Things happen."

Sid's mind got to wandering. Evidently all the talk of Boo being kin to an early gang of pirates wasn't just talk, and the present generation had continued the family business. Sasha, even Boo maybe—were involved in it, or at least knew about it. She'd resisted that fact as long as she dared.

Twenty-Seven

Sid and Alex drove along the coastline, Alex recounting tales her father told about the history of the area, including smuggling operations by pirate, Jean Lafitte.

Alex pulled alongside a boarded up beach house built up on stilts. Behind it, Sid saw a large weather-worn warehouse. Alex reminisced. "When I was kid, I remember my dad, who was also in law enforcement, saying something about the folks that lived here. I get the idea he suspected they were in some kind of shady dealings"

"Remember what their name was?"

"He mentioned some name in the middle of a string of four letter words, but for the life of me, I can't recall. I remember him getting out of the car and walking around the place. He seemed to be suspicious about something. The day is fuzzy in my head. I just catch these glimpses. He said something about Lafitte rolling over in his grave. I think this is the area where Lafitte's compound stood before he burned it to the ground."

Alex continued her tale from the past. "Even though Lafitte helped win the Battle of New Orleans, the U.S. government was fed up with his shenanigans. Gave him three months to break up and get his whole gang off the island. He told them he would, and waited out the three months. When they were about to come to shore and drive him out, the feisty man burned the whole place down to the ground rather than let them have what was left of his own little kingdom. The few remaining shacks went up like tinder, the story goes. He's also reported to have used a couple of aliases, Boutte, and Billot. I've heard oil companies paid royalties to family members based on land originally owned by Lafitte. Don't know if that means anything or not. A Boutte grandmother recounted how her husband would be gone for long periods of time, and after he died, they found some gold coins and other stuff buried under the corner of their house. Now that doesn't prove Lafitte used aliases, and if he did, that Boutte or Billot was one and the same, but it's fascinating speculation."

Alex switched off the motor, leaned forward and looked out the windshield. "Come on, let's walk around back and take a look."

Sid opened her car door along with Alex and they headed away from the gulf and around back. Soon as Sid rounded the corner and stared up at the top of building she noticed what was left of a large white L that had been painted on some time ago, and now only the mere outline of the letter remained. She squinted up into the sun, her hand shielding her eyes, trying hard to make out any other letters. The last one looked like an R, then a couple of E's.

"Look—up there." She pointed. "Can you make out the name?"

"L, E, G, E, R," Alex spelled out. "Leger?"

"No, look, there's an accent over the first E. It's Léger, same last name as George."

"Shall we try to get inside the building?" Alex asked, looking over at Sid as if she had all the answers.

"Why? What do you think we'd find in there?"

"Probably nothing. Maybe something, but at least we'd know there was nothing inside."

"This is private property. I'm going to have to ask the two of you to leave." A big burly man said. He'd walked up to them unnoticed while they had been in deep conversation.

Sid noticed a bulge under his jacket and wondered if he were a security guard. She didn't dare tell him who she and Alex were.

"No problem, Sir," Alex spoke up in her most innocent voice. "We're just exploring the island today, we're from out of town, and got turned around. At this very moment we were looking for a bathroom, and if we didn't find one, we'd be looking for a spot to squat." She smiled up at him.

"Humph." He muttered, obviously attempting to resist her charms. "No bathrooms around here." He pointed. "Head up the road a little further and you'll find a gas station. They'll let you use theirs. And I suggest you do that, this ain't a woman friendly place around here."

They headed back around the building and after several hours of driving around looking for anything that appeared suspicious, they headed to the ferry.

At the risk of sounding crazy, Sid blurted out. "Have you ever heard of a ghost ship?"

"A ghost ship? What do you mean? I've seen the movie by that name, but…"

"Okay, listen to this." Sid sat up straighter and half-turned to Alex. "Boo Murphy swears she not only saw a schooner out in the swamp that morning, but she also says she climbed up on it and stayed for awhile, right? Then the next day she and her cousin Sasha go out there and find nothing but a dead man. Quade goes out there and doesn't find a ship either. I go out with Shipwreck and his crew and we find nothing until I go off by myself. I see this schooner sailing along through the swamp. There is a line of fog just above the surface of the water, so I can't tell if the boat is actually in the water or floating above it, but I swear, it floated along until it was out of sight." Deciding against adding the vision of Mary Anne Radcliff onboard the schooner, Sid stopped short.

Alex sat behind the wheel focusing on the road. A line of consternation crossed her forehead, but she said nothing.

"Well?"

"I don't know what to say, Sid. I'm like you, it sounds crazy. I don't know what to think. I've never seen a ghost before, let alone a ghost ship. If you ask me, you imagined it." She glanced over at Sid. "Sorry, I just don't… I don't mean to insult you, it's just…"

"No, that's okay, I'm not insulted. I guess I'd feel the same way if I were you. Hell, I do feel the same way. I just don't know what to do with it."

After thinking about the situation overnight, Sid decided before she told anyone else about her suspicions of George, she'd first confront him. He'd been such a loyal mentor she couldn't imagine him being involved in something illegal. It was time to find out if what she suspected was true, and the best way to do that was to get it straight from the horse's mouth.

She drove to his office. But when she pulled into the parking lot and saw a City of Orange police car parked beside George's truck, she felt even more confounded. At first, she thought maybe she didn't have to worry about telling anyone her suspicions after all, maybe the police knew of George's involvement in some shady dealings. Or maybe they were in on something illegal themselves.

When she stepped into the lobby, it was empty, so she walked around the desk and headed straight to the half-open door to George's office. Two voices, one of them George's, sounded like they were close to arguing. The words grew heated, but they talked in half whispers and Sid couldn't make out what they were saying. She hesitated at first, but decided to knock anyway. Maybe they needed a breather. She gave a quick rap and stepped in. "Morning. Am I interrupting something?"

Both men's faces flushed.

"Sid," George stuttered, looking guilty as all get out. "I-I didn't hear you come in. Have you met the new Chief of Police that took Quade's old job? Chief, this is Sid Smart, a fellow PI. Warren Chadwick was her brother, you know—owner of the Third Eye? Sid, this is Chief Kitchen. He just got promoted to Chief of Police." It was the same detective that had investigated Hoke's death in Sid's living room. He carried the innocence of Colombo without the bumbling ways, the cigar-smoking, or the rumpled raincoat. The man stood a good six feet eight, but with a kind face and gentle nature—except for the anger behind his eyes.

"Nice to meet you, Chief. Sorry to interrupt," Sid said.

"That's okay." Again, both men spoke at the same moment. If she didn't know better, she'd think they were in cahoots on something, both of them sure looked guilty.

"We're just working on a case together, sharing some information, that sort of thing."

She'd never had any reason to doubt George, but that was before now. The air in the room smelled rank.

"I'm interrupting. I'll touch base with you later." She turned and headed out of the office while both men called her back. She walked straight out the front door, got in her car and drove to the Orange County Courthouse and to Ben's office on the second floor.

She entered his office, relieved he sat behind his desk, a pencil between his teeth. "Hey, handsome, you look busy. Got a few minutes?"

"Hey, Sid." He jumped up and headed around the desk. "I'm glad you stopped by. I noticed the contractors started hauling in material for your new office. It's looking good. I was just sitting here thinking about you—one part of me more than the other." He laughed at himself and smoothed his pants down as he headed her way.

She stepped toward him and was soon caught up in his arms. Lord he smelled good. "Love that cologne." She snuggled into his neck. "You're not worried your staff is coming in on us are you?"

"Could care less, let them."

She felt him breathe in, inhaling her shampooed hair, felt the rise in his pants.

"Are you wearing your ring today? He picked up her left hand and turned it up. "She is! Look here!" He fingered the ring then held her eyes with his. They sparkled with moisture as he came towards her, and she saw her own image reflected back. His lips looked soft as he opened them and came closer. "Wait, wait, I came here to talk business." She chuckled and pushed back on his chest.

He reached up and fingered her lips, "Darn, I thought you came to see me, not talk…"

"Business, Ben, business. Do you have any information about any smuggling operations going on in this area?"

"Drug smuggling, that's for sure."

"No, more than drugs. Artifacts and the like. Valuable art objects, that sort of thing. It seems some of Boo and Sasha's relatives used to be smugglers. Not sure if they are, or not."

"Not that I know of, but then again, I don't put anything past anyone. What you got?"

"Maybe nothing, but what I'm trying to figure out is why someone would kill Zeke, and then break into Boo's house. That one piece of information has eluded me from the start. If I can figure that out, I'll learn why they keep coming after me. What possible reason would they have if there wasn't a schooner resurrected in the swamp to start with? And do you have any idea why George would be in an angry confrontation with the new police chief?"

"Angry?"

"Yeah, I just walked in on them, and they sure were serious about something."

"That sounds scary, especially with our current concerns about George. I shudder to think we might have just hired a new police chief on the take."

After knocking around the situation with Ben, and getting nowhere, Sid felt like she'd missed something in Boo's story about the clan wars between the Cormacs and the Sweeneys. Even if she hadn't missed anything, maybe if she heard it again, something would click. She drove out to Boo's and found the woman sitting on the dock dangling her toes in the water. "Better watch out, an alligator's going to eat your toes," Sid said, walking up behind her.

"Oh, hi Sid, I didn't hear you drive up."

"Yeah, I thought you were deep in thought."

"What's up? Talked the sheriff into dropping my case yet?"

"No, not yet, but I had a couple of things I wanted to talk with you about. You still don't have any idea why anyone would break into your house? What they might be looking for?"

Boo shook her head. "Not a clue."

"Okay, remember you told me something about an ancestor of yours name Mary Anne Radcliff?"

Boo spit in the water and wiped her mouth with the back of her hand. "I reckon I do."

"Okay, I hate to sound like I have Alzheimer's, but I need you to tell me the story again. I think it relates to all this, but if it does, I've missed something."

"Well, Anne Cormac married this good-for-nothing named James Bonny, a scalawag if ever there was one. The two of them married against her pa's wishes, caused her pa a heap of trouble, and then fled to New Providence—now called the Bahamas. Later, she left Bonny and took up with *Calico* Jack. They sailed the Caribbean as pirates. Among Jack's crew was another woman pirate named Mary Reed—but that's a long story. Mary died, so when Anne—now a Radcliff—had her baby, she named the girl after her good friend Mary."

"Your story confirms what I read about her in a book from the library." Sid glanced at Boo and saw weariness creeping across her shoulders. "You're looking tired, sweetheart. Why don't we go inside?"

Boo pulled her feet out of the water and crawled to a standing position, yielding to the healing arm. Excited as all get-out from telling the story, she grabbed Sid's elbow and led her across the yard and into her house. Something told Sid she'd be there for a while.

For the next two hours, Sid listened to Boo recount stories handed down of her infamous pirate-ancestor Mary Radcliff, and how her granddaughter rode with Jean Lafitte. Interesting all, but Sid grew impatient, more interested in today than generations ago. She knew how to effectively change the subject.

"Remember when I borrowed your boat and went out into the swamp? I saw something I didn't tell you."

"What? You seen it didn't you? You seen the schooner!"

"Before I tell you, promise you won't laugh."

"Cross my heart." Boo gave the childlike gesture across her chest.

"I saw the schooner."

"I *knew* it. I *knew* it was out there." Boo squealed with delight. "Did you mark it? How come you ain't told no one about it? Did you touch it?" Boo leaned forward in her seat, eyes as big as two gold Spanish medallions.

"No, I didn't touch it, and to tell you the truth, it looked like what I'd imagine a ghost ship would look like sailing right above the water line, surrounded by fog and—"

"A ghost ship? Not even." Boo shook her stubborn head. "It's for real, I tell you."

"But wait—" Sid straightened in her chair. "Let me finish. The reason I think it was a ghost ship was because I saw your Mary Anne Radcliff on board."

"My who? You what?" Boo doubled over in laughter, holding her belly.

Barely containing her own, Sid admonished, "You said you wouldn't laugh."

"Yeah, honey, but that's before you started talking about ghost ships. Yeah, I've got a big imagination, but I ain't never imagined no ghost."

"Laugh if you want to, but I saw her!" She looked over at Boo and decided to change the subject again before she got herself thrown into a psych hospital. "I'm hearing you say that Bonny was the first husband of your ancestor, Anne Cormac Radcliff.

He wasn't kin to you then."

"Not even," Boo sputtered. And even if he was, that's one we wouldn't have claimed."

"But the family feud started a generation before Anne was born, is that right?"

Boo nodded. "Yeah, that started when Anne's pa, John Cormac, cheated on his wife, who was a Sweeney."

Sid swallowed before continuing with the biggie question she'd come to ask. "I keep hearing that your relatives have continued the family business begun by Anne and her granddaughter Mary Anne—smuggling."

The wind went out of Boo's enthusiasm. She hung her head and stared at her hands in her lap. Her voice shrunk to barely above a whisper. "So you found out. I hoped you wouldn't have to."

"Why, Boo?"

"Shame. And besides, that's only part true. Some of 'em do, but I ain't never had nothing to do with any of 'em. Don't even know who they all are."

"I can understand that. I'd feel the same way." Sid reached over and clasped Boo's hands. "What about Sasha? Is she involved with that side of the family?"

"I heard once that the Sweeny clan is their competition on the local market."

"What about Sasha? Think she might be involved in the smuggling business?"

"Not that I know of—but now from what we've learned about Zeke being a Sweeny, who knows what's true. And if that man was kin to us, it sure must've been a long way down the line."

"Have you talked to Sasha?"

"She ain't said a whole lot to me since we found Zeke out there dead. Despite what she might say to you, she still ain't sure I didn't kill him. Thinks he and I snuck out there while she was gone the day before, and I killed him to keep the whole thing secret. It ain't very comfortable living this close to a cousin who won't even nod morning to you." Boo held onto the chair arms and rose slowly.

Now, finally, all these clues were beginning to fit together. Hell, both families were in the smuggling business, and had been for over two hundred years! But how did her friend and mentor, George Leger fit into all this?

Twenty-Eight

Nathalee fought her way back up through the smothering mask of oblivion to the excruciating pain of a stinky-sweating man atop her, inside her, and urine-smelling hay beneath her. Only when she spied her torn running shorts and top piled on the muck across the stall did she remember she lay naked and that her hands were tied over her head and her feet tied somewhere below.

"Leave me alone, stop, stop, you're hurting me," she twisted, yelling, knowing he was too far gone to even hear her.

It was then she saw another man standing nearby, watching.

"Make him stop, help, get him off of me!"

Instead of helping, the other man stuck the barrel of a gun to her head. "You wanna see your brains splattered against that wall?"

The last thing she remembered before blackness returned was the hope that the horrible man had finished before she came to again.

But that didn't happen, for she roused to the same horrifying nightmare over and over for what seemed like forever. The only thing that changed was the man atop her.

Once, as she faded in and out of consciousness, she heard one of them say, "They haven't given up yet, and even if they don't, a girl like this? She should bring us a good hundred thousand on the open market now that we've broken her."

At one point she awoke with no one thrusting inside her. Forcing her eyes open, she saw a man sitting on a wooden crate reading a newspaper by kerosene lamp light.

She leaned up on one elbow, "When are you going to let me go? My family's looking for me you know—they won't stop till they find me."

"Honey, there ain't no family looking for you." He folded the newspaper and sauntered over to her. "I'm the one set to watch you, and no one gets to you 'cept through me. Best thing you can do is treat me nice, so I'll be good to you, find you a good owner."

"Owner? Who are you? Where am I?"

Twenty-Nine

Sid hated doubting George, but something just didn't feel right. She waited until close to midnight and drove out to George's house, parking down the street underneath an overhang of trees which shielded the vehicle from a bright, full-moon night. George was up to something he hadn't told her about, and it bothered her to no end. Not that she had to know all his business, but this *something* had driven a wedge between them. She didn't trust him anymore, and if she couldn't trust George…?

At first, she sat behind the wheel wide awake, tense, hoping he didn't go anywhere. When he didn't, relief moved in, thickening her eyelids, and making her head drop backwards. You're being ridiculous, Sid, she admonished herself. George is one of the few good guys. Go home and sleep. She reached for the ignition, deciding to do just that, when George's garage door started up and inside, the taillights of his truck glowed bright red.

Guilt eased into her consciousness as she started the motor, shifted, and eased out from the shadows a safe distance behind his black Ram. Since he'd taught her almost everything she knew, she had to be careful. How would she explain herself if he caught her on his tail?

She looked at the clock on the dash. Two a.m.

He left Bridge City, drove to I-10, and then turned on several county roads. But not until he passed the diner where Sid had first found Slider did she realize his destination. The barn with the turquoise balls painted on the side. "What the hell is it with that damn barn," she wondered out loud, pounding the steering wheel with her hands.

A few minutes later, George approached the drive that led up to the old farmhouse where Slider had once lived, and sure enough, his brake lights glowed. He turned and drove into the yard and on past the house, straight to the barn out back. The paint job on the barn now made sense. When you want to make a place inconspicuous, make it as conspicuous as hell.

Instead of following George, Sid turned off on a nearby private road, switched off her headlights and almost blindly drove down the darkened road toward the barn. When she got close enough, she shut off her engine and coasted the last few feet, wishing for her gun the police department still held since the Faulkner shooting.

She switched off the dome light and hustled the short distance to the barbed wire fence separating her from the barn. She slammed her boot down on the bottom row of wire, yanked up the top row and, carefully avoiding the barbs, stepped through the fence and right into a dried cow patty.

Shit.

She half-wiped the mess off her boot in the tall grass, crept around the corner of the barn and eased down its length, thankful now for the darkness of a new moon. But a light flickering through a large crack between two planks caught her eye. She stopped and peered inside. At first, all she saw was the low flame of a kerosene lantern perched on an overturned crate. But as her eyes adjusted, she made out the figure of a nude young woman sprawled on the floor, hands and feet tied. If she were still alive, she didn't look to be for long. Before, when Sid first found Slider, the barn had been locked and as far as she knew, the authorities had left it such, since the old woman's death had been from natural causes. But dead or not, this young woman had experienced anything but natural causes. And Sid had been looking for clues in all the wrong places.

George turned off the motor but left his headlights on to illuminate the barn door. No sense in tripping. There wasn't a soul within a couple of miles of this place. He got out of the pickup, wondering once again why in hell he was doing this. Martha would kill him if she knew. He stepped to the back of the truck, lifted out the big cardboard box and headed to the barn. Shoving the big door open with his foot, he stepped inside.

"Rodriguez," he said, when he saw his contact sitting on a bale of hay smoking a cigarette. The stupid shit. One ember and the whole, bone dry place, would turn into a fireworks display.

"Is that it?" Rodriguez asked, rising and walking over to stand under the fluorescent light fixture dangling from the ceiling.

"This's it. I told you me and Pete could get your guys in."

"Not that I don't trust you but—"

"—but you need to open it to make sure. Go ahead, see for yourself." George set the box on a bale of hay and stepped away, gesturing with his hands. "Be my guest."

Rodriguez smoothed down a head full of black hair, lifted the flap and counted the individually wrapped pieces.

"I'm curious as to why they changed the drop-off point." George had been thrown for a loop when, at the last minute, Rodriguez switched instructions from meeting at the Port of Orange to halfway into an adjoining county. "I thought the reason they planned this down to the second was so they didn't have to store the stolen merchandise and take the risk of getting caught."

Rodriguez cut a look over to George. "Change of plans. Coast Guard hanging around too close. We had to scrub that rendezvous point. This barn is our—what do you Americans call it—our Plan B. No need in walking into a trap." Rodriguez unwrapped a piece of crystal and held it up to the light. "Remember the Alamo," he read the words engraved on the crystal with a Spanish accent. "Yeah, right, remember the fucking Alamo! You Texans lost!"

He pulled a cell phone off his belt and pushed a button, waited a minute and then spoke into the phone. "*Steuben Collection* is in our fat little hands. Meet us at rendezvous point. Hasta la vista."

The door squeaked and George swung around, his hand automatically flying to the gun in his shoulder holster. "Sid? What the hell are you doing here?"

The man who had grabbed her from behind while she peeked through a crack, now twisted her arm tighter and shoved her inside and to the hard-packed floor. Her head cracked against the corner of a stall. Warm blood trickled down the side of her face.

"I told you to keep your nose out of this," George yelled.

"She followed you, that's what she did. You stupid jerk! And you mean to tell me you know this *puta*?" The man who had shoved her inside and to the floor, now stood over her panting, his mouth stretched into a sneer.

"Yeah, Lalo, I know her." George spat the words down at her. "I supervised her, taught her all she knows, and that's why she was able to track me." George stepped closer and shoved her in the stomach with his heavy work boot. "Guess she won't be tracking anyone from the bottom of the ocean. Did you see anyone else outside snooping around in our business?"

"She's it."

"Good."

As Sid's eyes adjusted to the bright light, she looked from one man to the other. Both of them, the one George had called Rodriguez, and Lalo, the one who caught her, were the same two men in the helicopter. She'd swear to it. For, even though she hadn't seen them up close, she would never forget those two. For it wasn't what they looked like that she remembered, but the darkness of their auras—that and the crawling sensation underneath her skin. Her guess was they were the ones who shot Hoke Faulkner dead in her living room. While she and Hoke were in the kitchen they must have come in through the open window and found her gun. If this was part of a Mexican cartel, then Homeland Security would certainly be tracking them and their activities, hence Hoke Faulkner's visit to Orange, and his death.

Finally the pieces were falling into place. Of course that still didn't fully explain who exactly killed Zeke, or who the young woman was in the back stall. Sid guessed it must be Nathalee Sweeny, Vi and Dexter's daughter.

"So what do we do with her?" Rodriguez asked.

"We feed her to the sharks. You think the man-eaters like the taste of *puta*?" George sneered as he snatched her by one arm and the little guy, Lalo, grabbed her other, and together they half dragged her outside and shoved her into the front seat of George's truck.

George stomped around the front and climbed in next to Sid. Asking him what the hell he thought he was doing begged to be asked. That and did he have anything to do with the unconscious, maybe even dead young woman in the back stall. Sid wanted to ask him all those questions and more, but for some reason George just didn't seem in the mood to talk to her. Besides, as heartsick as she was, she probably couldn't even get the words out.

Before the planets aligned for just such a conversation, Lalo climbed in beside her and slammed the door. Movement in the rearview mirror showed Rodriguez at the back of the truck. He put the box on the bed of the pickup, climbed in and sat beside it, bracing the Steuben Collection they'd stolen from the Stark Museum, from bouncing around in the truck.

When Rodriguez got settled, he banged on the truck roof. George turned the vehicle around and headed back into town.

Unable to resist, she cut her eyes over at George, wishing he'd signal her something, anything that might let her know he wasn't one of *them*. His jaws were locked so tight a small muscle twitched on the side of his face. When he turned a corner, his body leaned over and made contact with hers. The touch of his damp skin made hers crawl.

So absorbed with her sense of betrayal and an exponential fear in the pit of her stomach, she hadn't noticed where George drove until he pulled off the road and turned into the front yard between Boo and Sasha's house. Inside Boo's, lights shone through every window. Sasha must have retired, for her place sat in darkness.

George switched off the engine, coasted into the yard and stopped alongside a parked car with occupants inside who evidently awaited their arrival. As soon as the truck came to a stop, the car door opened and Pete Baxter stepped out, the same Pete Baxter who had driven the boat out to the swamp with Sid and Shipwreck.

Holy shit. This guy must be the same Pete that Winker called "Uncle."

George rolled down his window when Rodriguez climbed out of the back of the truck and stalked up, obviously upset. "What the hell is your security guard doing here? His job was done soon as he got our men inside the museum undetected. Does he think he won't get paid or something?"

George shrugged. "I don't know, but I intend to find out."

Where was Dog? She'd have thought he'd be alerted by now. And where was the damn sheriff's deputy who was supposed to be watching out for Boo? The commotion outside must have awakened Sasha, for her house lights switched on.

Rodriguez leaned over and looked inside the cab at Lalo. "Get that one in that house and bring her over here." Lalo made a move to go, but George opened his door. "Here, let me have the honors."

"Please, George, don't hurt her," she begged, knowing that had the old George been there, she wouldn't have even asked.

He bounded out of the truck, crossed the yard, and soon had Sasha by the arm leading her toward the others. In the darkness, Sasha's long nightgown looked no whiter than did the fear on her face. Loose hair curled around her sleepy eyes and a long plait lay down her back.

Lalo yanked Sid out of the truck and shoved her toward Boo's house. Half way there, Boo's lights went off. The screen door screeched open. "Don't a dang one of you come a step closer," Boo yelled, propping the door open with her foot. She steadied a shotgun by letting it rest atop the cast on her arm. At her side, Dog stood with his legs spread wide, growling.

"You may want to put that gun down, Miss Murphy," George called out.

"And don't call me Miss! It's Ms."

Rodriguez motioned Lalo to grab Sid while he grabbed Sasha's arm and yanked her away from George. "Well, Ms. Murphy, we've got your sister here and your private eye. Which one you want us to take out first?"

"Sasha ain't my sister." The words sounded more like a snarl than a statement.

"Whatever. We're coming in. Shoot if you want, but you'll kill your friends first."

Boo lowered the gun and the group proceeded up the steps. At the top, Lalo grabbed Boo's shotgun, struck the dog on the head with the stock, and pitched the gun out in the yard.

By the time everyone got inside Boo's tiny living room, it was standing room only. Rodriguez held his pistol on Boo and Sasha, staring them down. "Now cut out the innocent shit, *ladies*. We know smuggling is in your bloodline."

Boo threw back her shoulders in defiance, but Sid saw fear behind her eyes. "Well, if'n you know all that, then you know me and Sasha ain't never been involved in any of it."

"You might not have been, but Sasha's husband sure was."

Sid heard both women gasp.

"We know he smuggled goods from right out there," he pointed toward the swamp, "to get around your Coast Guard. So don't tell me you didn't know about that."

Sasha took a step forward. "How could I have, I didn't even know he had another wife until after somebody killed him, and that Vi woman came here and told me about it when she came to try to get his money. Said she was his legitimate wife, I was his bigamy wife. And I dang sure didn't know his name was Dexter Sweeney."

Boo turned and stared at Sasha, her mouth open wide enough

that a bird could fly in and make a nest. "Woman, what are you talking about?"

"I been meaning to tell you, but just so much has been happening."

"Tell me now, right this minute, before I spit in your eye." Boo's face had turned scarlet.

"There ain't nothing else to tell. While you was in the hospital, this Vi Sweeney came to my door. Said she was the wife of my late *husband* and she wanted whatever it was you and me took off the schooner or—"

"I keep telling everybody, I didn't take nothing—"

"—or she wanted whatever it was that Zeke hid out in a hollowed out tree." Sasha finally finished her sentence.

"And what the tarnation was that?"

By now, both Boo and Sasha's voices elevated several octaves and decibels. Sid feared any minute either of them would launch into the other, fangs bared. She wondered whether she should tell them about Zeke's younger double who lived over in Port Arthur with the rude son called Dutch. But she didn't have to. Sonny walked in the front door and let it slam behind him.

"Zeke?" Both Sasha and Boo cried out at the same time.

Stealing a quick glance over at Rodriguez, the man spoke, his voice barely above a whisper. "Name's Sonny. Dexter Sweeny was my pa, or was, till…till… "

Rodriguez stepped into the mix. "Till I found him out in the swamp stashing my merchandise in a hollow log. Now let's get on with it." He grabbed Boo's hair and yanked her half out of the chair. When Boo yelled out, Sid lurched forward, but Lalo caught her arm and squeezed it until she couldn't feel her fingers anymore.

"All right you old witch," Rodriguez said to Boo. "What did you do with the documents you found on the schooner?" When Boo didn't answer, he slapped her in the face so hard her cheek glowed with his handprint.

"But, but…" Sasha tried to get up, but George stepped over

and held her down by the shoulder.

Sirens wailed off in the distance.

"Who called the cops?" Rodriguez's eyes flashed from Lalo, to George, to Pete, to Sonny.

Pete Baxter stepped from the shadows and Sid caught some kind of signal between him and George, but before it made any sense, gunshots ripped through the window, shattering glass and slamming George and Pete to the floor in a heap. Rodriguez, now in defensive mode, released Boo and headed across the room. In her peripheral vision, Sid saw the two old women drop to their hands and knees and strike out for the bedroom. Lalo started toward them but Rodriguez called a halt. "Forget them," he said, and grabbed Sid's elbow. "This one will buy us a little time. Let's get to the truck."

Rodriguez slammed Sid through the door ahead of him, but just as they hit the yard, a dark figure came at Rodriguez, while a second one came at Lalo. A third grabbed Sid from behind and they both toppled backwards to the ground, him beneath her, his arms clenched around her waist. She floundered, kicking and clawing, and finally twisted sideways just enough to get a knee between her attacker's legs, and ramming him. Hard.

Instant release.

She leapt to her feet and turned, braced, ready to scratch, kick, bite, but the man—her man—roiled on the ground, helpless.

"Ben? Where the hell did you come from?"

"I had a feeling…something was…up. I figured if you're going to…do this job, I might as well be your back-up, so I followed…"

"But I don't need your help, Ben," she yelled.

"The hell you don't." He crawled onto his knees and slowly got to his feet, his hands holding his crotch. "Holy Mother of God, I'll never be the same again."

While Quade and the others fought for control of their captives, Sid looked up at the house, panicked now over Boo and Sasha. She raced up the steps and across the porch. When she opened the screen door, the first thing she saw was Boo, prone, on the bedroom floor. Sasha stood near the dresser, a knife in her hand and shock frozen on her face.

His back to Sid, Sonny stood facing Sasha, the sour smell of greed oozing out of his every pore. So intent on his mission, he hadn't heard Sid come in. "I've lost Ma and Pa over all this. Not that I cared much for either one of 'em, but I did care about Nathalee. I figure these guys took her, too. She was the only decent one in this whole fucked up family of ours."

"Nathalee?" Sasha took a step toward him.

"My baby sister, or was. She hated the smuggling business, and had just told Ma and Pa she wadn't going to be involved in it anymore. Then she disappeared. I reckon she's at the bottom of the river just like Ma."

Sid interrupted. "I think I know where she is, but I don't know if she's still alive."

Sonny swung around toward Sid, hope springing to his face. "You do? Ma'am, I know you don't owe me a favor after the way I treated you out at my house. But I'd be awfully obliged if you'd take me to my baby sister. She didn't deserve any of this."

"None of us deserved it." Sid turned and headed back outside.

The others followed her out to find Rodriguez and Lalo in the yard with their faces buried in the dirt, their hands cuffed behind their backs. Two other men leaned over them. Moonlight reflected off the backs of their jackets, and Sid squinted to make out the letters, FBI.

Ben had just limped over to Sid when someone behind her called out. "You okay, Sid?"

"George?" She swung around to see George and Pete standing behind her, neither one with a bullet hole in their back. "I thought you were both dead."

"Blanks and bullet-proof vests."

"Blanks? You mean you weren't in league with these devils?" Sid indicated Rodriguez and Lalo.

"Sorry, Sha. We were, but all under the supervision and advice of the FBI. They swore me to secrecy."

Boo and Sasha walked over, arm in arm. "Well, we know who these other guys are, but not this one." Boo stuck her hand out at Ben.

He took it. "Hi, I'm Ben Hillerman, Sid's new partner."

Sid's mouth dropped open, then, "Like hell you are!"

Thirty

The next evening, Sid sat on the sofa next to Boo, each of them holding a huge bowl of buttered popcorn in their lap and a Dr. Pepper in their hand, waiting for the final scene of Boston Legal where James Spader and William Shatner sit on the patio and discuss their day. Dog lay at Boo's feet with an ice pack tied around his head. The lump he'd gotten the night before was responding well to tender, loving care.

Boo grabbed a handful of popcorn. "I'm sure glad ya'll found Nathalee Sweeney in time. Poor girl. What she must've been through. Really pisses me off what those men did to her."

"Me, too. How she survived that ordeal, I'll never know. She must be a strong young woman."

Earlier that day they met in Quade's office, together with the FBI, George Léger, and a representative from Homeland Security. Quade assured Boo that the charges against her would be dropped. George apologized profusely for his inability to bring Sid into his confidence. They learned that Hoke Faulkner did have a Sweeney in his family tree, but he was also with Homeland Security because of the Mexican cartel's involvement with not only smuggling of artifacts, but also arms and ammunition to terrorists who had infiltrated the U. S. None of them, Sid realized, were concerned about the rumor of some stupid document aboard some non-existent schooner.

Now, the women sat and tried to make sense out of what they'd learned that morning.

"Oh yes, I meant to tell you," Sid said, turning to Boo. "I went by the store to pick up your photos on my way over here, but they all came back blank, the clerk said that the film had been exposed to light a long time ago."

"Well, dang, I was sure hoping pictures would show something me and Sasha didn't see when we went out there, maybe something sticking up out of the water, like a mast or…"

"Sorry. I guess you're just going to have to give up on the idea of proof and just let people think you're crazy." Sid laughed, thankful she'd kept her ghost ship to herself—mostly.

"I can't do that. I seen it, and I dang well know I seen it. I climbed up on the dang thing." Boo held her palms up to the sky in exasperation.

"Prove it. Give me something that shows you actually climbed up on the schooner."

"Don't rightly know if I can," Boo rubbed her chin with her hand. "Oh wait, here comes my favorite part." She settled back on the sofa and returned her attention to the TV show. The actors sipped their Scotch and puffed on cigars.

When the credits rolled, Boo sat her bowl down and returned to the conversation as if the break hadn't occurred. "Let's see, oh, yeah, I found some trash down in it."

"Trash? In the schooner? What kind of trash?"

"Trash, you know, like an old soda pop bottle. I throwed it away, though."

"Where? Where did you throw it?" Sid felt the smallest charge of excitement in her veins.

"I just pitched it in the bottom of the boat to get rid of when I got home. Really burns me up when folks litter like that."

"Did you?"

"Did I what?"

"Throw the bottle away?" Sid tried to keep exasperation out of her voice. "I was in your boat the other day, but I didn't see a bottle."

"I reckon it's still there, probably just up under the seat with all the other trash."

"Let's go look for it."

"Now? In the dark?"

"Right this minute. You have flashlights don't you?"

Energized all over again, Boo jumped up and fetched a couple of flashlights. They hurried out the door and down to the boat, giggling like two little girls on the adventure of their lives. At the dock, Sid held the boat steady while Boo climbed in and reached under the seat. Soon, all kinds of trash started flying up on the dock. Styrofoam cups, old license plates, bicycle chains.

"Good lord dog, Boo, you must be the bayou's one-woman litter control program." She flashed her light around in the bottom of the boat. "Well I'll be damned," she said when she spied a mud-coated bottle. "Is that it?"

Boo snatched it up and handed it to her. "Yep, this is it. This is the one I was talking about."

Sid exhaled every ounce of wind she'd held in her lungs. "Here, let's sit down."

They sat on the dock, legs spread wide, eagerness consuming their thoughts.

Sid turned the bottle around several times, her heart skipping six beats with every rotation. A cork, crammed deep into the bottle's mouth, was coated on the outside with some kind of heavy, discolored wax. Mud and barnacles and green slime covered the glass, but even in the dark of night, they spied what looked to be a yellowed piece of paper curled inside. "I've heard of a message in a bottle, Boo, but this is ridiculous."

"Here, let me get something to scrape off that wax. You'll need it for the cork, too." Boo scurried over to the pirogue on hands and knees, yanking at her skirt when it got in the way, and returned with a slim-handled fishing knife.

Sid eased the tip of the knife under the wax and peeled it off, saving each piece for later study. When the top of the cork was cleared off, she pushed the knifepoint down around the edges, trying to work it lose. Despite her care, the cork crumbled into pieces, falling partly inside the bottle, and the rest on her lap. She tried sticking her finger down inside to reach the paper, but to no avail.

"Here, I've got some wire in my fishing tackle box." Boo hustled back over to the boat and fetched a small roll of wire and passed it to Sid.

With one end of the wire down inside the bottle, Sid fished for the paper. "My heart feels like it's a snare drum." She looked up at Boo and now Sasha, who had heard the commotion and come running.

"Yeah, yeah, just get it out before mine explodes! This is too much for an old woman's heart." Boo held her hand on her chest.

Sasha patted Boo on the knee. "Hush, you've waited this long, you just be patient. We don't want whatever's in there to tear."

At last, one tiny edge of paper stuck up enough for Sid to reach. She put down the wire to grab it, but when she did, the paper slid back down in the bottle.

"Dammit!" She started over again, and again, until she got a big enough piece of the paper out to grab the edge and ease it out.

The other two women leaned over and watched as she unrolled the stiff, crinkly paper.

"It's a letter of some kind." Sid stared at the official looking document with the seal of the British government on it. "It looks like it's addressed..." Sid squinted... "to *Mr Laffite, or*—something—*at Barataria.*"

Making out enough words in the document to confirm her high school Texas history, Sid jumped up easier than she'd gotten down. "Oh my god, do you know what this is? It's one of the letters Lafitte received from the British asking him to side with them against Andrew Jackson at the battle at New Orleans. Yes, look, it goes on to say..." Sid struggled to make out the words.

"It *suggests* that he side with them and squash the break-away country. Wow. We're holding history in the palms of our hands. Priceless history!"

She stared at Boo and Sasha, who both sat with their mouths open.

"No wonder the cartel wanted what you'd found on the schooner. Lafitte always claimed letters like this existed, but he never knew what happened to them so was unable to prove it later. Well, someone preserved this one very well! Do you have any idea what this document is worth?"

"How much?" Boo and Sasha both spoke at the same time.

"I don't have a clue, but I do know you women will be quite comfortable should you choose to sell it."

Evidently Boo's pirate schooner hadn't been a ghost ship after all.

But what about Sid's?

From the dark swamp behind her, Sid sensed more than audibly heard a female and male voice beckoning her to turn toward them. She did so, and stared out into the bayou on a black, moonless night.

"Salute," the two voices said with deep respect, bowing at her as if a fencing match between masters had ended, and Sid scored the winning touch. "Salute," Sid offered in return then headed home to make those pickles.

Sidra Smart faces murder and dismemberment every day. So what does she do to relieve the stress? She makes pickles. Her pickles, like Sidra, offer a touch of sweet with a ton of sass. The delicious pickles are available for purchase at book events/signings, and speaking engagements.

Sidra Smart's Sassy Pickles

www.sylviadickeysmith.com

ingredients: cucumbers, sugar, vinegar, salt, yellow #5, alum and spices

Award-winning mystery author **Sylvia Dickey Smith**, although a native of Orange, Texas, has lived from one side of the state to the other, with a few years in-between spent on the Caribbean island of Trinidad, W. I. She has spent time in mental hospitals and leper colonies (just visiting!), explored shell mounds of the Atakapa Indians, and trekked across alligator-infested swamp, all in the name of research. Prior to writing mysteries, she worked as a Licensed Professional Counselor and Marriage & Family Therapist, as well as a regional director in long term care programs. She currently lives in Georgetown, Texas with her husband, a retired Army Colonel. You can learn more about Sylvia at **www.sylviadickeysmith.com**

Printed in the United States
142176LV00004B/19/P